No Way Down

No Way Down

Bill Bambrick

◆

Writers Club Press
San Jose New York Lincoln Shanghai

No Way Down

All Rights Reserved © 2000 by Bill Bambrick

No part of this book may be reproduced or transmitted in any form or by any means, graphic, electronic, or mechanical, including photocopying, recording, taping, or by any information storage retrieval system, without the permission in writing from the publisher.

Writers Club Press
an imprint of iUniverse.com, Inc.

For information address:
iUniverse.com, Inc.
620 North 48th Street, Suite 201
Lincoln, NE 68504-3467
www.iuniverse.com

ISBN: 0-595-12807-6

Printed in the United States of America

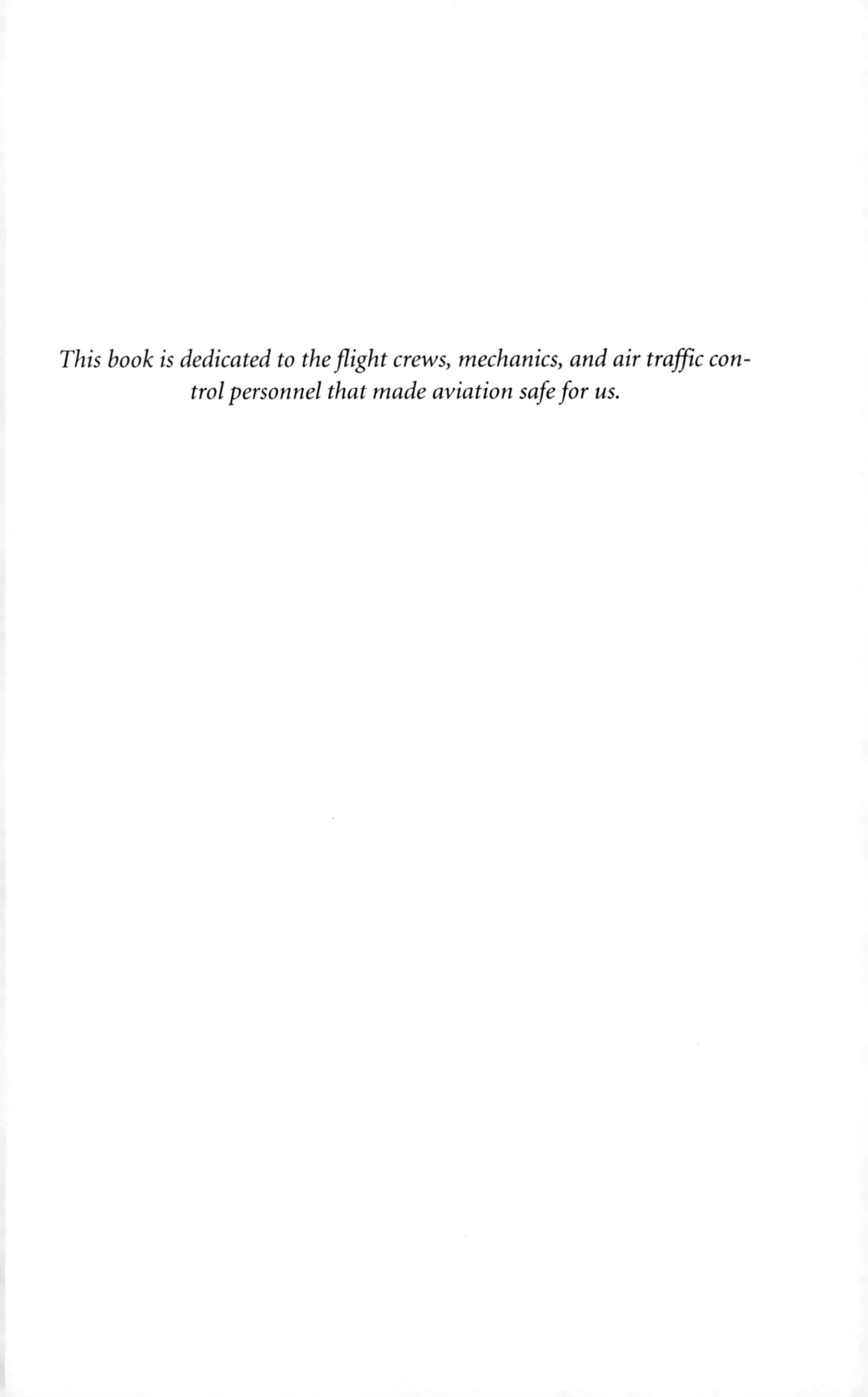

This book is dedicated to the flight crews, mechanics, and air traffic control personnel that made aviation safe for us.

Preface

◆

Technical note: The performance of the CH-12 trijet has been checked in a simulation constructed by the author. Every effort has been made to make its performance realistic and authentic. But remember, this is a work of fiction.

Prologue

◆

Tracy Wingate hurried to the elevators, pulling on her coat as she went. As she buttoned the coat she thought she could feel her baby stirring. She smiled. Just two more months to wait. She'd refused the doctor's offer of telling her the baby's sex. She liked surprises. So did Sam.

She hummed the first few lines of Bye-Bye Blackbird on the way down in the elevator. It was Tammy's favorite. Her four-year-old daughter was waiting at the day-care center. They were always good about it, but she knew they didn't like parents to be late. They had their own lives to get on with, just like she did.

"Thanks, Clancy!" She smiled at the elderly guard who was holding the door open for her. The act made her think of the snipping remarks of one of the women this morning about how she hated men that insisted on holding doors open for her. Tracy had never been able to understand that mind set. She liked being a woman. Liked men that appreciated that she wasn't just one of the guys.

"Watch your step now. It's been raining."

"What else is new?" Tracy laughed.

"Here. Take these for Tammy." Clancy thrust a couple of candy kisses into her hand.

"You're going to spoil her! Thanks, Clancy."

"You shouldn't be walking on a night like this. Take care, now."

"It's only four blocks. I'll be fine."

Tracy didn't mind the extra hours she was working. With the baby expected soon they needed the extra income. But they'd make it. They always had.

The traffic this time of evening was light. One of the few good things about working late. The streets were practically empty. A few people were waiting for the bus at the corner. Everyone's home having dinner, she thought. Tammy would be starving. She'd brought a cookie from the lunch room to tide her over until they got home. Better than the candy Clancy was always giving her. The light changed. She stepped away from the curb. A silver shape loomed out of the semi-darkness. A tremendous impact. No pain. Just shock. She had the sensation of flying. Her head slammed into something hard. She slipped mercifully into unconsciousness.

And then, after a while, her unborn baby boy tried to get born, but didn't quite make it.

And then Tracy Wingate died.

And Tammy waited...

And Sam waited...

* * *

A few pedestrians rushed over from the bus stop to see what had happened. A red-haired man, taller than the others, bent over the fallen woman as his finger stabbed the buttons of his cellular phone. The others gathered around her in a circle, silent, fearful in the presence of death. "Anyone see what happened?" one of them asked in a low tone.

The red-haired man finished his call. "I saw it," he said. "But I couldn't make out the license. It was going too fast. Anyone else see it?" The others shook their heads. The red-haired man continued: "All I could make out was a silver-colored sports job—a Jag, maybe—going like hell. He never even slowed down."

"Did you get a look at the driver?" a woman asked.

"No. It all happened too fast. But I caught a glimpse of the passenger as he went by. A man. Black hair, dark complexion. Sort of Latin looking."

"Looks like she's had it," one of the others observed. "No signs."

"Here comes the Aid Unit," the red-haired man said. The other two faded away, leaving him as the sole guardian over the still figure on the pavement. He felt it was the least he could do. Two paramedics jumped from the cab and slid a Gurney out from the back of the van. They bent over the body, checking for vital signs. After a couple of minutes they slid the lifeless body onto the Gurney, covered it with a blanket, and lifted it into the ambulance. The red-haired man disappeared around the corner just as a police cruiser pulled up, tires squealing. A uniformed officer jumped out. "Hit and run, looks like," one of the paramedics said, as he headed for the cab of the aid unit. "She's gone," he said as the policeman lifted the blanket.

"Any witnesses?"

"They all seem to have had other things to do," the ambulance driver said. "There was one guy—I thought he might stay—red hair, kinda tall, built like a bean pole. He didn't leave his name."

"As usual." The officer did a quick check on the woman's ID, then asked where they were taking her. As the ambulance left he leaned against the side of his car and took out his notebook to record the scant details he could observe. It wasn't much.

Friday

◆

0530: Anchorage

Number four was dead.

The blades of its propeller were feathered, turned impotently into the slipstream. The Orion's wings flapped like a frightened seagull as Lieutenant Commander Frank Russo struggled to get down through the fierce gusts. As the bucking sub-hunter staggered along he could just make out the gray sliver of concrete a mile ahead.

No warning. The plane slammed upward a couple of hundred feet in a fraction of a second, driving Russo down into his seat. "Jesus!" he gasped.

"Updraft!" Jenks yelled from the copilot's seat.

"No shit!" Russo pushed the yoke forward to get the nose down. He felt the plane trying to respond.

Then a downdraft slammed into them, driving the fragile ship down toward the ground. The collision alarm's electronic voice screamed at him: "PULL UP! GLIDE SLOPE! PULL UP! GLIDE SLOPE! PULL UP!…"

"Wind shear!" With the ground coming up fast he drove the throttles to the firewall and pulled back on the yoke as hard as he dared. "Please, God!" he moaned. The plane shook in agony as the roar of the engines vibrated the cockpit.

Still falling…

"Come on, you son-of-a-bitch! Climb! Climb!"

The ground still coming up fast…
Engines screaming…
Alarms shrieking…
"Come on, you bastard! Climb!…"
Ground filling the windscreen…

The impact jerked him awake. He was sitting up in bed, his heart hammering, the collision warning still boring into his brain.

"What the hell," he said, looking around. He was sprawled across a strange bed, the sheets entwined about his legs and arms like serpents. His body was drenched. He reached out and punched the offending alarm clock.

Silence.

He rose and staggered into the bathroom, and let the shower's warmth soak in.

Why did the dream keep coming back? So vivid, so real. He could still feel the jolt of the wheels biting into the concrete at the end of that nightmarish landing.

He dressed quickly and made his way down to the restaurant. Walter Harris was working his way through an impressive platter of ham and eggs as Russo joined him.

* * *

0955: The Board Room

The high double doors of the board room opened to admit a slender woman in a teal blue business suit. She was wearing little makeup, and her only jewelry was a small gold pin on her suit lapel, a pair of miniature pilot's wings. Her finely shaped features, high cheekbones, and the sculptured style of her dark hair combined to lend her a feminine air that contrasted with the business-like simplicity of her clothes. She was Janet Gordon, vice president and chief operating officer of Pacific Coastal Airlines.

The room was empty except for Josh Edwards, who was wearing the dark blue uniform and four gold stripes of a PCA captain. Edwards was the only other airline pilot on the board, a fact that gave the two a close bond. She took a seat beside him. "Hi, Josh. How's it going out there?"

"We miss you, Janet," he said, regarding her with a smile. "Any time you'd like your old job back, I'll go back to being a line captain." Josh Edwards was the airline's chief pilot, the post Janet had relinquished to take her present position a few months earlier.

"How long has it been now?" She suppressed a twinge of envy. "Almost two years. Too long!"

"If you ever get the urge to ride with me, I'll be happy to move over to the right-hand seat." Edwards remained silent for a moment before continuing in a softer tone. "Are you all squared away now, Janet? Anything I can do to help?"

She shook her head and smiled. "You've always been a close friend, Josh. I'm over it now. Thanks for offering." Janet's husband had died suddenly five months ago of a heart condition that no one had suspected.

She glanced at her watch. The meeting had been scheduled for 10 AM. It was now 10:07. Could the meeting have been rescheduled without her knowing? Half a dozen urgent things needed her attention.

She turned her gaze to the windows, where a line of glittering aircraft landing lights strung away to the south as far as she could see. A little too closely spaced for comfort, she thought. It was always like this now. No matter how much the Port tried to expand SeaTac, the traffic always managed to keep a few years ahead of them. She turned back to Josh, who was absently drumming his fingers on the shiny table's surface. She felt suddenly isolated and alone.

Josh laughed, seeming to read her thoughts. "The SOB's done it again."
Janet blinked. "What do you mean?"

"Santiago," he said. "Just like last Wednesday. He wanted to meet me for lunch. Urgent, he said. Something about a dropoff in load factors on the Denver runs. Told me he and Carter Wycroft wanted to meet me at the Thirteen Coins at one o'clock. I got there at one sharp, only to learn they'd been there at *twelve*."

"He did it—*deliberately?*"

"Ethyl had the message from his secretary on her answering machine. One sharp. Made me look like a damn fool in front of the Old Man."

"You think he's trying to make me look foolish?"

"Of course he is! Come on, Janet! He wants everyone to troop in here whenever the meeting's really scheduled for, and let them see the two of us sitting here waiting, wasting time, with nothing better to do than—"

"Really, Josh! I don't like the man either, but surely—he isn't Machiavelli!"

"He's doing a damn good job of impersonating him. Look at it. Everyone knows he'd do anything to discredit you. He couldn't while Richard was alive. But now? You're a real thorn in his side. Consider the facts: he's a failed pilot. Killed how many in that crash? And here you sit, the successful woman pilot. Three thousand hours in the left hand seat. A flawless flying career. You've crashed through the glass ceiling. And you didn't do it on good looks, although God knows you could have."

Janet felt a sinking feeling. Josh was right. Santiago *would* pull something like this. It was the way he operated. What she couldn't understand was that Santiago was a devout Catholic. He spent a lot of time working with orphans. *Mister Altruist.* No, that was unfair. He *did* spend a lot of time with them. There had to be something worthwhile in the man. The problem was, he seemed bent on wrecking her career, and doing harm to the airline in the bargain. She shook her head angrily. "We've got to do something about him, before it's too late."

Edwards spread his hands. "Tell me how. I'm on your side. But somehow we're going to have to take on Wycroft, too. They're thick as thieves lately. Cripes, the Old Man got the board to approve that wild-ass Costa Rican maintenance scheme of his."

"I know. I'm still flabbergasted over that one. It's unthinkable! No FAA inspectors, no licensed mechanics. Can you imagine what kind of work they do down there?"

"I hear they do it outdoors!"

Janet shook her head in disbelief. "We've got to fight it, somehow. I'm hoping I can get them to reconsider it today. The board ought to be able to see what's wrong with the idea. Any idea why Carlos and Carter are so cozy?"

"Search me. But I know for a fact they are. Whatever it is, it's serious."

"It certainly is."

Janet looked out at the incoming pattern of landing jets again. It was mesmerizing. One behind the other in a steady flow, they all touched down in exactly the right sequence. Just one little glitch—if an overworked controller were to screw up for an instant…But they didn't. The system worked. But only because a lot of dedicated controllers made it work. People always made the difference.

Her thoughts were interrupted by a commotion at the board room door as a file of suited men entered the room. At last the frail figure of Carter Wycroft entered. He took his seat at the head of the table. He was followed by Carlos Santiago, and lastly a couple of Santiago's assistants carrying an easel and a stack of pasteboard charts. Santiago was a delicately built man in his forties, average height, with dark skin and shiny black hair. His dark eyes had the glitter of sharp intelligence and a hint of arrogance.

Janet glanced at her watch again. Ten-thirty on the button. *Son of a bitch!* She avoided looking across at the blank face of Carlos Santiago. He was something of an enigma. He had come to Pacific Coastal a few years ago as head of public relations. No one else had wanted the job.

No one else would, in a company keyed to the fast-paced dynamics of modern transportation. But all that had changed just two weeks ago. In a surprise move that had everyone talking, Carter Wycroft had elevated him to even higher responsibilities as Vice President in charge of marketing, as well as PR. Janet was well aware that marketing was where the airline's vital sales campaigns were conducted, and where success could bring great financial rewards to the rainmaker.

Carter Wycroft rose to his feet. The room became silent as all heads turned to regard him. "Please forgive the delay, Mrs. Gordon and gentlemen," he said in a conciliatory voice. He glanced briefly in Janet's direction. "Apparently some of you forgot that the meeting time had been changed this morning because of Mr. Santiago's special presentation. I thought it would be timely, in view of the financial situation we're likely to be facing this fall."

A murmur went around the table. Janet turned to Josh. He rolled his eyes upward.

"We've got to do something!" she muttered under her breath.

On the surface she couldn't fault what was happening. Old Wycroft was accurate, at least. A recent oil industry announcement of a coming rise in the price of jet fuel was giving all the airlines cause for concern. The only thing that was bothering her was that Santiago was going to take up the board's valuable time on something that probably had no business being discussed here.

"Mr. Santiago will present his material after the break," Wycroft announced. Janet tried to reassure herself that whatever Santiago had concocted, if it would help the airline, she must keep a positive attitude. About as easy as catching soap bubbles.

She turned to Edwards. "Have you heard anything about what he's up to?"

Edwards shrugged and shook his head. "Big mystery. You should have asked Frank. He probably knows as much as anyone."

She nodded. Frank Russo was Janet's brother, and PCA's most senior captain. Pilots were generally pretty good at picking up on airline scuttlebutt.

As the meeting got under way, Janet glanced down the length of the long table. Despite her annoyance over Santiago she felt a stir of excitement as her gaze encountered the handsome features of Roger Greninger. He was the president of Zenith Enterprises, a large west coast holding company that owned a sizable chunk of PCA stock. She nodded and smiled briefly, then averted her eyes.

The first part of the meeting droned on through the usual committee reports and financial statements. Then she was called upon to deliver her report on the operating department, which was the main item of interest so far.

She went through the airline's load factors, revenues and operating expenses. "One of the major points I want to put before you," she said, looking around the room, "is concerning the financial trouble Mr. Wycroft mentioned earlier. The increases in fuel costs are real, and they are going to hurt us. There's only one way out of this that I can see, and it's a position I take reluctantly. I've already discussed this with the chief financial officer." She glanced at Mike Shea across the table, who nodded in agreement. "We're going to have to increase fares." Several of the board members registered surprise. "I know this is not welcome news nowadays," she went on. "But we aren't alone. All the other lines are facing the same situation. I know, there's bound to be a few that try to tough it out, cutting corners on maintenance schedules and other risky schemes." She looked directly at Santiago as she said the words. He didn't flinch. "But for us there isn't any way to cut costs below their present level. I think the conclusion is unavoidable: our fares are going to have to go up."

No sooner had she finished than Santiago was on his feet. "Mrs. Gordon, I respect your assessment of a serious problem," he said in a patronizing manner. "But I'm afraid you haven't considered all the facts."

"Such as?"

"Such as the possibility that there's a way to increase our revenues that won't require raising fares. It's called increasing ticket sales."

"And just how do you propose doing that, without moving fares in the opposite direction?" Janet felt the heat coming to her cheeks. She suspected he had nothing to offer. It was just a grandstand play. But this was combat, and she loved it.

"That's exactly what I'm going to show you in my presentation." Santiago kept his face expressionless as he took his seat again. Carter Wycroft took the opportunity to call for a break. Janet sat down, barely controlling her temper.

"What'd I tell you?" Josh Edwards said at her side. "He's got us. We've been set up. He knew you were going to ask for a fare hike, and he cut you off at the knees."

"I can't believe this."

"I can. Better head for the trenches."

Josh got up and headed for the door. She was about to follow when she was stopped by the approach of Roger Greninger. He was tall—six-two or so. His silver mane of thick, wavy hair framed a firm-jawed face with deep blue eyes that peered intently from under prominent brows. He was wealthy enough to be able to afford the time for golf and tennis that made his athletic frame belie his fifty-five years. He was considered a real catch in the black tie social set he moved through, she thought. As he approached he smiled. The smile caught her by surprise and brought a flood of emotions to the surface, emotions she had wanted to remain dormant.

"Hi, Janet," Roger said in a rich baritone voice. "Got a minute?"

"Hello, Roger."

"I just wanted to let you know that my Pacific Coastal stock is making me rich, despite old Wycroft's forecasts of doom. And I'm with you. I can't imagine anything the marketing people could come up with that would change your assessment of the financial picture."

"That's good to hear, Roger. I need all the support I can get."

"I doubt that you need it. There's never been any doubt about who runs this airline."

"Thanks. I try. But I know my limitations."

"You're just being modest. It's clear to anyone with eyes that you're the business brains of this operation."

Something about the look on his face told her he had been about to add something personal, but decided not to. She inclined her head. "It's nice of you to say so." She rose from her chair, feeling momentarily dwarfed by his height. She could almost fit under his chin in her bare feet, she thought. She turned to leave.

"Janet?"

"Yes, Roger?"

"Are you going to Santiago's party tomorrow night?"

She made a face. "I'd forgotten tomorrow was Saturday. I'd rather be anywhere but there. But I guess I'll have to. He's invited everyone. Are you going?"

"I wasn't sure. But if you are, I will too. I'd like to see you. After today, maybe you might need some moral support." He paused for a moment, appearing to choose his words carefully. "Janet, I know you're pretty independent. That's one of the things I've always admired about you. But sometimes, like today, things have a way of piling up. If you ever find yourself needing a hand—for any reason—I'd be hurt if you failed to call on me for help. I really mean that."

"I appreciate that, Roger. Thanks." She left ahead of him, puzzling over his offer. What ever could she need his help for? Apart from the obvious. Maybe he was making a pass at her. Was that what he meant? She found no answer.

* * *

1033: Flight 57

Frank Russo looked across at his first officer. "Ready, Walter?" Harris gave a thumbs up. "Okay, call it in." He looked down through the side window at the scene below. They were just crossing the silver snake of the Fraser River more than six miles below them, and ahead he could see the white peak of Mount Baker gleaming brilliantly in the morning sun.

Harris selected the correct frequency on the VHF radio and made the call to Auburn Center. Russo listened to the radio exchanges and went over the descent and approach sequence in his mind. The clearance to descend came through after a few moments delay. He reached for the thrust levers and reduced power. "Flaps five," he ordered, and adjusted the trim of the CH-12 to start the long glide down toward Seattle.

The mountain swam gracefully toward them. He adjusted his rate of descent slightly and eased the plane a little closer to the snow-capped peak. Great day for taking pictures, he thought. They were just a scant thousand feet above and half a mile to the right of it when his vision began to blur. Russo knew what it was. "Take it, Walter," he ordered. He took out a handkerchief to mop his sweating brow.

Walter Harris gave his Captain an inquiring glance as he took the control yoke. "Are you okay, Skipper?"

"I shouldn't have eaten those sausages for breakfast. Heartburn, I guess. Nothing to worry about. I'll take it back in a minute."

"No sweat. I'll take it all the way in, if you like."

Russo barely heard the last. His mind was a blank, and he was trying desperately to regain control. He didn't want Harris to think anything was wrong. But it was. This was the third time this year.

"…ought to see the flight surgeon, Frank? When did you have your last checkup?"

"What's that?" Russo glared at his First Officer. Who the hell did he think he was? "I told you, I'm fine! Just a little heartburn. Just watch the rate of descent. We're a little low. I'll take it again now."

"You're sure?"

"I'm sure. I have it," he said with authority. His eyes were clear again and he felt fine. It usually left as quickly as it came. So far he'd been lucky. He really would have to see the doctor.

The rest of the approach was routine. He made a textbook landing and turned off the runway onto the taxi strip, then passed control over to Harris again and relaxed as they made their way in to their assigned gate in the south satellite terminal. Harris pulled all three thrust levers back to the shut-off position. The whine of the turbofans died to a murmur, then became silent. Russo looked out through the cockpit windows at the brilliant sunlight and stretched. "That's that," he said. "Another notch on the belt."

"Who's counting?" Harris laughed. He was a younger man, of average height, slightly built, with Nordic blue eyes and blond hair, a contrast to Russo's dark Italian features. He also stretched as he released his seat harness. "It's good to be home for a weekend. Looks like we're in for a little Indian Summer." He rose stiffly from his seat. "We're taking the boat up to the San Juans for the weekend. Have you made any plans?"

"Afraid not," Russo said, rising from his seat. "I'm filling in for Mitch Degan on the Denver run tomorrow. He's come down with the crud, and the doc's grounded him."

"The crud?"

"Flu!" Russo laughed. "That's what we used to call it in the Navy."

"We're still on for Honolulu Sunday, right?" Harris asked.

"Count on it. And a nice layover on Waikiki Beach. Although we could probably do just as well on one of our own beaches this time. This weather is really something else!"

"Think it'll hold for a while now?"

"God, I hope so," Russo laughed. "Surely we're entitled to a little break. Remember Mark Twain's comment?"

"What was that?"

"He said he never knew how cold a winter could be until he spent a summer on Puget Sound."

"Pretty perceptive!"

Russo reached for the maintenance log books, thumbed through to the current page, and made his routine entries. The trip down from Anchorage had been without incident. Normal for the new CH-12s. "Can you think of anything for the log, Walter?"

"They were complaining about the audio for the music program back in the cabin," Harris said. "That's all."

"Just one channel? Or the whole system?"

"Just channel five."

"Which one is that?"

"The Hollywood film commentary, I think."

"Not a big deal," Russo laughed, making the entry into the logs. No matter how trivial, it had to be recorded. He closed the log book and returned it to its storage rack. "Are you hanging around for lunch, Walter?"

"Could be. What'd you have in mind?"

"I was thinking of that soup deal over at the Thirteen Coins."

"Sounds good to me." Harris followed his captain back to the exit leading to the portable metal boarding ladder. Pacific Coastal pilots entered the gate area from the ground level, where the mechanics waited to debrief them before they got away.

Russo stood on the small metal platform at the top of the ladder and avoided looking down. He would die if anyone ever discovered his secret, but he was terrified of heights. His palms glistened with sweat as he turned to face the ladder and descended backwards. It was weird, he thought. Flying at forty thousand feet didn't faze him at all. But any time he had to balance himself on an open structure that was more than five feet above the ground he felt dizzy, fearful of falling. He still remembered the job he had once had as a teenager working for a construction firm. The foreman had wanted him to stand atop a concrete wall and haul wooden joists up to lay them across from wall to wall for the flooring of the building. It was only a single story up, but he had frozen, unable to move, and the foreman had finally had to let him get down and work on less demanding jobs on the ground.

As he made it to the ground he wondered if this might be related to the dizziness and near blackouts he'd been experiencing. Could be, he thought. So far, no one, not even Walter Harris, had discovered his secret. He intended to keep it that way. But he would have to see his doctor. Today.

1040: The Board Room

Santiago glanced in Carter Wycroft's direction and the two men exchanged silent signals. He rose and went to the head of the table where an assistant was ready to flip charts for him.

"I'll try to keep this brief, so we can have time for questions," he intoned. "I suggested before the break that there was a way to avoid having to raise fares and still manage to survive the coming fuel price increases. Phase one of my cost-cutting was to cut our maintenance costs by having it done offshore. That's proving to be a wise decision. We're just getting the first planes back from Costa Rica now. Phase two is a new approach to promoting sales. And here it is." He motioned to his assistant, who uncovered the first pasteboard chart. It was entitled *THE EXCITING SKIES.*

"That's it: I call it the Exciting Skies. The reason people aren't flying more often is that we haven't tried to make it interesting for them. Flying today is about as exciting as riding a bus. What we need is to add a little spice to our passengers' fare. Get those retirees to spend a little of their kids' inheritances, instead of sitting on their duffs watching soaps."

There followed an animated description of several ideas that, to Janet, appeared laughable, except that some of them bordered on dangerous. What he proposed was that their pilots jazz up their flying by engaging in a few new gimmicks. Most of it was aimed at promoting a new image for the airline emphasizing youth, vigor, pizazz. "Our stewies need new uniforms," he claimed, and presented a color picture of what he had in mind. There were a few gasps around the table. Janet broke into loud laughter. There seemed no point in protesting. For once she was grateful for political correctness. No airline would dare promote such flagrant sexism. Then he got into some suggestions for flying practices. Snappy takeoffs and steep climbouts; faster enroute course changes where the passengers could "really feel like they were flying"; steeper descents and snappier flares on landing. The *piece de resistance,* as he put it, would be having pilots fly in close to the mountains, so the passengers could have lots of "photo-ops".

Santiago finished his presentation and returned to his seat. Janet looked down at the pages of notes in front of her, trying to control the revulsion that had been building all through the briefing. Never in her long career in aviation had she been exposed to such flagrant barnstorming. There was nothing fundamentally wrong with giving the passengers a little excitement for their money, within the bounds of rationality, she admitted. But what had his list of suggestions to do with rationality?

She rose to her feet and confronted Santiago. "Have you completely lost touch with reality?" she asked in a monotone tinged with barely contained fury. "Is this your own invention, or did you have help from some of those PR—"

"I think we ought to give the board members a chance to discuss these ideas, Janet, before we shoot them down cold." It was Carter Wycroft's voice cutting in. He had risen to his feet to face her.

She regarded him coolly. "Mr. Wycroft, I tried to stop him when he proposed that maintenance boondoggle with the Costa Ricans. But you intervened, and now we're stuck with a contract we can't break. Are you now proposing that we listen to *this* lunacy? Because if you are, you can have my resignation any time you want it. Pacific Coastal didn't get to where it is today following such inane policies."

"Let's examine it with cool heads, Janet," he said in the tone of a politician. "I'd like to hear the board's reactions."

"Mr. Wycroft, when I have a medical problem, I consult a physician, not an witch doctor. There are only two airline pilots on this board: Captain Edwards here, and myself. This is a discussion that belongs in the flight safety department. How can the two of us oppose the rest of the board members, who don't know the first thing about the seriousness of what is being proposed here? You might as well turn this airline over to Santiago's Public Relations ninnies and let *them* run it! And when our airplanes start falling out of the sky—which they may very well do, once we start getting our planes back from Costa Rica—maybe we'll let *them* explain it to the National Transportation Safety Board, and to the Federal Aviation Administration—*and* to the stockholders, who aren't going to be very pleased when they see their stock plummeting following our first disaster." She held her breath for a moment, pondering her words. Maybe she'd gone a little overboard. Most of her anger was at the man himself, not what he was proposing. She could easily countermand anything that was dangerous. She just wasn't about to let any cardboard executive tell her how to do her job.

"There's no question here of violating safety regulations, Janet," Wycroft said a little too quickly. He spread his hands in a gesture of conciliation. "I'll admit that perhaps some of Santiago's ideas go a bit far, but let's not throw out the baby with the bath water." A few snickers went around the table at the overworked cliché. Wycroft was not known for his originality. "Maybe we could vote on each one of the suggestions in turn." He looked around the board table for support. Heads were nodding.

"I'll submit my objections to the NTSB and the FAA if you approve this poppycock!"

Santiago jumped to his feet and cut in: "I wouldn't advise that. This airline doesn't need that kind of notoriety. You might find yourself suddenly alone, without any friends." Santiago avoided Janet's stare. Instead, he was looking at Wycroft. Janet couldn't believe it when a nuance of a smile touched Wycroft's lips. *The bastard!* she thought. *The spineless bastard is going to back Carlos! I can't believe this!* She resumed her seat in silence. Words were futile. She was damned if she could fathom what kind of weapon Santiago was in possession of that could make him so confident of his position, and so uncharacteristically arrogant in stating it openly. Usually he preferred the covert attack, without even the warning a rattlesnake would give.

As it turned out, however, her outburst seemed to have caught the critical attention of several of the board members, who were just as concerned about avoiding any hint of risky practices as she was. By the end of the voting the board had eliminated all of the more dangerous items. Rapid takeoffs and landings were felt to be defensible, since they would help to reduce the ever-growing noise problem at SeaTac, which would placate a lot of homeowners in neighboring cities under the approaches. She knew the FAA had already approved these procedures at most big-city airports. And Frank had told her that many of the pilots, himself included, were already buzzing the mountains to keep the camera buffs happy.

As the meeting came to a close Janet realized how cleverly she had been maneuvered by Santiago. She had wanted to get the board to approve needed fare increases, and to draw more attention to the riskiness of the Costa Rican maintenance scheme. Her plans had been shredded by all this exciting skies nonsense. Was he that clever? Or had she been lax in her failure to anticipate this attack? She avoided making eye contact with any of the other board members on the way out. She just wanted to get out of there without talking to anyone. She had not felt the need for Richard's help for a long time. She was feeling it now.

1145: The President's Office

Carlos Santiago poured a generous amount of Crown Royal from a cut-glass decanter. "May I pour you one, Carter?"

Wycroft cringed inwardly at the unwelcome familiarity, but forced himself to conceal his outrage. "I'll get my own," he said. Wycroft had invited Santiago to come to his office after the meeting. He joined Santiago at the sideboard that served as his wet bar and poured himself a glass of Perrier over ice. He needed a stiff drink more than anything right now, but he'd have to wait. The two men took their drinks into Wycroft's conference room and sat at a large circular table.

"That wasn't so bad," Santiago said.

"I wish I could share your enthusiasm, Carlos. Janet Gordon is nobody's fool. She knows what you've gotten us into down south. I'm not convinced we wouldn't be better off breaking that contract. We managed to keep her from bringing it up, but it was close."

"We did it. That's all that matters, Carter. Don't worry. The Costa Rican deal will save us a pile. And my exciting skies idea will fly, too, despite Janet Gordon's negative attitude. People love the excitement of flying. It brings out the Indiana Jones in them. There's no need to consider raising fares. That could be the end of this airline. Trust me!" He took a drink of his whiskey and pushed his legs out in front of him, head back, eyes half closed, a smile playing about the corners of his mouth.

"That's a pretty cynical attitude toward our customers," Wycroft retorted angrily. "They don't fly for excitement! They fly for a hundred reasons. They're businessmen, vacationers, school kids—anything but a bunch of thrill-seekers! They are the source of our revenues, and they're entitled to our best efforts to guarantee them what they've paid for: fast, safe, efficient transportation. That's how we pushed the railroads out of the passenger business. We can do it better. Faster. Cheaper. *Not more exciting!*" He forced himself to get control of his emotions. There was no point in lecturing someone like Santiago about business ethics. Nor himself, he admitted with shame, for this whole mess was his own doing. "I'd appreciate it if you would be a little more conservative when addressing the board. You're in a responsible position of authority now. Act like it! For the sake of the airline, if for no other."

"Naturally. And I do appreciate your support, Carter."

Wycroft recognized the patronizing tone of Santiago's voice. The underlying message was clear: *as per our agreement.* He wondered for the hundredth time why he'd ever allowed himself to get into such a predicament. But of course he knew the answer. He had to change the subject. "Let's get back to that Costa Rican venture. How's it working out? You're absolutely sure it's safe? The FAA's approved their work?"

"Sure! The only difference is it costs us a fraction of what it costs up here."

"How's that?"

"Easy! Their mechanics don't have as high living standards in Costa Rica. I should know. I used to live right next door in Nicaragua. Don't worry. The FAA's sent inspectors down there to look over their facilities, and they've given them a clean bill of health."

"They'd better not screw up," Wycroft grunted. Having maintenance done offshore had to be risky. Still, if they could cut their maintenance costs by that much…He knew they weren't alone. Lots of the small commuter lines were doing it.

"I know they won't. They have too much invested down there. It's an American venture, you know. Not a Costa Rican one. They know what they're doing."

Wycroft's mind had shifted to the really serious matter he'd wanted to talk to him about. Even now he hesitated bringing it up. But he had to know where things stood. "What have you heard about the other matter?" he asked.

"Not a thing. They don't have anything else to go on. How could they?"

"You never know," Wycroft said. He had seen the initial reports in the newspapers, then the follow-ups the next day. They all expressed outrage at the merciless killing of an innocent woman and her unborn child, and demanded that the police find the perpetrator. MADD had been demanding the death penalty if it turned out that alcohol had been involved. Wycroft shuddered at the thought.

"The cops're too busy with drive-by shootings and drug busts. Don't worry about it. Time is on your side. The longer it's been with nothing new, the better."

Wycroft noted Santiago's words. *Your* side. Not *our* side. "You'd better be right," he muttered. He took another sip of his Perrier and looked out the windows at the airport scene across the highway. Maybe Carlos was right. It had been two weeks, after all. With each passing day he felt a little safer. But how could he ever feel good about it? That, really, was what was plaguing him. "I keep thinking that perhaps it would be best to—"

"Don't even think it!" Santiago snapped, his voice tinged with icy hardness. "This is no time for nobility. If you start getting twinges of conscience, do like I do and donate some money to your favorite charity. The time for conscience was two weeks ago. It's too late now."

"As long as you keep your end of the agreement," Wycroft muttered. "You're in it as deep as I am, now."

"Oh, no! It was your doing. All yours!"

"You'd better keep quiet about it, for your own good."

"And if I don't? What would you do?"

Wycroft felt his stomach churn as he met the dark eyes of his adversary. He knew there was no answer. There never had been. It was hopeless, and he had known it from the beginning. If what he had done ever came to light his punishment would be severe. Carlos might get a light sentence as an accessory. He might even get off with nothing if he volunteered to testify against him. And what would it do to the airline? It would destroy it. He was beginning to appreciate that he was powerless to oppose Santiago. He had made a pact with the devil, and he would have to stick to it. That he was forced to lend support to such an opportunist went against everything he held sacred. But the alternative was unthinkable. He would never be able to survive a prison sentence.

As Santiago left Wycroft went to the bar. He spilled the liquor as he poured himself a stiff one. He took a deep draft of the smooth liquor and waited for it to hit his blood stream and soothe his tortured brain. That's more like it, he thought, and let his mind wander back to the night two weeks ago when the whole nightmare had started.

He couldn't remember the trip home. In fact, most of the evening was a complete blackout. All he knew was what Carlos had told him the next morning. They'd been at a cocktail party in Laurelhurst. Carlos needed a ride home. They were heading west on forty-fifth, on their way to the southbound on-ramp to I-5. A traffic light turned from green to amber at a pedestrian crossing. He floored it. The Jaguar leaped forward. Neither of them saw the woman's figure stepping away from the curb. Before they knew what happened there was a shriek and a loud thump. Carlos told him he had pleaded with him to stop, but he had refused, insisting they had to get the hell out of there. Carlos made him spend the rest of the night at his home on Mercer Island. Early the next morning he drove back to his own home in Hunt's Point. The car had remained locked in his garage ever since.

The evidence of his nightmare was there in his garage mocking him every time he looked at it. The beautiful silver Type E Jag he'd brought back from England two years ago was now an ugly mess, its front right corner mangled.

"You should have let me drive you home," Carlos had told him that morning. *If only you'd had sense enough to let him. He'd have done a lot better job than you did.*

He picked up this morning's *Post/Intelligencer* from the table they'd been sitting at moments earlier and returned to his desk to scan it for any new breaks in the case. Still nothing. A relief. He wondered what to do about the evidence. Was two weeks long enough to wait? Probably. Better to wait till Monday or Tuesday, though. By then there might be other solutions to his problems with Carlos Santiago. He was not without friends in high places, after all.

* * *

1400: The Doctor's Office

Frank Russo was apprehensive. The tests had gone on for a whole hour, and still his doctor hadn't voiced an opinion. They'd been friends too long for him to hold back. "What's the story, Doc?" he asked.

"I can't find anything that could be causing the vertigo, Frank. You say you've always had this fear of heights?" Russo nodded. "It's probably related, then. Lots of people have it. Even airline pilots," the doctor grinned.

Russo had been seeing Graham McFadden these past two years instead of going to the regular airline doctors. He'd considering trying to hide his problem from the airline, but knew he wouldn't be able to live with that. If push came to shove, he'd have to quit flying and take a desk job. PCA owed him that much.

McFadden seemed to be reading his thoughts. "Shouldn't you be seeing your airline doctor?" he asked.

"I thought I'd like to get your opinion first, Graham. Airline doctors don't work for the pilots. They get paid by the insurance weevils. But I'm not going to try to hide it, if it's serious. Am I going to have to quit flying?" He held his breath for the answer.

"I wouldn't think so. I can give you a prescription that will eliminate the blackouts. Just make sure you've always got them handy. Sometimes vertigo can be caused by a lot of stress, but since you've always had it I think I can rule that out. It isn't life threatening, and this medication will avoid any recurrence of the symptoms."

"Will this cure the problem?" he asked, looking at the prescription the doctor handed him.

"Nothing can take it away, Frank. All the pills will do is relieve the symptoms. Just keep them handy."

"I'll do that, Doc," Russo said, rising. He shook McFadden's hand. "Thanks a million. I couldn't stand having to give up flying while I'm still feisty enough to fly the midnight mail."

"Forty-five isn't young, Frank. You're going to have to slow down a little."

"I see your point. Thanks, Graham."

* * *

On the way home Russo called Janet at the office. She answered after several rings. "Jan, this is Frank."

"How's my intrepid flyer today?" she asked.

"Something wrong, Jan? You sound a little scratchy."

"Board meeting day. You've never had that experience. Consider yourself lucky!"

"Maybe I'm a little closer to it that you think. I just left my doctor's office."

"Your doctor? Haven't you been well?"

He told her about his dizzy spells and blackouts. They had no secrets from each other. "He did a bunch of tests. He doesn't think it's serious. But I'll have to go see our own medics. I'm sure they'll have a different perspective. Got a nice, comfortable desk job for me?"

"Any time, Frank. We could use you." She paused for a moment. "Should you be flying?"

"Sure, I'm okay. The doc gave me a prescription. But I'll be seeing our own airline doctor as soon as I get back from Honolulu."

"Want me to make an appointment for you?"

"Don't you trust me?"

"Within certain limits, yes. I just thought you might be busy getting ready for your flight. You're still taking Mitch Degan's Denver run tomorrow?"

"Yeah. Busy schedule!"

"I'll make it for next week, after you get back from Hawaii. Okay?"

"Okay."

"Make sure you get that prescription filled before you leave."

"I will."

"Promise?"

Russo chuckled. "Promise. Love you!"

"Me too. Take care, Frank."

"Bye."

* * *

1845: Hunt's Point

"Where are you going? I want to talk to you!"

Frank Russo had just risen from the dinner table. The tone of his wife's voice conveyed an urgency that surprised him.

"I have to get ready for my Denver trip, Marla." He regarded her with a questioning look. Surely she hadn't forgotten already? She looked terrible. Her normally attractive hair was tumbled in a disheveled tangle about her shoulders, and her skin had a pallor about it that suggested exhaustion. She'd told him she was coming down with a cold. Perhaps that was the reason for her appearance and the memory lapse. "Give me a few minutes to pack, then I'll join you for coffee in the family room," he said gently. "And maybe you ought to take some vitamin C for that cold. I'll have Louise make you some hot lemonade to go with it." On the way to the bedroom he summoned the maid and explained what he wanted.

Their bedroom was a large, airy room with windows running the length of one wall, the curtains now open to provide a panoramic view of Lake Washington. Across the lake he could see the glare of lights at Husky Stadium against a sky of crimson streaked with thin bands of dark gray clouds. The room was furnished with an eye to utility as well as beauty. Dominating the room were two custom-made king-sized twin beds. At first he had objected to the twin beds, but that had been long ago. He had since appreciated that it allowed him to slip in and out of bed without disturbing her, a frequent necessity for an airline pilot.

Their marriage had been troubled for a long time. Although they rarely talked about it now, their main problem was children. Or the lack of them, he thought sadly. Marla had become

pregnant during their early years, but there had been a complication, and the child, a son he had wanted dearly, had not survived. Afterward they learned that she could never conceive again.

From time to time the subject of adoption came up. At first Marla had been enthusiastic, but lately she had changed her mind. He wondered, with rising hopes, if she might have been having second thoughts about adoption. That might be what she wanted to talk to him about.

He packed what he would need for his trip, then returned to the family room. Marla was seated at one end of the huge, overstuffed sofa. He glanced at the half-empty wine glass on the end table beside her. "Did you take the vitamin C and lemonade?" he queried.

"I decided on a glass of sherry instead," she said. "Would you like some?"

"No thanks," he answered. "I'm flying tomorrow morning. There are no vitamins in sherry," he added dourly.

"I needed the stimulant." She sat upright, drained the wine glass, and refilled it. "Please sit down, Frank. We have to talk."

It sounded like a command. Evidently it wasn't going to be about adoption, which he had to admit was now becoming a little too late for them. "Your nickel," he said, taking a seat in an easy chair across from her.

She looked at him for a long moment, took a deep breath, and announced in a level voice tinged with hardness: "Frank, I'd like a divorce."

He sat there staring at her wide-eyed, unable to think of an appropriate answer. Anything but that, he thought, his mind rebelling, refusing to accept such an impossible turn of events. "Marla...Marla, why?"

She ran her fingers through her tangled hair, and a trace of a smile played about her full, sensuous mouth. "You really had no idea, had you?" He neither nodded nor shook his head. He just continued to stare at her, unable to believe this was really happening. "Poor, dear Frank," she went on. "You just thought everything would work itself out for us. But how? On what basis? We don't do anything together any more. Haven't for years. We don't even make love any more!"

"That isn't exactly my fault," he protested. "I'm not the one that pushes you away." A flicker of an emotion crossed her face. He couldn't tell whether it was guilt or mockery. "Why now, of all times? Why not long ago, if you haven't been happy?"

"Something has changed, Frank." She straightened all the way up, seeming to square herself for an effort she did not want to exert. "There's someone else now. Has been for some time."

There was a long silence as he tried to quell the churning of his insides. He tried to tell himself he'd been expecting something like this, but without much success. His heart was pounding so loud he wondered if she might be able to hear it. "Is it—someone I know?" He had to ask, but he was fearful of the answer.

"No-ooo." There was no trace of emotion on her face, no telltale flushing to tell him she could be lying. Just the tiny break in her voice. "No, there's no chance of that." She paused for a moment, as though struggling with a question she didn't want to drag out and examine. At last she said, "I'm not going to tell you who it is. Except that he's someone that knows what I need, and has promised to get it for me."

"And what, may I ask, would that be?" He was overcoming the initial shock, and now he felt himself succumbing to growing anger at the effrontery of her demands.

She flared angrily. "To get out of this God-forsaken frontier hick town! Back to civilization, where there's more to do than go to God-damned Husky games!"

Frank rose slowly. He looked down at her for a few moments without speaking, his arms hanging limply at his sides. A kaleidoscope of emotions surged through his brain. For a moment he struggled with the impulse to strike her. At last he forced himself to respond with a leaden heaviness: "I guess I've known this was coming. It isn't a bolt out of the blue. Okay, if you want it that bad, you can have it—if you think that's the answer. You aren't a Catholic, so I guess you can do it without any qualms. As far as I'm concerned, I'll have to see about having the marriage annulled, and that's going to be very difficult. But I want you to understand one thing clearly, Marla: since this is your idea, and you've admitted you're involved with another man, you're not to expect any settlement." He held up his hand to quell her sudden protests. "You asked for this! You may take whatever is yours. But this," he said, spreading his arms to indicate the house, "is mine. I'm not letting your lover take my home away from me."

"The courts may have something to say about that," she countered, her eyes suddenly flashing venom. "This is a community property state!"

"Don't count on that, Marla," he said. The tone of his voice was final, conveying nothing of the inner turmoil he was experiencing. "That only applies in divorces. An annulment means we were never married. Never married!" he repeated. "So there's no community property to split. I hope you enjoy your new friend. As for me, it's going to be hard. I loved you, Marla. I guess you never appreciated how much. Maybe that's partly my fault. I can't hate you. But the love…I guess we lost that somewhere along the way. I wish—I wish it could have been otherwise." The break in his voice was the only hint he would give her of the devastation he was feeling inside as he left her.

Saturday

◆

1230: Ballard

Karen Braun opened the back door and whistled sharply. An answering bark and the scampering of paws in loose gravel came from the backyard as a large, multicolored dog of mixed ancestry came bounding and wagging up to her. The dog jumped up and it was all Karen could do to keep from being bowled over.

"Felix! Stop it!" Laughing, she tried half-heartedly to fend him off. As she wrestled with him Felix barked happily, clearly recognizing the leather leash in her hand and its significance.

"Wanta go with me for a cup of coffee, Felix?" she asked. "Naw, you don't want a cup of coffee! But you do want a little exercise, don't you, fella?" She ruffled the thick fur about his neck as she snapped the leash to his collar. Felix's tail doubled its wagging rate and he let out a few excited yelps. "Okay, let's go! We're going to meet the guys and talk about our big event," she explained, as she opened the gate leading to the front of white Cape-Cod home.

Her home was the only thing she allowed to conflict with her work. Renovating it absorbed most of her off-duty time. She thought about that for a moment and smiled. "The home and you, Felix," she said, and turned to the right at the sidewalk. Karen firmly believed that when she talked to Felix the communication was two-way, because she understood her dog's moods and facial expressions as well as she might have known those of the children that she'd always wanted.

Karen was an attractive woman with a brilliant mind, but all through her college years and afterward her shyness had kept her from meeting men. Then her research job in the U of W's molecular biology lab had become uppermost in her life, pushing her longing for a family into the background. She paused for Felix to mark a hedge with his scent.

The 'big event' was one she had been looking forward to all summer. At last she was going to get a chance to climb Mount Rainier, the highest peak in the state of Washington. It was Mark Svenson who had gotten her interested in mountain climbing a couple of years earlier. Feeling left out of things when he went off without her on his frequent climbs, she had coaxed him to teach her. It was much preferable to sitting at home with nothing to do. So she got him to register her for a course with the Mountaineers, and after spending all their weekends this spring and summer reconnoitering the foothills and lower peaks of the Cascades, Mark had taken her along on a climb up one of the more difficult peaks with his climbing team. She had returned an avid disciple.

A problem had surfaced during her first climb. She became aware of the extra deference being accorded her because of her status as the only woman on the team. There was a succession of little acts of kindness: letting her carry the lightest pack, helping her tie into the rope, and a host of other special concessions they wouldn't think of had she been a man. The old-fashioned part of her felt honored at all the pampering, but her new woman side rebelled at the implication of feminine weakness. It became clear to her that she was going to have to work hard at being accepted as a mountaineer, and not some sort of softie that had to be carried up and down the hills. She was resolved to achieve that victory on this climb.

Karen was twenty-eight, of average height, but had a body that looked deceptively fragile. This may have been the reason for some to view her as incapable of tough physical challenges. Actually, she was incredibly strong for her size. Her body was remarkably well tuned from the rigors of her mountaineering course. But long before that, her fondness for long bike rides had eliminated every trace of fat, including from her face, leaving it somewhat gaunt looking. But she made up for the gauntness with a warm smile, a rosy complexion, beguiling blue eyes, and platinum blond hair that she wore in a single, shining braid, usually coiled atop her head. "Heidi the goat girl," Mark would say, to tease her.

Karen had to wait again for Felix to decorate a fire hydrant along Market Street. As she approached Starbuck's she could see Alex Papoulis's teddy-bear shape through the front windows.

Alex came outside to greet Karen and Felix. He was a stocky man, about five feet five or six, very powerfully built, with the neck and shoulders of a wrestler—which he was, as an amateur. Under his bushy black eyebrows his large, dark gray eyes sparkled with humor, but at the same time they mirrored a great intellect and a genuine compassion for others. He had a grin that extended from one side of his round face to the other. What was left of his hair was jet black, as was his luxuriant mustache and full beard. He was of Greek ancestry, a second-generation American, and was working on a doctorate in math at the university. Alex and Mark alternated as leaders of the team, although Alex's resume as a climber far exceeded Mark's. He had climbed extensively in the Alps.

"Hi, Karen," he said with a grin. He slipped his arm around her slender waist and gave her a scratchy peck on the cheek, then bent to greet Felix with a pat on the head. He took Felix's leash from her and made it fast to the leg of a circular sidewalk table. None of their group were part of the latte-and-croissant crowd that usually populated Starbuck's, but that wasn't necessary. Starbuck's had plenty of other options.

He turned to her. "What'll you have? Tea?" She nodded. "Can I give Felix a biscuit?" He took one from a stash in his jacket pocket.

"Just one. You guys are going to spoil him."

"The others should be along any minute," he said. He left her at the sidewalk table and went into the coffee house, returning after a few minutes carrying two steaming mugs and a paper sack. As they talked, Felix lay under the table crunching happily.

Fifteen minutes later she saw a pair of husky youths waiting for the light to change across the street. Eric Whitely and Malcolm Krouse waved as they crossed the busy intersection. Felix stretched his leash to sniff the legs of the newcomers.

Eric's husky frame topped Alex's by a good eight inches and twenty or so pounds. Twenty-three years old, he had just graduated from UCLA the spring before as a journalism major. He had joined the northward migration and now made his home in Seattle. He met Papoulis and Svenson at a meeting of the Mountaineers, and Svenson helped him find a job on the *Seattle Globe*, where Svenson worked as a columnist.

Malcolm Krouse, the youngest member of the team, was an undergraduate student in mathematics at the university, where he had become friendly with Alex at one of Alex's math labs.

Alex rose and shook hands with the two. He grinned broadly and said: "We knew you two would make it if we met at a place where there was food."

The two laughed. Eric said: "We just had lunch. Mark's coming?"

Alex shook his head. "He's going down to LA for a few days. There'll just be the four of us. Oh, by the way, I thought we might meet over at Karen's house tonight. She's offered to let us check over our gear in her basement."

"We'll buy the groceries, if we can talk you into cooking dinner for us," Eric proposed, grinning boyishly.

"You guys!" Karen laughed. "Why don't you find wives to look after your bellies? Okay, but never mind the groceries. I have plenty."

"Then I'll get the dessert," Eric insisted. "There's a great Danish bakery just north of here, and you wouldn't believe the stuff they put out."

Karen laughed again. "We know all about Larson's! It's Seattle's only compensation for the nine months of rain."

"Nine months?!" Eric Whitely looked at Karen in amazement. His face gave the impression that he might be regretting his decision to move north.

"You'll get used to it," Papoulis assured him. "And you won't need to worry about sunburns. We just rust up here."

"You're kidding me, right?"

No one cracked a smile. Eric bore it good naturedly.

The four companions sat round the circular table. Eric and Malcolm ate their way through an impressive array of pastries as Papoulis dug into his jacket pocket and unfolded a plastic-coated contour map of Mount Rainier, which he spread out flat on the table. "I've been thinking about an assault up the north side…"

* * *

1815: The Princess Maria

Carlos Santiago watched the caterers putting the finishing touches to a long buffet table. There was a mound of jumbo shrimp over a bed of crushed ice, a chilled glazed ham surrounded by pineapple rings, and a baron of beef being trimmed by a white-jacketed server. All of this was flanked by trays of exotic hors d'euvres and an assortment of raw vegetables and dips for the health freaks. He grinned at the thought. He was certain they wouldn't be passing up all the free booze, which was hardly the healthy complement to the raw veggies.

Santiago had been planning this party for weeks, but now that it was about to begin he felt his anticipation building. He strolled over to the wet bar that was part of the yacht's permanent furnishings and poured a generous amount of Crown Royal over crackling ice cubes. He let his fingers move sensuously over the crystal. He loved fine things. They were possessions, and Santiago valued material possessions highly, not so much for their aesthetic value as for the feelings of envy they would produce in some of his guests. He owned the yacht for the same reason. It was the kind of thing he had heard that wealthy men possessed, and he yearned to be counted among that fellowship.

He thought about his long, twelve-year struggle since leaving Nicaragua. He'd had to fight his way up the rungs of the corporate ladder against the resentment and bigotry of the Anglo pilots. They regarded his slight physical stature as definitely un-macho. That he wasn't an active airline pilot was viewed as a shortcoming, though he had been one in Nicaragua—about that part of his past he was content to keep silent. And of course they sniped at his Latin heritage, of which he was intensely proud. But all that had changed just two weeks ago when fortune had smiled on him in a way he never could have anticipated. Now, with the grudging—but so far willing—help of Carter Wycroft, his success seemed assured. There had been moments when he wondered whether he could pull it off. But Carter Wycroft was an intellectual, and guilt in the mind of an intellectual was a powerful toxin.

He gazed about the opulent interior of the yacht. Its sixty-five-foot length allowed room for a galley and three luxuriously appointed staterooms below and an upper deck that was dominated by the huge main salon, which extended aft from the wheelhouse to the rounded stern. The interior was beautiful in its functionality. It was paneled in oiled teak, with port holes framed in dark mahogany with polished brass fittings. The salon floor was of oak parquet, and the white leather lounge chairs were all securely bolted in place. The salon had an open area that was large enough to serve as a dance floor, which was what his guests would be using it for tonight.

There was one other aspect of the evening that was giving him a sense of accomplishment, and more than a little anticipation. Marla was coming. He had addressed the invitation to Captain and Mrs. Russo, of course, but he knew perfectly well that the flying half of the family wouldn't be back from Denver in time to interfere with his plans.

He took a slim cellular phone out of his shirt pocket and dialed. Marla's voice came on after two rings. "Hello, darling," he said, and listened to the vibrant excitement of her voice.

* * *

1823: Hunt's Point

Marla Russo hung up the telephone and returned to her place before the large vanity mirror. She picked up a fine-tipped brush and applied the finishing touches to her mouth. Carlos had been pleased when she told him she would be coming alone. But of course he must have known Frank would be in Denver.

She rose and inspected the sweep of the black silk gown in the full-length mirror, turning to one side and then the other, tilting her patrician head to emphasize the glitter of diamonds that graced her delicate ears. She had once been considered beautiful. Now, having just passed the age of forty, she was beginning to show a little wear. Her figure, once the envy of the New York jet set, was a little over-generous around the hips. She always wore long, flowing gowns to hide the evidence. It was working tonight.

Her face was beginning to show her age, too. She was on the verge of considering a facelift to correct the crows' feet and slight puffiness about her tired-looking gray eyes. Her hair was still her crowning jewel. That part, at least, was easy. Regular visits to a good hairdresser kept it looking lovely. She was wearing it up tonight in a new style that she knew Carlos would admire. He was one of the few men she knew who really enjoyed the sight of a woman dressed in a formal gown. The rest of the men in Seattle seemed to prefer tank tops and blue jeans. Par for the northwest, she thought.

She hated Seattle. To her it was the end of the cultural trail, an uncivilized wilderness town populated by bearded graduates of the sixties, Bill Gates's software nerds, and of course the chain-saw-wielding "K-Mart cowboys" who thought they were living on the frontier. As far as Marla was concerned, the word frontier fitted the northwest perfectly. She yearned for New York's soaring towers, its theaters, the Philharmonic, the Met, and of course the shopping. And that, she hoped, was where Carlos would be the answer to her aspirations. Carlos said he shared her contempt for Seattle. He'd told her he was just marking time here, waiting for a chance to make a move to one of New York's large advertising firms, where they would appreciate his novel marketing intuitions. And when he did, he had promised she would go with him, if she wanted to. And she would, too. Either as his wife or as his mistress. She didn't care which. Marriage could come later, if that was what they both wanted. But first she would have to divorce Frank and get out of this one-horse town.

The thought of the divorce gave her a momentary stab of guilt—as close as Marla ever came to that feeling. Frank had loved and cherished her, and she had responded to his love in the beginning, although that had been a long time ago. He had been very good to her in his way. She knew how much her demand for a divorce had hurt him, despite his attempt to hide it last night. But then she thought of his refusal to consider any kind of settlement, and her feelings of guilt gave way to angry frustration. She'd have to consult her lawyer about that. Washington was a community property state, and half of everything should come to her. What the hell was an annulment, anyway? Her lawyer would know. There had to be a way she could block it.

She called a taxi. Another boring party. But not so boring later, she thought, giving her lustrous hair a final pat. Dear Carlos. He really was a godsend. A genuine Latin lover.

1855: Ballard

"There's just one thing missing," Karen mused, looking over the mountainous pile of pack boards, rucksacks, multicolored ropes, ice axes, pitons, piton hammers, karabiners, boots, crampons, extra clothing, food, canteens, and all the other odds and ends they had piled on the floor of her basement.

"What's that?" Malcolm asked.

"The helicopter to lift it up to the summit." She laughed at her own joke.

"We'll take it in to White River by truck," Alex Papoulis explained. "There won't be that much to carry. About thirty pounds each, I figure. A little less for puny little Miss Goldilocks." He gave her a nudge and a grin. Karen took his jibe good-naturedly.

Back upstairs, they sat round her kitchen table while Karen prepared dinner. "Have you picked out a route yet, Alex?" Eric asked.

"I haven't decided on the exact route yet." He spread out a contour map of the Rainier park area. "I've always wanted to try Liberty Ridge."

"Think we're up to a climb like that?" Malcolm wondered.

Alex grinned. "Sure! As long as I don't get too tired hauling you kids up the rocks and ice cliffs!"

"Cut it out, you guys!" Karen scolded. "Let's eat."

"All *right!*" the two younger members of the team chorused.

Karen served one of her famous German banquets—wiener snitzel, red cabbage, and potato pancakes—to the acclaim of the three hungry climbers. Alex and Eric departed right after dinner, but Malcolm remained for a few minutes, apparently concerned about something. "Do you really think we can handle a climb like that?" he asked.

Karen studied him for a moment. She thought she understood. Malcolm was the youngest, and had less experience. It was natural that he would be worried. And natural that he wouldn't want to show it before the others. She wasn't quite old enough for the role, but she was having motherly feelings as she thought about his fears. After a moment she found the answer. She just pretended she was Mark, and it was she who had asked the question.

"None of us climbs alone, Malcolm," she said. "Never forget that. Alex has climbed mountains that would make Rainier look like a walk in the park. And he really knows Rainier. Been up there more times than I can count. He knows what he's doing. But the important point is that we're a team. Each of us has strengths and weaknesses. I may have a little more experience, but you're way stronger. Never forget: climbing isn't one against the world."

Malcolm broke into a smile. "Thanks," he said, rising. "I guess I forgot for a moment."

"You'll be fine," she said, grinning. She wondered privately if she would be too.

2047: The Princess Maria

Janet Gordon deposited her coat in the pilot house forward and looked about the crowded salon of the yacht. Small groups were chatting gaily about nothing in particular. From the loud laughter and noise she guessed the party had been under way for some time. Free booze will do that, she thought, smiling. She spotted Roger Greninger's tall figure standing by the bar, and strolled over to join him. "Great place for a party," she said, surveying the rich ambiance of the salon.

"If you can afford it," Roger agreed, his voice reflecting mild skepticism. "Carlos isn't a captain, is he?"

"Not likely!" She laughed. "He doesn't even have a pilot's license. He used to have a captain's rating before he moved here. Something happened down in Nicaragua. I've never heard the details."

Roger appeared startled. "Losing your license is pretty serious. I wonder what happened."

"Nobody seems to know for certain, but there've been rumors." She glanced about to be sure they couldn't be overheard. "Apparently his plane was involved in a runway collision in Managua one night. Hit by another plane. There were a lot of deaths."

"His fault?"

"It's usually the pilot's fault. Jetliners are designed to survive. The only unpredictable part is the pilot. Anyway, Carlos isn't flying any more. No one knows the details."

"Someone must know," Roger thought aloud. "A good investigative reporter ought to be able to sniff it out, if there's a story behind it."

"I'll keep that it mind. We may need some ammunition." She moved a little closer and lowered her voice. "I still can't get over that Costa Rica venture he put over on the board."

"Is it that serious?"

"Anything that compromises the safety of our passengers is serious," Janet replied. "I've seen pictures of their operation. I'm not impressed. And now he proposes this silly Exciting Skies nonsense!" Then she caught herself and broke into a broad smile. "Sorry! I hardly need to tell *you* about this. You were there."

"Don't apologize. I enjoy seeing you excited about things you're passionate about. The look in your eyes a moment ago was quite breathtaking. You're really quite a beautiful woman."

"Thank you." She felt her cheeks flushing, but it was the flush of excitement, not of embarrassment. She felt beautiful tonight. She had always been keenly aware of her positives—and her negatives. To have either confirmed was neither flattery nor criticism. It was the simple act of identifying and naming the truth, and that required an act of morality she was not accustomed to discovering in people. Finding it in a man like Roger pleased her.

He steered her over to a couple of easy chairs. As they sat down his voice took a serious tone again. "Look, tell me to get lost and I'll never mention it again, Janet, but—are you seeing anyone?"

"Not in the way I think you mean it," she said. "Why? Are you suggesting you'd like to date me?"

"I've been wanting to ask you, but I wasn't sure how you'd react. I'm not a kid any more. Maybe I've lost the knack."

She chuckled. "I'll confess it's something I haven't given much thought to, either. Frankly, I haven't had the time, with all the demands of this job. I promised myself when Richard died that I'd dedicate all my time to the airline. It was easier to just forget the socializing." She paused briefly and looked up into his eyes, concerned about hurting his feelings. "I'm flattered you'd think of asking me, Roger. I mean that."

"I wondered—maybe we might have dinner sometime?"

She guessed this was probably the most difficult thing he'd had to do all week. The look in his eyes told her that her answer would mean much more to him than he was likely to admit. But she wasn't ready for that yet. Would she ever be? She wasn't sure. But she didn't want to turn him down flatly. After all, she might change her mind, and men like Roger were rare.

"Let's put it on hold for a while, shall we?" she said gently. "I'm very touched, Roger. Just let me think it over."

"Okay," he said. "I hope it'll be soon."

Their eyes met again and held. It was one of those electric moments. She took a deep breath and forced herself to keep from revealing her true feelings, which went a lot deeper than she was admitting—to him, or to herself.

She smiled. "I think it will be. Don't lose the thought."

* * *

2245: SeaTac Airport

Russo completed his turn to the north and prepared for his descent into Seattle. The moon was full, well up over the Cascade Mountains to the east, turning the white peaks into ghostly shapes that floated above the mists covering the valleys. "Flaps five," he said to Walter Harris.

"Flaps five."

"This is one trip I'm glad to put behind us."

"I'd say you can say that again, but I'm afraid you would!"

Russo chuckled. "Take her in, Walter. I've got to pay the man a visit." He released his harness and rose out of his seat. Harris nodded. Once inside the lavatory he took a small bottle of pills from his pocket, took one out, and poured himself a glass of water to wash it down. *Damn,* he thought. *Pilots shouldn't be doing this. I guess I'm headed for the pasture.* He replaced the bottle and returned to his seat.

"Everything okay, skipper?" Harris asked, glancing across at him.

"Of course!" *Does he suspect anything? Jesus, I'm going to have to watch it.* "I'll take it now," he asserted, and waited for Harris to relinquish control of the airplane. Was he being too curt? Walter doesn't deserve this, he thought. "See about finding us a parking space, Walter," he chuckled. It's been a long, long day."

He'd been in close shaves before, but the incident over the mountains coming out of Denver this morning had really unnerved him. His thoughts went back to that nightmarish landing that night on Whidbey Island. He'd had a premonition of something ominous about to happen that night. He was experiencing the same feeling now. No reason that he could put his finger on. Just a feeling. He shook his head to clear it and focused on the routine of landing the plane. But he couldn't shake the feeling.

*　*　*

2311: Seattle—The Princess Maria

"I can't believe you're really serious!" Josh Edwards, his tone reckless after a few more martinis than usual, glared into the smirking features of Carlos Santiago, who was doing his best to emulate the successful airline executive in an impeccable white dinner jacket. They had been discussing Santiago's new offshore maintenance deal, and Edwards, not the sort of man to keep his opinions to himself, had been venting his disgust to the author of the scheme. He was wishing Santiago would take a swing at him, but knew it was highly unlikely, in view of the difference in their physiques. Besides, Santiago was standing beside Carter Wycroft, and the airline president was clearly taking Santiago's side. Edwards was just sober enough to realize what a colossal blunder it would be to start a fight with Wycroft watching.

"You guys just don't get it!" Santiago said, his voice tinged with sarcasm. "You know we're in deep trouble financially!" He lifted his champagne glass and drained it, then summoned a waiter for a fresh one. He seemed to be enjoying the duel, well aware of his advantage. "You flyboys never give economics a thought. You just bumble along from day to day assuming that somehow we'll save your asses. How naive can you be?! Somebody's got to work the financial end, or you'd be out of a job. And with the rising cost of fuel these days, that won't be far off."

"That's not the point, and you know it!" Edwards flung back, his temper rising again. "There are lots of ways to improve profits without taking unnecessary risks."

"Oh? And what might those be?"

"Well, for one, we could ask some of you senior executives to live on a little less. You guys aren't exactly starving!" He took another swallow and glanced around the lavish interior of the yacht. "You didn't pay for this with food stamps, Carlos. And I'll bet you're writing it off on your taxes, too."

"He's entitled to that," Wycroft interjected. "He uses this yacht for entertaining. This party, for example."

"Oh, sure! Suppose we have the next one in my house!" Edwards flared. "Can I write off my house as a business expense?"

"You're not in marketing," Wycroft replied. "But that's beside the point. You know as well as I do that Carlos's idea makes a lot of sense. Besides, the board approved it."

"*Your* board!" Edwards cried, raising his voice. A few guests turned to regard the group with annoyance. His hands bunched into fists at his sides, ready to smash into Santiago's gloating face, when he felt a hand touch his elbow. He turned to see Janet Gordon looking up at him with a conspiratorial smile. "Hi, Janet," he said, grinning sheepishly. "I'm in trouble. I need moral support."

"Why don't you buy me a drink?" Janet suggested, tugging at his arm to draw him away from the two men.

"*Buy* you one?" He studied her eyes for a moment before her words registered. "Oh! Sure, okay." He grinned again and let her lead him away from the other two. He turned to look at the two executives over his shoulder. "Tell you what. Why don't you guys come on a flight with us some time. Maybe we'll have an engine fall off because those nitwits down south forgot to check the mount bolts. Oh, and while we're at it you can see what your Exciting Skies crap is all about, too. We'll show you what one of your low-noise descents are like, and maybe scare up a mountain goat or two as we swoop down past Rainier."

"Josh, leave it alone!" Janet pleaded. "It isn't doing any good. We can manage, despite what they're trying to do." She wished she could believe her own words, but the last thing she needed was to lose her best line captain to these bean counters. As she led Edwards away, the thought came back to her again. Why is Wycroft so willing to stand behind this arrogant little upstart? What's Carlos ever done for him? She could find no answer.

* * *

It was five minutes short of midnight. Janet had just poured Josh Edwards into a taxi, with Roger Greninger's help, and given the driver a twenty-dollar bill and Josh's address. "I'll be right back, Roger," she said. "I have to get my coat."

The yacht was quiet. The other guests had left. She went forward to the boat's wheelhouse and picked up her well-worn Burberrys, which was lying across the chart table next to a lovely fur stole. Apparently not everyone had left. The wheelhouse and the rest of the yacht were almost dark. The only light was from the dim illumination coming through the cabin windows from the dock lights outside. Leading down from the center of the wheelhouse was a companionway that led to the staterooms forward. One of the stateroom doors was open, and in the doorway she could make out two back-lit figures, a man and a woman. She could make out a white dinner jacket and a full-length black evening gown, but couldn't make out the faces. Sudden recollection came to her. Marla Russo. And the white dinner jacket had to belong to Carlos.

As Janet watched, her brother's wife moved into Carlos's arms and when she kissed him there was no doubt about the feelings being exchanged. Janet wondered whether they were just about to enter the stateroom, or were just leaving it. In either case, she didn't want to be seen. She had to get out of there. Suddenly she felt weak, almost nauseated. She wondered if Frank knew. She made her way noiselessly to the outer door.

Still shaken by what she had seen she slipped her arm into Roger's for support as they walked back to where she had parked. "Let's get out of here!" she cried.

Roger looked at her. "What's wrong, Janet?"

"I just saw Marla and Carlos outside his stateroom. They were kissing."

"No kidding! Frank's wife?"

Janet nodded. "And it wasn't just one of those 'So glad you could come over' kisses, either. "It was either the prelude or the finale."

"Prelude, probably. They couldn't be that fast. I saw Carlos just a few minutes ago, while you were putting Josh into the taxi. He was saying good night to the Wycrofts. And boy, was he stoned!"

"Who? Carlos?"

"No, Carter Wycroft. Paula was helping him off the boat. I hope she's a good driver."

"No kidding! He couldn't drive home?"

"No way! Good thing Paula was along. But that's his problem. I'm more sympathetic toward your brother." He shook his head sadly. "I've heard everything. She was trying to project the image of a woman with real class. One that was above anything so sordid as a quickie with the host while her husband was out of town. Where is Frank, anyway?"

"He took the Denver run this morning. He's probably back by now, but couldn't come to the party. He's off for Honolulu tomorrow. You know the drill. No drinking for twenty-four hours before a flight. Carlos probably knew all about it, and invited the two of them, knowing full well that Frank wouldn't be here."

"Someone ought to let him know what's going on while he's away."

"Maybe he already knows," Janet said. "No one could be that blind. But I suppose it's possible."

"Don't I know it." Roger's face clouded over. Janet saw the look, and knew what had caused it. She got into her car and started the engine. She looked up at Roger. "It's still early. Would you like to come up to my place for a nightcap?"

"You're sure?"

She laughed as Roger broke into a grin. "I need someone to talk to. I still can't believe what I just saw. God, how could she?"

"It happens," Roger commented. "Where's your place?"

"Just follow me. I'll keep the flaps down." She laughed as Roger made a dash for a gleaming black Type E Jag. No way she could lose a car like that. Not that she wanted to.

* * *

0045: Sommerset

"You almost lost me climbing this bloody mountain!" Roger exclaimed, as Janet ushered him inside. "I may never find my way back to Normandy Park."

"Wishful thinking?" she grinned. "How do you ever manage to navigate when you're flying?"

"Easy. I don't have to try to follow any maniac women pilots!"

"You'd better watch that sexist stuff." She laughed musically. "Come on out to the kitchen. Coffee, tea, or—"

"Or?"

"Or something a little stronger. Remember, I was a pilot, not a stewie. Still am," she corrected. "So, what'll you have?"

"Whatever you're having."

"I'd love a glass of sherry. Sound okay?"

"I haven't had sherry for ages. It's almost an anachronism today." He followed her into the living room where she placed a bottle of Harvey's on the coffee table, and filled two glasses. "Do you have a plane now?" he asked, as they sat together on the sofa and sipped their wine.

"No. I've never owned one. But they let me sit in the left-hand seat of a CH-12 once a month, to keep my rating up."

"Maybe you'd like to try mine sometime. Have you ever flown a float plane?"

Her eyebrows arched. "You have a float plane? What kind?"

"A vintage Otter—bought her two years ago. I keep her on the lake over at Renton. I've been reconditioning her."

"Mmmmm! Maybe you can teach me. I've always wanted to try floats."

"Love to."

"I'm going to hold you to it, so don't forget."

"Jan, the last thing in the world I'd do is forget about you!" His eyes studied hers for a moment as she refilled their wine glasses. "You were pretty badly shaken up, seeing Carlos and Marla on the boat."

"I guess so," she said after a pause. "Frank and I have always been close." She wanted to change the subject. Anything but Marla's sordid little affair. "I hope Josh doesn't have a big head in the morning. I had to get him out of there, before things got out of hand."

"He'll be fine," Roger said. "Apparently tonight wasn't the first time he's had a run-in with Santiago, though."

"How's that?"

"Josh told me earlier—before he got stoned—he'd seen Santiago and Wycroft together at a party recently."

"What party?"

"Some soiree over in the U district. A fund raiser for one of the Democratic hopefuls, I think."

"When was it? I never heard about it. I'm usually on their hit list when they're after money."

"Two weeks ago."

"Really?"

He nodded. "Edwards said the two of them were thick as thieves all evening. Every time he tried to speak to them he found Carlos banging Wycroft's ear about that Exciting Skies crap. Josh finally told him to cut out the shop talk, and Carlos started throwing snide remarks around, the way he always does. Josh told Carlos what he thought of it at one point. He said it was really strange: Wycroft seemed to be really angry— totally opposed to what Carlos was suggesting."

"That *is* strange. Carter's not one to reverse directions that easily."

"Josh said Carter was pretty drunk."

"Drunk? At a party?"

"Just like tonight. They say he's an alcoholic."

Janet looked at him, astonished. "An alcoholic? Wycroft?"

"It's common knowledge at the JC."

"Good Lord! Is it bad?"

Roger laughed. "It's like being pregnant. There's no such thing as being a little bit alcoholic."

"I hadn't the slightest idea," she said slowly. "Poor Carter. He ought to try to get help." She paused for a moment to think about the implications of what she had just learned. "That could explain his behavior. He's never been one to back frivolous ideas. First there was the maintenance contract with the Costa Ricans. Now he's backing Carlos on this Exciting Skies nonsense. Completely irrational. Maybe that's the hold Carlos has over him. A man might do anything to conceal an alcohol addiction."

"It happens."

"It's so frustrating! The airline's in bad enough shape with all our financial problems. If Carter's really sick, and he's being used by that little..."

"That really bothered you, didn't it? The confrontation with Santiago yesterday?"

She nodded. "The airline—I guess in a way it became my family when Richard died. It meant a lot to us. That's why Santiago's bullshit really gets to me."

"You really care a lot," he observed. "I'm not surprised. You seem to really throw yourself into things that lift your kilt."

Janet laughed at the image. "I used to think everyone did," she said, pushing a strand of dark hair back from her face. "I've become convinced that modern airline management—ours included, apparently—needs its corporate head examined. That offshore maintenance lunacy is typical."

"It isn't the brightest thing I've ever heard of."

"It's symptomatic of the modern Harvard Business School attitude," Janet fumed. She could feel her fury rising again, just as it had yesterday in the board room, and again tonight at Santiago's party. "God help us, I think the whole industry is riddled with this new bean-counting mentality."

"I agree. But is it that serious?"

"It's a matter of complaisance. We've enjoyed a long, steady trend toward better and better safety in the air. But all that could come crashing down around us if we let them get away with cutting corners on maintenance. We could wind up with the same kind of safety nightmares they've got in the Third World countries." She felt her cheeks flushing as she looked up at Roger. "I'm sorry! I guess I do get a little carried away. As you said, it really lifts my kilt!"

"You're talking to a believer, Janet." He grinned. "Maybe I'm in the wrong business. Maybe I ought to come and join you. Tell me: how do you reach the next plateau?"

"What do you mean?"

"You said you've made a lot of progress in safety. How do you improve it, when it's already so good?"

"It'll take a lot of money," she said thoughtfully. "You're right: we're already damn good. At least we are as long as we have our maintenance done here, where it's controlled by the FAA. It's essential that we get back to that."

"Agreed. Then what?"

"Human factors are the prime cause of accidents now. We need to spend a lot more on crew training. And on better air traffic control facilities. We need a whole new generation of equipment in the towers and control centers. You wouldn't believe some of the equipment the FAA is still using! It's coming, but it takes time—and a lot of money. But somehow we've got to take air traffic control back from the government. Let the FAA look after their regulations, let the NTSB look after accident investigations, but let us run the ATC system, like we did in the beginning."

"In the beginning? I thought it was always a government operation."

"No way! Well, it started with the government, of course. But air traffic control didn't really get started until it was taken over by the airlines back in '35. And it was working great. Then the government took it back, and you can see the mess we have today."

"Sounds like a familiar story," Roger said, grinning. "You just get something to work and the government comes in, takes it over, and screws it up."

"At enormous cost!" Janet agreed. "We could do it much more efficiently. But I'm sure you know that." She offered him another sherry, but he declined. "Anyway, that would be the first place to start modernizing. Get rid of the old vacuum tube and transistor technology of the sixties. Then start using GPS, which is common in many third-world countries now—but not here! Then we could start modernizing our own equipment on the ground and in the planes. We could really do a job on them."

"How do you get the money?"

"Simple! Stop these bloody price wars! Start charging a decent price for air travel. That's what I was trying to explain to the board yesterday. How the hell does the public expect us to fly them from here to New York for a measly two hundred and fifty dollars return? Good God, it cost twice that back in the fifties, when we flew DC-3s and it took several stops for refueling. The cost of everything else has shot up by a factor of five or so since then, thanks to Jimmy Carter. But somehow we're supposed to keep flying them for peanuts! Sure, we've come a long way in fuel efficiency with the big turbofans, and these wide bodies let us make up for it on high-density seating. But we ought to be getting twice what we're charging for fares. Then we could really do something about putting in the kind of safety measures that would all but eliminate fatalities."

"Couldn't you take that message to the public?"

"They'd never listen! It's the dumbest thing I've ever heard of. The flying public is so used to cheap fares they never think about what cost-cutting and price wars can do to safety. They force us to look for ways to cut corners. And then, when anything does happen, they descend on us like a plague of locusts with law suits for unheard-of damages, which our courts rubber-stamp with never a thought to what it's doing to us. It's the craziest business I've ever heard of."

"And you love it!" Roger laughed. "You ought to see yourself right now. Like I said earlier: Your face takes on a special glow when you're excited."

"I do love it, Roger." She felt her exhilaration of a moment ago returning to normal. "Oh, I guess somehow we'll find a way. God knows, we'll never get all the airlines to stick together and insist on higher fares. There'll always be a few holdouts that want to cut corners and make a few extra bucks by taking chances. And what chances! Some of them are buying bogus airplane parts from a thriving black market. Parts that have never been inspected by the FAA."

"Good Lord! What airlines are doing those things?"

"I could tell you, but then I'd have to kill you," she said, and then laughed. "Actually, the practice is not at all uncommon. But as long as you stick with the big American carriers you're fairly safe. It's the little startups and the commuters and charters you have to be careful with. Watch for the ones that are in financial trouble."

"Or ones with alcoholic presidents?"

"What a terrible thought! We've got to do something about that, before it's too late."

"You know you can count on me to help." Roger glanced down at the Rolex on his wrist. "It's getting late, Jan. I guess I'd better be going."

She rose with him and accompanied him to the door.

"May I call you?" he asked.

"Of course, Roger."

"Count on it."

She let him draw her into a light embrace. Long-suppressed desires surfaced quickly as she felt the strength of his arms about her. Before things could get out of hand she pushed herself away.

"Thanks for the sherry," he said, and left with a smile and a wave.

Janet watched his retreating figure from the door and wondered if she had been a little too standoffish with all her airline talk. Could she be using the airline as a safeguard against involvement? She knew it was possible. Her mind drifted back to the thoughts she'd been experiencing during the board meeting yesterday. In a brief fantasy she had imagined the two of them alone at his cabin on a lake somewhere. There was a fireplace and a pair of wine glasses, like tonight, and he had taken her into his arms and kissed her. But in her fantasy she had not resisted. She smiled as she turned out the lights and went down the hall to her bedroom. *I wonder if he really does have a cabin on a lake?*

Sunday

0716: SeaTac Operations

Russo balanced a styrofoam cup of coffee in one hand and his black leather flight bag in the other as he backed crab-like through the Ops Room double doors. He made it to the counter and deposited them without dropping either. He removed his gold-encrusted cap and sun glasses and set them on the counter beside his coffee. Ralph Carlson, the Pacific Coastal operations official, was spreading out a sheaf of charts and computer printouts for his review. "Morning, Ralph," Russo said.

"Good morning, sir. Everything's ready for you. Give a yell if there's anything else you need." Ralph Carlson turned back to his work.

Russo scowled at the pile. He was still fuming over the notice he had read on the company bulletin board downstairs. Coming right after the confrontation with Marla the night before, it had double the impact on his normally cheery outlook. He was poring over the weather data when he heard the ops room door open again.

"Morning, FDR."

Russo looked up. Walter Harris was one of the few people that he allowed to address him using his initials. Frank David Russo was a life-long Republican. His views had always been more in line with Teddy Roosevelt's than with those of the famous wartime president. He nodded and smiled half-heartedly.

"You look like someone's just taken the last jelly donut," Harris said. "I gather you've seen the bulletin downstairs?"

Russo grunted. "It's not the brightest thing the board's ever produced." He unfolded a sheet of paper on the counter and read it again. "Laughable, really. Lots of airlines are already adopting steeper descents and climbouts. The rest of it is just PR bullshit! The Exciting Skies! When are they going to learn? Our passengers don't want excitement. They want low fares, a safe, on-time flight, cheap booze, good food, and maybe a decent movie. *Period!*"

"I couldn't agree more," Harris said quietly.

Russo glanced in the direction of Ralph Carlson, who was busy processing another flight plan, but still within earshot. He didn't care who heard his outburst. He had enough seniority. Besides, this could be his last flight, once he'd seen the airline medics.

"Anyway," Russo continued, "I don't imagine they're willing to listen to reason. It looks like Santiago's gotten his way again. I still can't believe they went for that maintenance contract with the sleepy Gonzales outfit down south." Russo finally moved out of earshot of the ops chief. "Damn it! When is Wycroft going to develop balls enough to slap that arrogant little pup down? You'd think this was a travel agency, not an airline!"

"I'd be happy to take that duty on for our gutless president any time," Harris agreed.

Russo chuckled. Harris could always dispel his dark moods. He glanced up at the array of ops room clocks. It was 7:28 Seattle time—5:28 in Honolulu. They were scheduled to push back at nine. He consulted the weather chart and computer printouts for their trip to LA and Honolulu.

He summoned the ops room chief as he studied the weather chart for the north Pacific. "What's the scoop on this, Ralph?" He pointed at a large low pressure ridge out over the ocean.

"Storm coming in," Carlson remarked. "It's expected to hit B.C. and Alaska tomorrow. Nothing for you to worry about, though. It won't come this far south."

The two pilots went over the seemingly endless details of their flight. Finally satisfied with the arrangements, they headed for their gate. But satisfied was not what Russo was feeling. He still had that premonition he'd felt coming back from Denver.

* * *

0800: SeaTac Main Terminal

The man approaching the Pacific Coastal ticket counter was over six feet in height, with the sturdy build and appearance of one accustomed to hard work outdoors. He was in his mid thirties, with blond hair that had been bleached under the same sun that had caused the fine wrinkles about his blue eyes. His hands were large, powerful, and like his face, deeply tanned. His neatly tailored Harris tweed sport coat and wool slacks didn't match the rugged outdoorsman image.

He stepped up to the counter and smiled at a young woman wearing the navy blue tunic and gold buttons of Pacific Coastal Airlines. The girl returned his smile and waited for him to finish fumbling for his ticket envelope. She looked at the ticket, then back up. "Welcome to the exciting skies of Pacific Coastal, Mr. Svenson. Off to Los Angeles for a business trip?"

"And a little pleasure, I hope," he answered. "How's the weather down there?"

She laughed. "Do you need to ask? Clear and sunny, almost eighty degrees. But watch the smog."

"We have lots of that here, so I guess we can't laugh at them any more."

She finished writing on his ticket with a black marker pen. "Any luggage to check, Mr. Svenson?"

"No. Just this garment bag and my briefcase. I'll manage."

"You are flying on Flight 47, boarding at Gate S-22 in the south satellite terminal at eight-thirty. Your airplane is one of our new CH-12's. Enjoy your flight, and thank you for choosing Pacific Coastal."

Mark Svenson started to leave, then turned back again. "What's a CH-12?" he asked. "Not one of those noisy foreign turboprops, is it?"

"It's a new design, by Crawford-Hiltz Aircraft—their newest tri-jet. It has a lot of features you may find interesting. And no, it doesn't have props." She handed him a pamphlet with a picture of a large jetliner on the cover. "Ask the crew when you board, Mr. Svenson. They'll be glad to tell you all about it. We're pretty proud of these airplanes."

Svenson nodded, turned to go, and narrowly avoided colliding with the next customer in line. He decided it might be better to wait until later to read about the CH-12. He spotted a large green and white sign that pointed the way to the S gates. He headed for it in a strident gait that would leave all but the very hardy behind.

As he arrived at his gate he thought about his mountain climbing team, who would be beginning their ascent of Mount Rainier tomorrow morning. Normally he'd have been along with them, but he had to cover an air show and convention at Burbank for *The Globe*. They'd be in good hands with Alex, but nevertheless he worried about Karen, who never seemed to know her own limitations. More than anything else, he wanted to be up there with her. But his job had to come first.

After checking in at the gate Svenson followed a young couple along the jointed boarding ramp. Newlyweds on their honeymoon, he guessed, noting the longing looks they were exchanging and the bits of confetti the bride had failed to brush out of her hair. He found himself envying the man. He wanted a wife. Not just for the sex he wasn't getting, either. It went beyond that. He wanted the companionship of a woman, and he wanted to start a family. Sometimes he wasn't sure which he wanted most. But he'd had to put those needs on hold. Too many mountains to climb, he thought with an inward chuckle, as the line shuffled forward. He needed a break, something to catapult his career toward the kind of success he needed to be able to support a family. Not in luxury necessarily, just in a little comfort. When he married he didn't want his wife going off to work every day to help pay for the house he couldn't afford to buy. His wife was going to be the mother of his children, and she couldn't do that if she had to park them at a day care center every morning. Somehow, he must find a way.

He cast a quick glance down the side of the aircraft fuselage as he boarded. Impressive, he thought. Mark Svenson loved airplanes. It made his job as an aerospace columnist a natural for him. *The Seattle Globe* was a newcomer to the northwest's media scene, and it was already giving the other two Seattle newspapers, which were notoriously liberal and frequently wildly sensationalist, a run for their money.

Svenson stowed his luggage in the overhead bin, took his seat, and began reading the pamphlet describing the CH-12. His mind automatically began to translate the advertising agency's hype. The airplane was impressive. It could fly 8,000 miles with a load of 275 passengers. It was the newest and largest of the tri-jets, which Svenson had always regarded as the most practical arrangement for an airliner, and had the same engines as used on the giant Boeing 747-400. But the feature that really caught his attention was its short takeoff and landing performance. It was really an impressive airplane.

* * *

0815: The Main Cabin

Although she was the cabin crew supervisor, Megan McLain was the latest addition to Frank Russo's crew, and she was just getting used to the routines. At thirty-five, after producing and raising a twelve-year-old son, she was still trim for her five feet five, but at the moment she was plagued by a conviction that she had been losing her battle against the pounds. She had to pass the next weigh-in. She always did, but the worry was always there. She wasn't given to worrying about such things, normally. She had inherited her Irish father's stoicism and quiet humor. But as a single mother she had to be concerned about holding her high-paying job. Her good looks helped. She had been blessed with her mother's blue eyes, dark hair and creamy complexion, and she possessed a simple, understated poise and manner that was impossible to hide, even in a tailored uniform.

On the way forward toward the first class section she noticed one of the girls struggling with a passenger's heavy carry-on bag and stopped to help her stuff it into the overhead rack. "One of these days our management will start enforcing the carry-on regulations," she said, once they were out of earshot of the offending passenger. "But till then, keep working out with the weights every night."

"They never told us about this at the flight attendants' school!" the girl complained.

Megan laughed stoically. "How else could they get you to take a job like this? Where you have to take all the abuse of your passengers, work long hours in a bone-dry environment that turns you into a prune, and have to leave your kids at a boarding school because you're away so often?"

"You just ruined my day!"

"Ah, but the pay makes up for it," Megan consoled. "At least we have that."

She continued forward to the galley to supervise the stowing of the first class meals, leaving the girl to ponder the great equation of modern airline business. We all have to do it, she thought. Prostitute ourselves to make the big bucks so we can retire before it destroys us. But Megan didn't mind it. She had Sean, and he was worth any discomfort she had to endure on the job. Besides, she'd always been enchanted by aviation. It made Rodney's death a little more bearable to be part of the world he had loved.

* * *

Russo sat crossways in his cockpit seat and finished scanning the maintenance log. He replaced it in its rack when he saw Megan McLain approaching. Despite his lingering dark mood, Megan's arrival was an event that was difficult to ignore.

He had not had time to get acquainted with her in the week she'd been with his crew. He made a practice of knowing each crew member well enough to know his or her strengths and weaknesses. When emergencies came up, you had to know. There would be no time for explanations.

He returned the maintenance log to its rack and moved aft to where Megan was just stowing her overnight bag into the crew luggage compartment.

"Hello, Megan," he said in a crisp, professional voice. "Ready for our first exciting skies adventure?"

Megan looked up, annoyance clouding her features. "Hello, Captain," she said, forcing a smile. "I wish they'd fire the clot that thought up that slogan. It's creating problems. Everyone wants to know what makes our skies so exciting. I have a feeling they'd rather have *less* excitement, not more."

Russo laughed. "I'm sure we'll manage, despite the annoyance."

"I guess you're right."

"I've been trying to guess your accent," Russo said, happy to change the subject. "Are you English?"

"Some might consider that an insult!" But her eyes reflected amusement, not anger. "I'm Irish."

"Yes, I see your point. Sorry," he apologized. "Where in Ireland?"

"A tiny little town on the seaside just south of Dublin." Her brogue became more pronounced as she spoke of her home. "I'm sure you've never heard of it."

"But I'd like to," he said with genuine interest. "You must tell me all about your home some time. Perhaps we could have dinner together in Honolulu?"

"I—That would be lovely!" He noted a flush of excitement as she lowered her eyes. She looked up again. The professional smile had returned. "How nice of you to invite me."

"Wonderful. I'm so glad to have you on our crew. Meanwhile, I've got to get back to work or this bus'll never make it out of Seattle."

As she left Russo experienced a twinge of conscience. Could it be he was just on the make after Marla's bombshell? It'd be a natural reaction. And not too hard to believe, given Megan's obvious charms. But it wasn't that, he was certain. Still, he ought to be careful. If Marla ever got wind of it she might be able to hold him over the barrel in divorce court. Was there any chance of her learning about this dinner date? Not much, he reasoned. Besides, Marla was having her own fling. He dismissed the idea without further thought. He really wasn't on the make, anyway. His intentions, as they said back in days when it meant something, were perfectly honorable. He really did make it a practice to get to know his crew well, and this trip would provide a good chance to do that.

He was deeply troubled by the mess waiting for him when he returned to Seattle on Wednesday. Dealing with Marla's demand was going to be the hardest thing he'd had to do in all their married life together. He'd spent an agonized night pondering every side of the situation. It was tearing him apart. Thank God we'd never had children, he thought. What an ordeal to have to thrust upon sons and daughters. Had they had any, he knew he would never be able to allow her to leave him. They'd have to find a way to make it work. But with no children, and with her admitted involvement with another man, he knew he'd have to let her go.

He rejoined Walter Harris, and together they worked their way through the long checklist prior to starting the engines. But it was difficult. He kept seeing two visions. One was of his own wife in bed with another man—a man without a face. The other was of a pair of deep blue eyes, a beguiling smile, and a lilting Irish accent.

0825: The Main Cabin

Megan joined Beth Winslow, who was getting the first class section ready to serve breakfast. Beth and Megan had become close friends when Megan had joined Pacific Coastal. It was Beth who helped her get settled into this crew's routine when she transferred from another crew a week ago.

"I think I just caught the brass ring, as you Americans say," she confided to Beth.

"How's that?"

"The captain's asked me out to dinner tonight."

"*No!* Did he?"

Megan nodded, smiling.

"Megan, maybe—I'd go a little cautiously, if I were you."

"Why?"

"He's married."

"I know that. I'm not husband hunting!"

"I never thought—I'm sorry, Megan. But apparently you don't know. There's a rumor that his wife is having an affair with one of the airline executives."

Megan's eyes reflected dismay. "Are you serious?"

Beth looked around to make sure they couldn't be overheard and said in a lowered voice: "Everybody's talking about it. It's a wonder Russo hasn't picked up on it yet. But the husband is usually the last one to know." Beth looked at her superior closely. "Be careful, Megan."

"Why?"

"He's a Catholic, for one reason."

Megan laughed. "So am I. What's that got to do with the price of eggs?"

"An *Italian* Catholic. A good one, at that. I've never heard of an Italian Catholic divorcing his wife. Their priests are too conservative. He may put out a contract on her, but no divorce!"

Megan laughed at the image. Then she sobered. "Irish Catholics have just as domineering priests, but there are ways around it. They're granting annulments nowadays."

"Aren't you getting a little ahead of yourself?" Beth said with a wondering look.

"Sorry! I guess I was, at that. A little wishful thinking, perhaps. Please keep this to yourself, Beth."

"Okay, okay. Just be careful."

"As always," Megan said resolutely. She was about to leave when she asked: "Does he have any children?"

"No, not that I know of. Why?"

"No particular reason," Megan said.

* * *

0848: The Tarmac

Outside gate S-22 the gleaming shape of the CH-12 waited in the morning sunlight as the ground crews finished their pre-flight checks. The fuel hose had been disconnected from the aircraft's belly and allowed to rewind into its underground reel, leaving the aircraft many tons heavier. The caterer's truck was just completing its task of loading the inflight meals, and the train of baggage carts was nearing the end of its semi-automated process of stuffing huge aluminum luggage containers into the ship's hold.

Glen McDougall, the ground crew supervisor, watched over the preparations from his perch on the side fender of the squat towing tug that was attached to the nose gear of the plane by a stout towing bar. He knew enough about the CH-12s to be impressed.

The fuselage was a long cylinder, about twenty feet in diameter, artfully tapered fore and aft, with the tail rising upward in a sweeping curve at the rear to reach the enormously high tee-tail above its rear engine pod. The two wing engines were suspended on pylons from its high shoulder-mounted wings. It resembled the old Air Force Starlifters, except for its three engines and the distinctive downward slope of its nose section. The ground crews called the latter a "droop snoot," a term that some of its designers viewed with less than enthusiasm. It was intended to give the pilots better visibility.

The airplane's most significant aspect was not apparent from a casual observation. Along the upper and lower surfaces of the wings were rows of slots that augmented the flow of air over the wings. This provided a large increase of lift at low speeds. The result was that the CH-12 could take off and land on very short runways, a decided advantage at some of the smaller airfields Pacific Coastal had to visit.

The hand-held VHF radio beside McDougall broke into a rapid staccato of voice instructions, interrupting his thoughts. He stood and summoned the rest of his crew, who at his signal plucked the ground safety pins with their long red streamers from the undercarriage joints and removed the chocks from under the main wheels. Flight 47 was ready to start its engines. McDougall figured there was just time for a quick bagel if this flight didn't have to wait to push back.

* * *

0849: The Flight Deck

Captain Russo signed the loading manifest presented to him by the gate agent. At this stage it was all serious business on the flight deck. Walter Harris worked the radio controls to obtain engine start-up and push-back clearance from the ramp controller. Once it was granted Russo gave the signal to the waiting ground crew. He initiated the automatic start sequence. The number one engine under the left wing slowly pressurized and spooled up to twenty-five percent RPM. The low rumble of the fuel catching flame quickly gave way to the whine of the engine coming up to idle speed. The procedure was repeated for the number three engine on the right, and finally number two, back in the tail.

"Seattle Ground Control, Pacific Coastal Forty-seven, ready to push back," Harris said over the radio.

"Coastal Forty-seven, Ground. Cleared to push back. Proceed to runway sixteen left. Position and hold. Contact Departure on one-one-niner-point-niner."

"Coastal Forty-seven, sixteen left, position and hold."

Russo signaled to the crew chief below and released the brakes. The plane rolled backwards, pushed in a wide turn against the thrust of the engines by the tug.

There was the usual confusion of traffic out to the taxi strip. An MD-11 made an attempt to cut them off at the first intersection, almost forcing Russo to come to a halt, but the offending pilot raised his hand in salute and allowed Flight 47 to take the honors. Russo grinned and saluted back. It was then that he noticed that the MD-11 pilot had his middle finger extended. "I'll be damned!" he said to Harris. "Did you see that? I can't believe it!"

"Maybe his air conditioning is on the fritz," Harris offered.

"I hope so!" Russo advanced the throttles to inch forward again. It took the CH-12 ten minutes to reach the north end of the runway. He had foreseen a busy morning, and had requested an extra couple of thousand pounds of fuel for taxiing out. It was costly, but essential. The alternative, running out of fuel in a holding patterns over Los Angeles, was unthinkable.

Harris changed to the tower frequency. "SeaTac Tower, Coastal Forty-seven Heavy. Ready for takeoff."

The SeaTac tower controller answered immediately: "Coastal Forty-seven Heavy, Roger. You're next in line. Please stand by."

"Forty-seven."

The two watched a United 737 accelerate down the runway ahead of them, and Harris again took the call from the tower that cleared them for takeoff. Harris acknowledged. Russo released the brakes and steered the plane around in an arc and lined up for the takeoff run. He advanced the thrust levers to takeoff power. The CH-12 leaped forward as Russo released the brakes.

Walter Harris monitored the air speed indicator as they hurtled down the runway. "V-One," he announced, and then, shortly after, "Rotate!" Russo felt the contraction of his viscera as he hauled the control yoke back. The rapid rise was part of the new Exciting Skies nonsense. Although it probably frightened some of the passengers, Russo knew it was harmless, especially in CH-12s, which loved high-angle-of-attack takeoffs. For him it brought back memories of the takeoffs from Whidbey Island in the Navy Orions. Great fun then, great fun now.

He glanced across at Harris. "Flaps and gear up," he ordered.

Harris complied. The whine of the retraction motors and loud clunk of the wheels coming up into their stowed position confirmed that everything was doing what it should be doing. He busied himself with obtaining their radar vectors for the trip south.

The gleaming snow cap of Mount Rainier slowly emerged out of the brownish haze to the south. Their path would ordinarily take them a few miles west of the snow-covered summit. But these were not ordinary times. He adjusted his course to bring their flight path closer to the white dome. He glanced across at Harris. "We're supposed to get them in close enough to grab a handful of snow," he said. Harris grunted.

As they continued their climb up to their assigned cruising altitude Russo's thoughts went back over Marla's shocking revelation, and the dismal prospect of going through the sham of getting the church to perform an annulment. He had to admit that for a long time he had been vaguely aware of something wrong between them. But that's the way of marriages, he thought. They'd gotten caught up in the day-to-day routine. He'd been aware something was off kilter, but not serious enough to take the time to get to the core of it. So he just let it slip into the background and promised himself that some day they'd get away for a weekend, just the two of them, and confront the problem. But "some day" never arrived, and the problem kept fading in and out of focus as time drifted quietly by.

Nevertheless, Marla's sudden demand for a divorce had been unexpected—and devastating. He would never have guessed that the problem had gone far enough that Marla would regard their marriage as beyond saving. It was obvious she must have been feeling this way for some time. She'd taken a lover. He wondered if it had been her idea, or whether it had just been a chance encounter between two lonely people. He felt a sharp stab of guilt over that. His job kept him away from home too much. Marla was only human, with a stronger-than-average libido. He could empathize with her. He imagined it would be the same for a man married to a woman pilot or flight attendant. But it must be harder for a woman—the prospect of the gradual dimming of the flower of youth and the looming insecurity of old age.

Now he must face a similar kind of future. He would be alone for the first time since his twenties. That made him think of his dinner date with Megan McLain. He found himself smiling, despite his depression. There could be compensations.

* * *

0919: The Main Cabin

The seat belt sign was off, but Mark Svenson left his secured. He was watching the scene outside. He never failed to feel thrilled by the awesome grandeur of Rainier's summit. He knew this peak as only a mountaineer could know it. Unlike most mountains, Rainier had three crests, all over 14,000 feet in height. The Liberty Cap, lowest of the three, crowned the steep and forbidding rock face of the Willis Wall on the north side. A little over a mile to the south was Point Success, which overlooked a number of glaciers fanning out into the valleys below. And between these two, about half a mile to the east, was the highest, Columbia Crest, 14,411 feet in height. Columbia Crest marked the sites of two ancient volcanoes, and surmounted the massive Winthrop Glacier to the northeast, the Emmons and Winthrop Glaciers to the east and southeast, and the Nisqually Glacier, which wended its way south and west like a gigantic toboggan chute, finally becoming a formidable river that fed into the Puget Sound. The summit had the appearance of two giant saddles joined at the pommel, as though two ancient warriors had collided and were forever locked together in mortal combat.

Svenson had never been able to view the mountain top from this vantage point. On his few flights to Los Angeles it had either been too cloudy or the plane had passed too far away to be able to see much. Today he could even make out the "snow cups" that covered the surface, caused by the heating of the sun. But as the scene came closer and closer, and the separation closed to a scant few hundred yards, he began to experience an icy fear deep in his stomach. The nightmare was there again, impossible to ward off.

You're on the Kautz Glacier. It is mid-morning, and the sun is so brilliant your eyes hurt even behind the dark goggles. Conrad, the youngest member of the team, has stopped to adjust his pack and harness. You lean into the strong wind and feel its biting cold trickling down through the open neck of your wool shirt. The others have paused too, waiting for Conrad to signal that he is ready to go on. Suddenly there is a deep moan. You look up, but you know what that sound means. A gust lashes down from the ridge above with too little warning. You yell, but your words are whipped away before they can travel five yards. You look back to see if the others are braced for it. Alex is all right. So is Eric. But Conrad is still on one knee, fumbling with his harness. At that moment you realize with horror that for some unknown reason, oblivious to the danger, Conrad has disconnected himself from the rope. He is caught like a feather and lifted off his feet. Before any one can get to him he is fifty feet down the icy slope, his body hurtling toward a yawning crevasse. And then he is gone. Gone where no one can reach him. Gone where no one will ever find him. Gone to become a permanent part of the mountain he had yearned to conquer.

Svenson shook himself to banish the nightmare. He saw a flight attendant moving past him and beckoned to her. "Miss—Miss McLain?" he said, reading her name tag.

Megan McLain stopped and leaned across the vacant seat beside him. "Yes, sir? Is there anything I can get for you?"

"I wouldn't turn down a good cup of coffee," he said, momentarily deflected by the sight of a beautiful woman. Gently, he explained: "You may think I'm some kind of nut, but I assure you I'm not. I'm an experienced mountaineer. I have to complain about your pilot's getting this close to that." He indicated the mountain peak just sliding past their left wing. "Do they always come in this close?"

"I'm not sure, sir. I've only been with this crew for a week. But I'll certainly relay your complaint to the Captain, and I know he'll appreciate your concern. Thank you so much. And I'll send someone with your coffee."

* * *

0951: The Flight Deck

Megan McLain motioned to Beth Winslow and told her to take a cup of coffee to the man in 16-A, while she went forward to see to the needs of the flight crew. She rapped on the door separating the crew compartment from the first class cabin. There was a moment's delay, and Walter Harris opened the door to admit her. It was standard practice to keep the flight deck door locked during flight to hamper would-be hijackers. It wouldn't stop them, she knew, but any delay could provide time for the crew to make a quick change of their squawk signal to alert the controller on the ground.

Megan paused behind the two pilots, who were engaged in an animated conversation about the Huskies and the Cougars, Washington's arch rival football teams. Walter Harris noticed her and smiled. "Thank God, a normal person that isn't a football freak!" he exclaimed, laughing. "Pull this guy off me!"

Megan waited respectfully, not wanting to be the one to throw cold water on the light-hearted mood that prevailed on the flight deck. When Russo turned to see what she wanted she said: "I'm afraid we've had a complaint, Captain."

* * *

1034: Flight 47 Main Cabin

Mark Svenson became aware of a gentle tugging at his arm. He opened his eyes sleepily and looked up into the smiling blue eyes of Miss McLain. "I'm sorry to spoil such a lovely nap," she said. He grinned at the sound of her Irish brogue. "We'll be landing in Los Angeles in a few minutes. Can I get you anything before we land? You were sleeping so soundly, I hated to wake you for breakfast."

"In my dream, I was asking for your telephone number," he said, still grinning. "But I guess your husband wouldn't approve."

"I'm a widow, actually."

"I'm sorry. Please forgive my rudeness."

"Perfectly all right, Mr. Svenson. You had no way of knowing. It's been a couple of years now." She smiled again. "So technically I'm not married. But definitely not giving out telephone numbers, either."

"I love the way you say *eye*-ther," he said. "I was hoping I might see you again."

"That's easy. Just keep flying the Exciting Skies of Pacific Coastal! Oh, and Captain Russo asked me to tell you he appreciates your complaint, and apologizes for any anxiety it may have caused you. He said it's the result of a new airline policy, and he must comply with it, as long as the weather is clear. But he said to thank you for your thoughtfulness, and suggested that if you would like to make a formal complaint to the airline both he and his first officer would be very appreciative." She turned on the public relations smile once more, and then went forward to begin preparations for the descent.

As she departed Mark began to ponder what Miss McLain had told him—and what she hadn't told him. This "Exciting Skies" thing was new. Apparently the pilots didn't think much of it. Neither did he, as a mountaineer. It could bear looking into when he returned. He usually had a newspaperman's sense about things like this. Could this be the big scoop he was looking for to advance his career? And to settle down with someone like Miss McLain and start making beautiful babies? That part, especially.

Svenson, almost alone among the hundred odd passengers in the plane, remained in his seat until they had docked at the gate, in silent obedience to the largely ignored request from the cabin crew. A few passengers nearly lost their footing as the pilot applied the brakes. Stupid fools, he thought, as he released his own seat belt. They weren't gaining more than a second or two by leaping to their feet, because the exits could only handle a fixed flow rate—usually a lot slower than they were hoping for.

He made his way out through the passenger ramp into the gate area. He caught a glimpse of the honeymoon couple he had noticed earlier, arm-in-arm, oblivious to what was going on around them as they listened to the announcement for the departure time of their ongoing flight to Honolulu. He smiled wistfully. Some day.

He stopped at the Pacific Coastal information counter where he was greeted by a silver-haired woman of fifty-odd years. She confirmed that his return reservation was in order. Fortune smiled on him at the Avis counter. A pretty black girl informed him that they had no compacts left. "Would you mind taking a Camaro at the same price, sir?"

"I guess I can deal with that," he grinned. He checked the free map they gave him and studied the route to Burbank. It was beginning to look like a pleasant trip.

* * *

1259: LAX—Flight 78

"Pacific Coastal Seventy-eight Heavy, cleared for takeoff. Have a nice flight, sir."

"Seventy-eight Heavy, cleared for takeoff. Thank you and good day." The two pilots advanced the thrust levers in unison. The plane accelerated down the runway toward the broad expanse of the blue Pacific. The big tri-jet lifted effortlessly off the black-streaked surface and shot upward into the cloudless blue sky, which was free of LA's characteristic "brown death" this close to the ocean. "Gear and flaps up," he commanded, and adjusted the airplane's trim to compensate. They continued to climb as Harris worked the radio to obtain their route clearances to Honolulu.

* * *

1735: Ballard

Karen was unloading her dryer when the phone rang. She knew who it was. She charged up the steps up from the basement two at a time. She barely made it before the fourth ring, when her answering machine would have cut in. "Mark?" she said, out of breath.

"Hi, Kitten!" Mark Svenson exclaimed. "What were you doing? Out running with Felix?"

"No. The laundry." She laughed happily. She was always lifted by Mark's calls. She sat down on one of her chrome and vinyl kitchen chairs. "How was your flight?"

"Uneventful. Except that I had a great view of your mountain on the way past. Did you meet with the guys yesterday?"

"Yes. And they were over here last night for dinner. Those guys! They just about cleaned me out! I hope they'll have enough to eat on the climb."

Mark chuckled. "They'll probably be packing an extra ten pounds of candy bars and goodies. Did Alex select a route yet?"

"Yes. We're going up Curtis Ridge."

"Curtis Ridge? That's—a little ambitious."

Karen could detect an edge of concern in his voice. "Quit worrying! I'll be fine. I'm going to show you all! I'll probably be the last one standing up there when we hit the summit. Except Alex, maybe. He's pretty solid. Those other two are just like puppies!"

Mark let out a chuckle. "Pretty big puppies!" His voice became serious again. "Be careful up there, Kitten. Remember, it's not the terrain. It's the *weather*. I worry about you."

Karen laughed again. "Quit worrying! The weather's great, and I'm going to be fine. Don't forget, you taught me all I know." Changing the subject, she asked, "What are you doing tonight?"

"I thought I'd do a little shopping. I need a new pair of boots. There's a great mountaineering store down here. How's the weather look for your climb?"

"Alex says it'll be fine. There's a weather system 'way up north, but it won't come anywhere near us."

"Alex ought to know," Svenson agreed.

They continued to chat about the climb for another couple of minutes, then Mark made her night by telling her he missed her, almost causing her to blurt out "I love you." But not quite.

1658 local: Honolulu

Walter Harris released his seat belt and stretched. "Layover time!" he announced with a broad grin, looking across at Russo, who was busy filling out the maintenance log entries. "Where's this bird headed now, Skipper?"

"Nowhere. We'll take it back to LA tomorrow, then it goes off to Denver while we get another break. Our airplane'll be coming from San Jose Tuesday morning, and we'll take it over and fly it back to Seattle."

"San Jose? What's it going up there for?"

"Not *up* there. *Down* there. San Jose, Costa Rica. It'll go into the barn for a B Check."

"Is that what you meant this morning? Santiago's new maintenance contract?"

"Yes. They claim it costs a whole lot less than it costs up here."

"God! I hope they know what they're doing."

"Between you and me, I doubt it. Santiago's probably got friends down there. Or maybe he owns a share of the operation. He's from Nicaragua, you know."

"Somebody ought to look into that. I don't like the idea of someone working on our plane where there's no FAA inspectors looking over their shoulders."

"Me neither," Russo snorted. "We'll have to do a really good walk-around Wednesday morning. Make sure there's nothing missing."

"I hear that." Harris rose from his seat. "What's up tonight? Are you eating alone?"

"No, I'm not, actually," Russo answered slowly. He thought about his response for a moment. Walter had to know, and it would be better if he got it straight from the source, instead of through the gossip mill. Besides, he trusted Walter completely. They were good friends. "I'm taking Megan out for dinner," he announced. "I haven't had a chance to get to know her yet."

"Oh, I see," Harris said, grinning.

"It's nothing like that!" Russo felt the color coming to his face. He wondered if he was just kidding himself. Walter apparently wasn't buying his story. Maybe he'd been mistaken in revealing his plans. But in his own conscience he knew it wasn't like that, despite appearances to the contrary.

Harris broke into his thoughts with an apology. "Sorry, FDR. I didn't mean to imply that—"

"No need to apologize, Walter." He glanced over his shoulder. The crew had already deplaned. "Ordinarily, I'd have been reluctant to take her out like this. But last night things changed radically in the Russo nest. You might as well know: Marla wants a divorce. It was quite a shock. You may have heard rumors already. I know these things have a way of getting around."

"No, I hadn't heard. I'm sorry."

"Thanks, Walter. It was quite a shock. So I guess I needed a little diversion tonight. But that's all there is to it."

"I know that! You're one of the last straight arrows," Harris chuckled.

"Well, I wouldn't go that far. But I'm sensitive to the situation." He retrieved his overnight bag from the crew locker on the way out. "What are you doing for dinner, Walter? Did I abandon you?"

"I think the girls are planning to eat together at the hotel. I'll probably tag along."

"I hope you have a good time. See you tomorrow?"

"You bet! I guess I don't have to wish you a pleasant evening."

"I'm sure it will be," Russo said.

* * *

1938: The Four Seasons Hotel, Seattle

Marla Russo was alone and bored. Carlos had helped her to move into her temporary quarters in downtown Seattle's luxurious Four Seasons Hotel. But then he had abandoned her for a business trip to Spokane. Having nothing else to do, she decided to take in an art exhibit in the hotel. She was strolling through the throngs of art patrons, not paying much attention to the paintings. She doubted that more than half a dozen of the hundred or so "patrons" could appreciate art the way it was meant to be appreciated—the way it would be in New York, she thought bitterly. A waiter appeared bearing a tray of champagne glasses and paused to offer her one. She accepted with a bored smile and strolled on.

She glanced about the crowd in silent appraisal. There were only two or three other women wearing formal gowns, attended by tuxedoed escorts. The rest were dressed in an assortment of casual attire. Men in business suits, sport coats, and the usual few in Bohemian sweaters and baggy pants. Women in cheap cocktail dresses, pant suits, and equally Bohemian sweaters and jeans. Marla had spent two hours getting ready for this affair, and she liked the result. A glittering tiara held her elegant coiffure in place. Matching earrings hung from her small ears, and a diamond pendant graced her throat. Her gown was a genuine Givenchy in burgundy silk that had cost Frank two thousand dollars.

One of the paintings caught her eye. It was the work of a northwest artist who appeared to have more talent than she was used to finding in this frontier town. It was while she was leaning forward to study the boldness of his brush strokes that she heard a voice at her elbow: "Pretty good for this part of the country, isn't it."

The man was just above average height, with straight chestnut hair, blue-gray eyes, a strong jaw line, and a thin, hard-looking smile. He was casually but expensively dressed in a light brown camel's hair sport coat and brown wool slacks. He wore a good broadcloth shirt and paisley tie, held in place with a gold tie bar, and she caught the glint of matching gold cufflinks at his wrists. She felt her cheeks coloring with excitement.

"I like his style," she answered.

"So do I," he said, his smile broadening. "And that isn't all I like." His eyes swept over her in silent appraisal. "I see you're alone."

"How did you know that?" she demanded. Then she realized she had missed a move in the game as she saw the thin smile broaden. "So what?" She decided the game wasn't worth pursuing anyway.

"Then perhaps you wouldn't mind some company?" He said it as a question, but his tone left no room for objections. "My name is Warren. Warren Smith."

As she took his hand, she wondered if the Smith was genuine. "Martha Jones," she said. Two could play that game. His hand felt strong, vibrantly alive. He was young, a good ten years younger than she. She released his hand and studied his eyes. Why not? she reasoned, excited by the feeling of power she knew was hers in an encounter of this kind. It was a perfect opportunity. She had been feeling depressed and lonely, with Carlos out of town. A knowing smiled played about her mouth. "What did you have in mind?" She was perfectly aware of what he had in mind, but she hadn't quite decided to play along yet. She needed a little sparring room.

"I thought we might escape this farce and find some place where we could talk quietly over a few drinks, and just see what develops."

"What develops?"

"Perhaps nothing," he grinned. "And perhaps we'll make it to the stars and beyond."

"You sound like a poet."

He laughed. "I'm a writer. I'm doing some research for my next novel."

"And you think you'd like to have me in it?"

"I can't imagine anything I'd like more." He let his eyes linger over her gown's décolletage. "You're very beautiful. And I have a feeling that you'd be very, very exciting." He didn't need to add where and in what way she would be exciting. She studied his eyes for a hint of mockery, but saw none. Damned audacious, she thought. Probably an enormously inflated ego, but maybe he was sincere, after all. She inclined her head gracefully. "And where would this little fantasy take place? Are you staying here in the hotel, Warren?"

"Yes."

She hesitated. Did she really want this? She certainly had no scruples about a little casual screwing, but one had to be careful these days. And yet she suspected that he would be the kind to be discreet. His body had a firm, supple, animal-like grace. And he was clean and well groomed, which was important. She felt the color coming to her cheeks again.

"Why don't you give me your room number," she murmured. "Go on ahead. I'll join you in a few minutes. I'd rather not let anyone here know about our meeting."

"Room 409."

As she watched him disappear through the crowd her thoughts were a confused jumble. He had awakened in her a primitive desire. She wanted to be taken by this audacious predator. But along with the desires came even more powerful warnings of impropriety and possible danger. About the impropriety, she admitted that her affair with Carlos had already put her reputation at risk. Another casual affair wasn't likely to erode it much more. What about the physical danger? She doubted he was interested in doing her harm. But there was always the fear of diseases these days. She could take precautions against infection, but nothing was fool-proof. In the end her desires got the better of her. After another round through the exhibits she made her way out to the hotel gift shop in the lobby and picked up the essentials for safe sex.

On the way to the elevators, she glanced out through the glass entry doors. It was raining heavily, and she could see tree branches whipping wildly in the wind. A good night to stay inside, she thought, smiling secretly, and pressed the elevator button.

1908 Local: Honolulu

Megan McLain opened her brocade suitcase across the bed and took out the plain black dress she always packed on overnight trips and hung it on one of the hotel's hangars. Her years of flying had taught her to choose clothes that would survive a suitcase unwrinkled.

As she showered she thought of Sean. He was spending the three days with one of his friends, whose mother was also a Pacific Coastal flight attendant. She wondered what the two were doing right now. Probably watching a horror movie, she thought. At least she hoped it was one of those, and not one of the R-rated bits of trash being doled out via cable TV. So far she'd been able to shield Sean from such horrors, but sooner or later she would have to let him decide on his own what constituted decent moral values. She felt she'd given him a good foundation.

She missed him, and that brought concern to her as she thought about her dinner date with Frank Russo tonight. She knew she would be walking on eggs if she were to start dating him. As a single woman with a young son, she had to be careful. She wasn't sure how Frank would react to Sean. Or how Sean would react to Frank.

She sat down before the vanity mirror and drew her hairbrush through her hair. It helped her think. She wondered again if there was any truth behind the rumors of Frank's marriage breaking up. Perhaps tonight he would open up a little.

Her thoughts were interrupted by the telephone's sharp ring. She made a lunge across the bed for it and almost knocked it off the night table as she scooped it up and lay back across the bed.

"I hope I'm not disturbing you," Russo said.

"No, not at all."

"I've made reservations for eight-thirty. Okay?"

"Sounds great. Give me fifteen minutes. By then I'll have myself put together." She glanced at the red numerals on the clock radio. "Eight-fifteen?"

"Eight-fifteen," he agreed. She thought she could hear a "Roger" at the end. Pilots had a way of talking that was unique. It was part of the excitement she always felt around aviators. "I'm looking forward to this," he said.

"That's sweet of you, Captain," she said. "So am I." She dressed and finished doing her face, which didn't require much attention. She used makeup sparingly. At last she stood before the mirror, debating whether to leave her hair down or to do it up. She decided to wear it up, not wanting to project the wrong image.

* * *

2030: Diamond Head Beach Hotel

"Exquisite!" Megan exclaimed softly, looking out at the scene outside. The sun had already made its plunge, and now the full moon was tracing a glittering path of gold that extended out to the horizon. Snowy linen and the sparkle of crystal and silver greeted them as they were shown to a table overlooking the ocean scene.

Frank had changed into a neatly tailored blue blazer and gray slacks. The blazer, Megan noted, did wonders for his broad shoulders. Or was it the other way round?

"I'm so pleased you asked me, Captain," she said, smiling across at him.

"Frank, Megan. Let's relax the formalities here."

"Gladly." She smiled again. She felt full of smiles tonight.

"I'm so glad we had this chance to get acquainted, Megan," Russo said. "I was a little dubious when I asked you, afraid of what you might think of my motives. But I was serious about what I said this morning. I think it's vitally important for a crew to work together as a team. And I've found there's no better way for people to get to know each other than by breaking bread together."

"No need to explain," Megan replied. "I feel the same way." As he continued to explain she wanted to laugh, but managed to keep her face composed as she listened attentively. She found herself believing that he really was as square as the image he seemed to be trying to project. His formality was too rigid to be a front. But she suspected that the formality could mask passions that would be fun to explore, should a relationship develop.

As they ate and talked, she continued to ponder the question of what she really wanted. Her life had been so full before Rodney had been taken from her. She knew she could never find that again. But was that really necessary? In her marriage to Rodney, she had discovered that one of the key ingredients was the simple observance of good manners on a day-to-day basis—of not allowing mundane problems to become blown out of proportion. It was so powerful she couldn't understand how anyone could approach an intimate relationship like marriage from any other basis. But in this she had discovered that her views were rare. Manners, it seemed, were usually the first thing to go when tempers flared.

"This has been wonderful, Megan," he told her as they relaxed over liqueurs. "I had to be careful, though. I didn't want you thinking I was coming on to you. After all, I'm still married."

Before she could think of a reply a small group of native musicians started playing a sentimental love ballad. "Would you like to try it?" he asked, glancing at the tiny dance floor.

"I'd love to."

She moved lightly into his embrace on the dance floor. The mood was romantic. The music, the semi-darkness of the lounge, the supple movements of his body close to hers. She closed her eyes dreamily, letting the music envelope her as they moved slowly about the floor. "This is lovely," she murmured.

"Very," he said. "I love the old songs. Why aren't they still writing this kind of music?"

"I know what you mean. What we need is a musical renaissance—another Rogers and Hammerstein."

"I know. We've grown up, and so has our world. It isn't at all like it was when the world was young. Young and innocent and lovely. The way you look tonight," he added.

She smiled. "That's a line from one of those old love songs. Thank you for your gallantry, but I have to remind myself that I'm the mother of a teenager."

"A teenager? Impossible!" He held her at arms' length for a moment, his eyes moving over her as though for the first time. "I don't believe it."

She wondered briefly whether he was sincere or just handing her a line. He seemed to mean it. A *very* straight arrow, she thought. "It's the truth," she insisted. "Of course I was married at the age of twelve." He laughed at her joke. "And I do play a lot of tennis."

"Good for you!"

"Do you have any children, Frank?"

"No," he said hesitantly. "Marla—my wife—can't have any. We thought about adopting, but she...well, that's a long story," he said, a shadow of sadness clouding his face. "And now, I'm afraid it's too late. But please, tell me all about your teenager."

"His name is Sean."

"How old?"

"Twelve." She saw doubt in his eyes. "I told you, I was a child bride." They both laughed again. "I'm thirty-five."

"You shouldn't have told me. I was certain you were ten years younger. I'm forty-three."

"So I've heard. The girls keep stats on all the pilots. Even the married ones."

Again they laughed. He seemed to have a genuinely spontaneous sense of humor. And so easy to talk to. As they continued to dance she told him about Sean's difficulties in adapting to American schools. Because of the educational differences Sean had had to skip two grades, which made him the youngest in his class. As a consequence he was frequently having to defend himself against assaults from larger boys. This was making him much tougher than she would have liked. As she finished explaining the musicians decided it was time for a break.

"That was wonderful!" he said, escorting her back to their table. "You're a superb dancer, Megan."

She smiled over her shoulder as he held her chair for her. "I love dancing, but I'm afraid I don't get a chance very often."

"It's been ages for me, too," he admitted. "Another liqueur?"

She inclined her head graciously. "I guess we may as well enjoy not having to fly tomorrow." She looked across at him. "We've been talking about me all night. Now it's your turn."

He fidgeted with his napkin. Finally, apparently coming to a decision, he said: "I don't know whether you're aware of it, Megan, but my marriage isn't in very good shape." There was a pause while he seemed to be debating whether to go on, and how much he should reveal of his private life. She hoped she was projecting the kind of warm empathy that would encourage him. At last he said quietly: "It's been developing for some time now. You've probably heard rumors about it, but I guess I really wasn't aware of it myself until just last night. My wife wants a divorce."

"Oh, dear!" Megan fought to keep her face from revealing her feelings, which were a mixture of sincere caring and relief—relief that it was out in the open now, and no longer had to be hidden. She knew from his expression that this must be the first time he had talked about it to anyone. That he would choose to reveal his innermost feelings to her, she regarded as an extraordinary compliment.

"I'm so sorry, Frank," she said softly. She reached across and touched his hand lightly. She sat back in her chair. "Would it help to talk about it?" Then she wondered if the question was a little too forward. They were hardly close friends yet. But he didn't seem to resent it.

"I'm afraid it's still too fresh, Megan," he murmured. "Perhaps another time. I'm sorry. I didn't want to spoil your night out. In fact, I probably should have put this off until later. I'm sure I'm terrible company tonight."

"Not at all! It's perfectly all right. And please don't be embarrassed. I have to remind myself that few couples enjoy what I once had."

"Your husband was killed, wasn't he?" he inquired, apparently relieved that she had changed the subject. "I heard you'd suffered a tragedy."

Megan nodded and decided to open up with him, hoping it might help to ease his pain. "Rodney was a pilot, too. A fighter pilot with the RAF. You'd have liked him. Everyone did. I'm sure we were the happiest little family in the British Isles—at least so we thought. He and little Sean had become my whole world, and it was a very happy world, indeed. Sean was just a little boy when Rodney got his call to active duty. He was a Harrier pilot, flying with his squadron in the Balkans."

"Were you allowed to go along with him?"

A smile flickered over her face as the waiter returned with their liqueurs. She waited until he had left before answering. "Not officially. Rodney moved us on his own, and we found a lovely little flat not far from the base."

Russo was suddenly serious. "What happened, Megan?"

Her smile flickered out as rapidly as it had come. "We were about to return home to England the night of the accident. It was very quick. I don't imagine Rodney even knew what was happening. I learned about it from his CO later. One night, on the approach to a landing, his plane was struck from above by another Harrier. The cockpit was crushed, killing him instantly. The pilot of the other aircraft ejected, but his chute never opened. He was killed too."

"Dear Lord!" Frank murmured. "What a tragedy."

Megan lowered her eyes briefly. "It almost destroyed me. If it hadn't been for Sean, who was absolutely devastated and needed me more than ever, I'd never have survived." She went on to tell him how she had to keep going for her son's sake, day after day managing to gather a little more strength. "Then one day a friend suggested that maybe a new career might help pull me out of the dumps, and how easy it should be for anyone with my—well, with my physical and mental qualities—to succeed as a stewardess."

"I couldn't agree more," he said gently. "You're easily the most unusual woman I've seen in this business. I'm thinking there's quite a remarkable mind hidden behind that beautiful exterior. One that I think I'd like to get to know better when my own problems are out of the way."

"Thank you, Frank." She smiled. "I think I'd like that, too." She felt her heart stir, but kept her face composed. "Anyway," she continued, "my friend's idea sounded appealing. I'd always found aviation exciting, so I decided to try my hand at it. It appeared to solve two problems at once. It would help me over my bereavement, and it would provide an income to augment Rodney's Air Force pension—It was generous, but not enough to let me raise Sean the way Rodney would have wanted me to."

"What gave you the idea of coming to America?"

"Circumstances. I was doing pretty well at British Airways. In five years I'd been promoted to supervision. But there were just too many memories tearing at me. One day I saw an ad from a new airline in America that was looking for a flight attendant supervisor." She smiled across the table at him over the rim of her liqueur glass. "That airline was Pacific Coastal. On an impulse I answered the ad, not really thinking I had much of a chance. How wrong can you be?! Pacific Coastal offered to bring me over for an interview, with all expenses paid."

"And you got the job! Congratulations, Megan. It's really heartening to hear a success story like yours. But it's really our good fortune. Where are you living now?"

"We have a lovely town house in Bridle Trails, and Sean is happy in his new school—learning a whole new collection of bad habits, I'm afraid."

Russo laughed. Then his face became serious again as his dark eyes studied hers. "Have you managed to put it all behind you now, Megan?"

"Yes, I think so. But there've been times when I needed a strong shoulder to cry on." She looked up at him, wondering whether the remark had been too forward. He didn't seem to mind. "I've been doing most of the talking, and I'd really like to hear about you now, if you feel you could."

"Later, perhaps. First I'd like to hear more about that son of yours."

"Okay. But I'm afraid it isn't a very happy story." She told him how the tragedy of Rodney's death had left one part of her new life still in a shambles. "Sean was very close to his father. Absolutely idolized him. So in many ways the loss was even more traumatic to Sean than it was to me. I hadn't thought about it from Sean's viewpoint, but soon I began to appreciate how much Sean needed someone to teach him masculine things. So I realized that sooner or later I'd have to make an effort to find someone to be a father to him. But that's easier said than done." That was as much as she could tell him. What she had to hold back was her despair of ever finding one as wonderful as her Rodney.

"I'm touched that you've been willing to share all this with me," Russo said softly. He motioned to the waiter for the check.

They walked out into the balmy night air. "Let's walk along the beach for a while. It's so lovely," she sighed. The moon, now higher in the sky, was casting feathery blue shadows on the sand from the palms above as they strolled along the boardwalk bordering the white sand. They paused to lean on a railing and look out over the glittering path of gold across the water. When she looked up his eyes were studying her, and the look in them was pained.

"Frank? What's wrong?"

"I—I'm sorry, Megan. It's nothing. I was just thinking…"

"Was I in your thoughts?"

"I can't answer that."

"I think you just did. I'm sorry. I won't try to pry into your private life, Frank. I have no right, as long as you're married. But if you need to talk—*ever*—I'd be honored. I mean that. You see, I—I rather like you." She was suddenly aware of the source of his pain. He probably loved his wife a great deal.

"We'd better go," he said.

They continued their walk back to the hotel and rode up to their floor in the elevator without saying anything more.

"It's been wonderful, Frank," she said, fitting her key into the lock.

"Good night, Megan. See you tomorrow."

"Can I buy you breakfast?" she asked on an impulse.

He regarded her with a crinkled smile for a moment. "We'd better do that another time," he grinned. "I promised to have breakfast with Walter, and I'm not sure he'd understand!"

"Roger that!" she laughed, pushing her door open. "Thanks again, Frank—or should I say Captain now?"

"Save that for tomorrow," he chuckled. "Sleep well."

Monday

◆

0710: White River

"We have to register here," Alex announced.

"Register?" Eric asked.

Alex grinned. "You haven't been exposed to our Governor's red tape yet. But that's not quite fair to the Evergreen State. I'm sure California climbers have to register when they're on Mount Shasta, don't they?"

"I suppose so," Eric replied.

Alex stopped the truck beside the park office at the White River campground. He saw Karen and Malcolm pull up behind him in Malcolm's battered blue Ford Bronco. "Registering is something all climbers have to do at the start of a climb, Eric," he explained. "In the early days they had no such formality. So no one knew who was on the mountain at any given time, or where. That meant no one knew where to look for them if they weren't heard from after a few days. There were a lot of deaths."

"I guess it makes sense."

"Sure, but now a lot of climbers are complaining that things have gone too far in the opposite direction—moaning about the loss of the freedom of the hills. But I appreciate the extra safety that filing a climbing plan gives me. There'll always be grumblers."

"There're probably a lot of private pilots that grumble about having to file a flight plan, too," Eric observed.

"Exactly. And many of them don't—Like JFK Junior a while back. Not a nice thing to do to the relatives—and to the poor crews that have to go out and risk life and limb trying to find them when they're overdue. So we do what they ask and don't grumble." Alex went into the park ranger's office, and returned after a few minutes with a copy of their registration form. They parked their vehicles and helped each other hoist their packs into place for the short hike across to the Sunrise camp, where the Burroughs Mountain Trail began, and where they would begin their ascent.

1300 Local: Honolulu

Megan answered the telephone after the second ring. It was Beth Winslow. "What's on for this afternoon?" Beth asked.

"I'm up for anything—within reason!"

"The guys were talking about taking a boat out for the afternoon. I'd like to go for a swim first. Did you bring a suit?"

Megan laughed. "Sean made sure I had one. I'm not sure I want to wear it around the pilots, though."

"A little skimpy?"

"Sean helped me pick it out. He said I needed a little advertising. But I'm afraid this one's like a blazing billboard!"

"This I've got to see! I'll stop by your room and pick you up."

"Okay. I'll be ready." Megan slipped into the suit and was just tying her hair back when Beth arrived. When she opened the door her friend just stood there gaping.

"What on earth is wrong?" Megan asked. "For heaven's sake, come inside! Is it too revealing? Maybe I should change."

"It's sensational!" Beth exclaimed. "It isn't—no, it's not too revealing, if that's what you're worried about. It's just—I've never seen you in a swim suit before. It's your figure. You could be on the cover of a magazine."

"It's not that fantastic! I have a pot belly," Megan protested, touching the slight bulge that she had never been able to get rid of after giving birth to Sean.

"Pot belly my foot! If mine looked like that, I'd die happy. The only thing I'm worried about is—no, forget it! Surely they'll have cops patrolling the beaches in Hawaii!"

Megan snorted and shook her head as Beth dropped into a chair. "Before we go, I'm dying to hear about your dinner with the captain last night. Feel like talking?"

Megan broke into a smile. "I guess you can tell from my silly grin that it was pretty terrific. We had a wonderful dinner together, a little dancing, lots of conversation, and I think we know each other a lot better now. But that was really all there was to it."

"I hope you didn't think I was suggesting…"

"I'm only teasing, Beth!" Megan laughed. "Sometimes I forget that this British reserve makes people think I'm hiding something. I know you'd be the last person to think I'd hop into the sack with a man on a first date. Especially a married man." She put her hand out to touch Beth's arm. "I'm sorry, Beth. Really, I am. You're my best friend. I've always felt a real closeness between us."

"You don't have to apologize, Megan."

The two women found a reasonably private part of the beach and spread their beach towels out on the hot sand. "Hungry?" Beth asked. She opened a styrofoam cooler stuffed with things she'd bought at a deli.

"Not terribly," Megan said. "I think my body's still trying to recover from that big dinner last night."

"Mmmm! Tell me!"

Megan told her as much as she could about her evening with Frank, leaving out a few of the more personal parts. She was slowly learning to appreciate the differences between Britons and Americans. She was discovering that Americans were a generous people, and that generosity extended to a willingness to share their innermost feelings with one another. She was coming to the realization, as so many of her countrymen had, that America was truly a new world where old taboos could be safely put aside. She was gradually falling in love with her adopted country.

"Did he give you any hint whom Marla is seeing?" Beth asked.

Megan shook her head. "He did say his wife's asked for a divorce," she admitted. "But no hint of whom she's fooling around with."

"He probably doesn't know." Beth snapped open a can of diet soda. "How did he feel about it? Did he seem crushed?"

"I'd say he is, but he keeps it to himself. My guess is he's a very private person. I think he really loved her. Still does, probably. He's really hurting."

"It must have been difficult for you."

"No, not really. He's not the kind to break down, though I think he probably will in private. It was just—a couple of times I could see the strain in his face. He wanted to talk about it, but he couldn't."

Half an hour later Russo and Harris came striding along the beach toward them wearing Hawaiian shirts and shorts. The two women waved to attract their attention.

"Hello there, haven't we met somewhere?" Harris quipped.

Russo laughed. "I think it's a good thing the crew don't dress this way all the time." He averted his eyes after a few seconds. "Say, I was thinking this morning—they rent sailboats here. Anyone game for an afternoon on the briny?"

Beth and Megan exchanged looks. "I'm in!" Beth announced.

"I've never sailed," Megan admitted. "Does that matter?"

"Let me see your arm," Russo said, frowning. He took her forearm in his hand. "A little soft, but I think you'll do as a winch wench."

"Winch wench?"

Harris laughed. "That's American for a slave to do the sail trimming. You put the handle into the winch barrel and crank like hell. It has been known to ruin marriages. But you're single."

The boat they rented was a sleek thirty-foot sloop named *Luisa*. Frank was the only member of the little crew that had any experience sailing, since he owned a thirty-footer similar to the one they rented. Walter had crewed for a couple of races in Seattle, but had never taken the helm. Beth and Megan were novices.

1013: The Trail

Karen swung her walking stick and swayed to the tug of her pack straps. She looked ahead to where the trail descend into Saint Elmo Pass. Beyond that was the rise up to Curtis Ridge. She was walking at the tail of the line, the place she enjoyed most. From there she could go at her own pace, unconcerned about holding anyone up behind her if she chose to stop and admire the flashing color of an upland bird or take a sip of water from her canteen.

As she plodded along she hummed a song to herself. Her head nodded happily in time with the song, causing her single braid to swing from side to side. The motion made it catch golden glints in the brilliant sun, which had now dispelled the morning mists. The warmth on her shoulders was a welcome relief from the morning dampness.

Alex had caved to her insistence that she be allowed to carry her share of the provisions with an amused chuckle. Karen, well aware that she had chosen a sport that saw relatively few feminine enthusiasts, was determined to take whatever this climb could throw at her. All of her prior climbs in the Cascades had been in preparation for this assault up the fourteen-thousand-foot flanks of Rainier. It would be her greatest challenge. Her only regret was that Mark couldn't be here to watch. But she knew Alex would tell him—the good parts and the bad, she thought, and strengthened her resolve not to provide any reason for criticism.

A hundred feet ahead Karen could see Eric and Malcolm walking along the path together. Occasionally one would have to drop back as the trail narrowed to pass through an outcropping of rock, but they returned to walking abreast as soon as they could so they could maintain their constant chatter.

A hundred feet or so ahead of Eric and Malcolm strode the short, bearish figure of Alex Papoulis, who was leading the team. As was his custom, he planned to let each of the others participate in selecting the route to give them the experience of leadership, in preparation for the day when they would lead.

He went over the route he had selected in his mind. It would be easy going until they reached the beginning of Liberty Ridge. Soon the trail would drop down and cross over the icy stream that issued from the tongue of the short Inter Glacier, where they would stop and refill their canteens. Then there would be an easy ascent up through the gradual incline of the pass. They would cross over a ridge onto the Winthrop Glacier at an elevation of 7,500 feet. Before crossing they would stop for a break and eat lunch. The afternoon would be spent traversing the glacier, then climbing up over the lower extremity of Curtis Ridge, down onto the Carbon Glacier, then across to their first night's camp at the base of Liberty Ridge. From there he planned to make it up to the summit and back the next day, and return to White River on Wednesday. "God willing," he said to himself.

He glanced up into the sparkling clearness of the blue sky as they broke out of the trees to cross an open stretch of gaily flowered meadow. Seven thousand feet above he could see the gleaming white of Liberty Cap, and above that there was a stack of pancake-shaped clouds, the result of the collision of warm, moist air from the Pacific with the cold, dry air of the upper reaches. He knew that the meaning of these frequent visitors to the mountain crest was ambiguous. Sometimes they simply dissipated after a few hours. Sometimes they brought heavy precipitation. And sometimes they descended down the mountain sides, bringing heavy snow and a white-out to the upper slopes, making the lives of unfortunate climbers miserable until the clouds moved off.

"Maybe we'll be lucky," Papoulis muttered into his shaggy black beard. He hitched his pack board higher on his massive shoulders and turned to see how the others were making out. He could see Eric and Malcolm chattering away like two blue jays. Karen's golden head was just visible bobbing along at the rear. He grinned as he turned back to face the beginning of the rocks. "Mark's a lucky son of a gun," he said to himself, then added: "I wonder if he knows."

* * *

1500 Local: Honolulu

Russo scanned the white-flecked surface of the bay as he neared the end of a long starboard tack. There was a forty-foot ketch they'd been dodging all afternoon a hundred yards to their right. He judged that it was far enough along to allow *Luisa* to pass astern. He glanced at his crew. Walter Harris was on the starboard sheet winch, and Megan and Beth were working the port winch. He yelled, "Ready about!"

"Ready on starboard," answered Walter.

"Ready on port," Megan and Beth yelled. Their voices were not quite as confident.

"Helm's a-lee!" Russo spun the wheel all the way around to execute a ninety-degree turn. He watched the boat's bow swing across the brisk wind. Something was wrong. The big Genoa hadn't started to luff. The boat heeled hard over on her starboard side. The two women were struggling with the jib sheet. It was jammed. The sail had caught the wind on the wrong side, driving the boat hard over.

"Take the wheel, Walter!" Russo sprang over to help. He gave the sheet a vicious yank and released the tangle. The sail caught the wind and went flying to leeward with a loud crack, taking the sheet with it in a sudden jerk. Megan was pulled off balance before she could let go of the flying rope. Frank grabbed her waist and held her. "Gotcha!" he said with a laugh.

"Good Lord!" Megan exclaimed. "What happened?"

"It's what we call a wrap," he explained as he took the wheel back from Walter. "Got it now, Walt?"

"Roger!" Harris called. Russo pulled the dancing sheet in and secured it. The boat settled into a less dramatic heel as it took off on the port tack. He turned to Megan. "It happens a lot," he said, smiling. "The sheet gets fouled on the winch if you're not careful. It's like trying to untie a knot with someone pulling on the rope. Sometimes it's so bad you have to cut the sheet to keep from broaching."

"What's broaching?"

"That's when the bow goes all the way down and digs into the water, and you wind up on your side. Not a nice experience." He looked into her frightened eyes. "It isn't a strong enough wind to do that today," he assured her. "Don't worry! You'll get the hang of it."

"I'll never learn!"

"Yes you will! Just keep at it." He gave her waist a squeeze and released her. "The way you make sure it doesn't happen is to have the sheet ready before we start to turn." He showed her how to do it.

"You're a real sailor!" she exclaimed, smiling approvingly. "I hope you'll be patient with me."

He laughed. "Of course! We don't flog the crews in America!"

Megan and Beth joined in the laughter. "This is all new to me," Megan said. "I've watched Sean sailing on Lake Washington. But from the shore they looked so slow and serene! Not at all like this!"

"It's the distance," Walter Harris explained. "An airplane doing aerobatics looks graceful from the ground, too. But when you're sitting there gripping the stick, it's anything but graceful."

"You guys really love it, don't you? Flying, sailing, all this physical stuff?"

"Sure!" Frank chuckled. "You will, too, in time." He wanted to say he'd love to teach her. Once he was free there might be time. He knew Megan would be an enthusiastic pupil. And an easy one to look at, too, he thought. He glanced at his watch. "Guys, I think we'd better head for the barn, or we're going to be half way to Tokyo."

"Roger that!" Harris answered. "I'm hungry enough to eat a wild pig—which may be what they're serving at the luau tonight."

"Okay, let's let her run free. Ready about?"

They all chorused: "Ready!"

"Helm's a-lee!" Frank yelled, and spun the wheel as Walter released the tension on both sails. The boat came around stern to the wind, heading back toward the shore. He let Megan and Beth each take a turn at the wheel on the way in, to give them a chance to experience the thrill of guiding four tons of charging energy with the flick of a wrist. The day seemed much too short when they finally returned to land.

"We have to do this again," Frank said to Megan as they walked back to the hotel. "My boat's a lot like that one."

"I'd love that," Megan said. The excitement he saw in her eyes was a little more than just the anticipation of another afternoon of fun on the water. He was sure he was projecting similar feelings. Looking good, he thought. But then he thought of Marla, and felt his spirits plummet.

* * *

1928: Curtis Ridge Camp

As Karen slipped the heavy pack to the ground she felt as light as a bird. But the sensation didn't last long. She was suddenly aware of the aching weariness of every muscle and tendon. For the first time since leaving White River she felt ready to collapse. She found herself grabbing for air in quick gulps, experiencing the effects of the altitude. It wasn't yet sundown, but Karen was ready to roll into her sleeping bag and forget about supper. But the last thing she wanted was for them to see her collapsing like a rag doll. She squared her slender shoulders and set up the folding camp stove on a flat rock.

Alex joined her and tuned his portable radio in to the local weather broadcast. The report wasn't encouraging. An unexpected storm had rolled in off the Pacific. The whole district down below was experiencing heavy winds and rain. Already power lines were coming down. Eight thousand residents were without power, and more were likely to join them as dusk approached with no abatement of the storm's fury.

"Grim!" Papoulis muttered, and snapped the radio off.

"How could this happen?" Karen wondered aloud. "They weren't forecasting anything like this yesterday."

"It's a freak. It happens sometimes. Probably a shift in the jet stream."

"What's the jet stream?"

Malcolm joined the group. "That's a band of very high velocity winds up where the jets fly," he interjected. "They don't understand them that well."

"That's right," Alex agreed. "All they really know is they play hell with the weather. The jet stream doesn't have to change much to cause havoc. A shift of a few degrees in the wind's direction out at sea can do it. This storm was supposed to hit the coast up along northern B.C. and Alaska. It just got deflected."

Karen and Alex moved over to the edge of the ledge and surveyed the broad white blanket of fluffy clouds below them. The clouds were moving up the side of the mountain. Where they were camped it was still a fantasy land. The mountain was catching the slanting rays of the setting sun. From down below, had anyone been able to see, the snowfields would be taking on glorious shades of pink. As Karen watched she could feel the strength of the wind in her face. It was getting colder.

"We may be in for it," Alex said as they returned to the camp.

Karen filled a pot with snow and put it on the stove to make the soup. "Will we be able to go on?" she asked, suddenly apprehensive.

"We'll see how it goes in the morning," Alex said. "Sometimes the clouds just dissipate without dumping. If not, we can hole up here and wait it out."

"It's a good thing we aren't up on the top then."

"A very good thing. Could get nasty up there." Papoulis squatted in the shelter of an overhang and began to light his pipe. He glanced up again. The lenticular clouds had moved downward.

Tuesday

◆

0830 Local: Honolulu Airport

The big tri-jet thundered down the runway. Russo lifted its nose and headed out over the white-flecked ocean, while Walter Harris looked after the radio transmissions to get their route clearance.

As they passed through ten thousand feet, above which they could relax the "sterile cockpit rule" forbidding unnecessary flight deck chit-chat, Russo glanced over at Harris. "Walter, would you do the travelogue this morning, please?"

"Are you serious?" Harris's jaw dropped in mock surprise. "You're actually giving up a chance for another of your monologues?"

"You're going to get yours one of these days!"

Harris chuckled. "What's our ETA?"

Russo glanced at the computer display. "Make it fifteen-forty-five LA time," he said. "Just in time for Happy Hour."

"And another layover! This is too good to believe." Harris picked up the handset and began to talk.

Russo found it impossible to believe that just a few days earlier he had been facing a marital Pearl Harbor. But after dinner with Megan Sunday night, and yesterday's sail, he was feeling years younger, his outlook completely altered—decidedly for the better. What an enchanting woman! He wondered if there might be something in the future for them. Could be. Megan had been more than casually sympathetic when he'd poured out his problems. But what about her son? That was something he'd have to ponder. He'd always wanted kids. But someone else's? Could be a handful. Still, with a woman like Megan, life could be pretty wonderful.

He wanted to ask her out again when they got to Los Angeles. Would she think it too forward? Would it run the risk of giving her the wrong slant on his intentions? And what *were* his intentions? One-night-stands weren't his style. And it was much too early to be thinking of anything serious. Still, there had been an attraction. Mutual, he admitted. Still, the last thing in the world he wanted was to scare her off. He'd better go carefully.

1115: Liberty Ridge

The rope joining her to the rest of the team slacked. Karen dug her toes into a narrow ledge and clung to a knob projecting from the steep rock face as she craned her neck back to look up. She saw Alex's bright red stocking cap against the gray rocks as he searched for a way around the bulging overhang that blocked their way. Eric and Malcolm were clinging to toe and hand holds below him. Above Alex the mountain was shrouded in a thickening white mist. As she waited she heard the metallic clink-clink of Alex's hammer driving a piton into a crack. Then came his deep baritone voice: "Okay!"

Once again she faced the wall, hands groping upward for a hold, following the slowly rising length of rope that joined her to the rest of the team. During their brief contest with the steep wall she had been feeling a growing sense of confidence she'd not felt before. All the practice climbs with Mark were paying off. She knew how to cope with the rigors of this mountain. The metallic glint of Alex's piton came into view. She gripped it and thrust herself upward. The overhang slowly moved on down past her.

The others were waiting on a gently sloping ledge, squatting on their haunches. The air was thick with snowflakes, and the wind was stronger.

"Can we find our way through this snow?" Karen asked.

"The wind will make a difference," Alex replied. "It's increasing. Good news and bad news. It'll keep the snow from accumulating, but it will make balancing tougher. We'll shorten up on the rope from here on. We're over the worst of the rocks. We'll be onto the snow slope soon. Then the crest in a couple of hours."

"Will we camp up there? asked Eric.

Alex laughed. "No way! That could be a battleground up there. We'll just go up, sign the register, and come back down before we get caught in a white-out. There's a nearly flat ledge just a couple of hundred feet below Liberty Cap. We'll set up camp there and spend the night. Hopefully, this storm will pass over us by morning, and we'll be on our way back down."

"The snow might accumulate and be too soft to travel," said Malcolm.

"Don't be such a pessimist!" Karen forced a laugh. But the thought of powdery snow sent a chill through her. She remembered Conrad, who had fallen into a crevasse hidden under a snow bridge.

"Don't worry about it," cautioned Alex. "If it snows hard we'll just wait it out. The wind and cold will harden it. By the next day at the latest it will go. We've enough food for that long."

"For bare survival!" Eric protested.

"Quit worrying!" Alex laughed. "We'll get you back down to Larson's soon enough. Or maybe we could radio them and get them to make an emergency air drop?"

"Now you're talking!" Eric chirped.

"Meanwhile," Alex grunted, rising.

"Meanwhile," the others echoed.

* * *

1530: Los Angeles

"Where are we staying? The Marriott?" said Megan. She retrieved her overnight case from an overhead bin.

Walter Harris shook his head. "No. They have a big convention this week. They've booked us into the Marina International." He'd finished going through the post-flight checklist with Russo and was searching for his overnight bag. "Where did I put that thing?" he muttered.

"I put it in here." Megan opened another of the overhead bins and lifted down two bags. "The other one is the Captain's. Would you give it to him?"

"Why don't you save it for him? He'll be right along. I think he wanted to talk to you."

"Roger!" she said. She felt her cheeks flushing as the first officer moved past her toward the exit. Good Lord! she thought. Maybe they all know. It was bound to happen. An airplane crew didn't have many secrets.

Russo emerged from the flight deck, interrupting her thoughts. She glanced around. The rest of the crew was back in the main cabin, getting ready to deplane.

"Hi, Megan. Is that mine?" Russo reached for his overnight bag. "Did Walter tell you about the hotel change?"

She nodded. "I like that. Sounds like more fun than the big city hotels."

"It's not as fancy, and a lot older, but I like it. And it's right by the marina. Maybe we can find another sailboat."

"Not on your life! I'm still recovering from yesterday. I just want a nice deck chair and a cool drink. I think my arms and shoulders are still in a state of shock."

"I guess we were a little rough on you girls," he laughed. "But we warned you." His face went serious again. "Megan, I was wondering—we had such a lovely time last night—do you think you could tolerate another evening? If I promise not to bang your ear with my personal problems again?"

"I was hoping you'd want to," she said. "And please don't mention banging my ear! That's what friends are for. Besides, I think I did more ear-banging that than you did." Again she glanced about them to be sure no one could overhear them. "As a matter of fact I was going to ask you. I'd like it to be my treat tonight."

He registered surprise, then something between amusement and pleasure. "I like that," he murmured.

"What? My asking you, or my picking up the tab?"

"I think you know which," he chuckled. "Your choice, but I know a lovely little French restaurant up in the Valley."

"Sounds wonderful."

"Shall I make reservations?"

She nodded. "Let's meet in the lobby."

"See you later," he said as she turned to go. "And Megan: Thanks."

"What for? It's what good friends do."

"Good friends. I like that."

"Me too."

Wednesday

0752: The Mountain

Through the raised nylon flap, Alex Papoulis looked out on the wintry scene. It was bitterly cold. He slipped on his parka and moved outside quietly to avoid waking Eric, who was still curled up in his sleeping bag. This morning the storm appeared to have exhausted its high-altitude rage. Overhead the sky was the incomparable deep blue that only mountaineers were privileged to see. Twenty inches of fine powder had accumulated on their ledge during the night. There was still no sound of stirring from the other tent, where Karen and Malcolm were sleeping. He decided to let them rest. They would need their strength.

He lit the stove and heated a pot full of snow. As it melted he thought about the nightmare in the snow the previous evening. He'd had them rope up close as they groped their way down the upper snow slopes through the blinding fury of the storm. They had managed to find the haven of the ledge because he knew it was there from past expeditions. Otherwise, they'd never have found it.

He planned to remain on the ledge for another day. Then they might continue, if the storm remained down in the lower altitudes. He peered down over the edge. All he could see was a sea of woolly clouds spreading out in all directions like a vast quilt. He could only guess what lay beneath.

He dumped powdered hot chocolate mix into his mug, filled it with boiling water, and wrapped his hands around it for warmth. From his vantage point he could look down into the broad sweep of the Sunset Amphitheater, a huge natural cirque on the west face of the mountain. Above, from that angle, Liberty Cap appeared forbidding: a white-rimmed cap that surmounted a two-hundred-foot-high ice wall. The wind was strong, out of the southwest. In another twenty-four hours, the wind and biting cold should harden the snow enough to give their crampons something to bite into.

Rainier looked like a gentle mountain today. But Papoulis knew only too well that it was never a gentle mountain, except in the minds of those who had never tried climbing it. Many of the novices he'd trained had thought Rainier was little more than a weekend stroll, because of its gently sloping flanks and rounded summit. More than a few unfortunates had become permanently frozen into the mountain's glaciers, which radiated downward like the spokes of a giant wheel around the mountain. The glacier ice was hundreds of feet thick in places, with deep fissures that could snatch at unwary climbers and draw them down into the death grip of frozen silence. He thought of Conrad and shuddered.

However, Rainier's most serious danger was from an unexpected quarter: the mountain's unpredictable weather. The peak was a battleground where raging winds and snows fought it out with a fury that only experienced climbers could appreciate. All the people down below ever saw was the endless parade of winter rains that marched through the northwest for three seasons out of four. But up on the summit the temperatures could drop to well below zero even in the summer, and sixty-mile-an-hour winds were not uncommon. A man could freeze to death in minutes in such weather. And then there was the altitude itself. At over 14,000 feet the air was rarefied, and made climbers fight for every breath. Pulmonary edema was a frequent but little-known malady that had taken many lives on the mountain. The disease could strike even experienced climbers, rendering them weak, disoriented, and foaming at the mouth. The victim died unless he could be brought down quickly.

Yes, it was a terrible battleground, Papoulis thought. But to the victor came the mountaineer's pride of conquest. And that said it all. It was enough to draw men to it like moths to a flame.

Alex Papoulis went down on all fours and crawled back into the tent. Eric opened his eyes as he entered and let out a grunt. "Time to eat?"

Papoulis chuckled. Things were back to normal.

* * *

0810: Wally's Garage, South Seattle

Roger Greninger parked in front of the garage and got out, juggling a cup of coffee, a jelly donut, and the latest issue of *FLYING*. Wally's was the only reputable shop that handled Jags in the city. Wally Knight had been trained in England, and really knew his business.

"How's life, Wally? Anything wrenching?"

Wally broke into a belly laugh. "A little busy this morning," he said, wiping his hands on a red rag.

"Will you have time for me?"

"Sure, if you don't mind waiting 'till I get this body job out of the way. It just came in. I had to call in a specialist from the dealership."

"What kind of car?"

"Type E, like yours." He pointed toward the last bay, where a man in white coveralls was kneeling in front of a gleaming silver sports car.

Roger went over to look it over. He crouched down to examine the damaged front fender. "Hey, this fender's got blood where the bumper joins the sheet metal."

"Yeah, I know," Wally said. "The owner said he hit a big dog out on the freeway. Couldn't avoid it. Poor thing was probably trapped. You know how it happens. Probably fell out of some guy's pickup, and then it couldn't get off the highway. Sooner or later somebody was bound to cream it."

The man in the white coveralls joined the conversation: "I'm not so sure it was a dog," the man said. "Usually you'll find some animal hair when you hit one. There's none of that. Looks like the guy took pains to wash away the evidence, but I guess he missed that bit. You oughta get the police to come down and have a look at it."

"Gee, I don't know," Wally said, scratching his temples. "The owner's one of my best customers. What do you think, Roger?"

"I'd say you have to. If you don't, and it turns out there's been a crime committed, you could be charged too."

"That's right," the body repairman allowed. "Body shops have to report anything suspicious. It may have been involved in a hit-and-run."

"I doubt that. Not this guy. He's not the type. Too damned square."

"I doubt we know anyone that well," the body man observed. "We've all got our secrets. Anyway, I think we have to let the police know, and let them decide. Want me to do it for you?"

"No," said Wally. "I'd better look after it." He walked back to his tiny office with Roger Greninger. "I'll just be a minute, Roger. Then I'll get onto your car. Okay?"

"No hurry. I've brought some reading material."

Wally picked up the telephone and dialed.

Greninger took a seat in the small waiting room. He opened his magazine as he ate his donut and sipped the coffee. He found his attention wandering. His mind kept revisiting the party on Carlos Santiago's yacht Saturday night. Not the party, really. The hour he'd spent with Janet afterward. He wondered what she was doing for lunch.

* * *

0940: LAX

Calvin Bronson glanced at his watch. "Jesus!" he muttered. Departure time was twenty minutes away and the line in front of the check-in counter was stalled. Not hard to see why. A blond twit at the head of the line was having a problem with her tickets. Three blond-haired brats clutched at her skirts, making a fuss.

"Typical," Bronson sneered to the man behind him. "They never bother to look at the signs. Ticket sales are down at the other end of the counter. Easy to see why she didn't want to get into *that* line. We were moving before she butted in. Not any more. She's seen to that. They'll probably have no aisle seats left by the time I get up there, and I'll wind up sandwiched in between two fat-asses all the way to Seattle."

"You should have reserved a seat ahead of time," the other man pointed out, showing signs of exasperation.

At last the woman got her ticket problem straightened out. She departed for her gate, followed closely by her three little ones, who were all linked together hand to hand like chicks following a mother hen. The check-in line inched forward.

Calvin Bronson was an experienced hand at air travel, and had the routine down pat. He wouldn't have to check any bags. He had a garment bag slung over his shoulder, and was carrying two other pieces: a fat suitcase and a briefcase. The limit was two items, but the airlines never complained. They didn't want to annoy business travelers.

At last his turn came. He presented his ticket to the agent and drummed his fingers on the counter as he waited for her to check it.

"Are you checking anything today, Mr. Bronson?" the agent asked, eyeing the three pieces of luggage he was guarding.

"No, I'll manage."

"You might be more comfortable checking the large ones, sir. You might have trouble stowing them in the overhead compartments."

"There should be lots of room. I want to be sure they get there. Is that an aisle seat you've given me?"

The agent handed him his ticket, forcing a professional smile. "Yes, sir. You're in seat 33-B on Flight 74, now boarding at gate C-12. Have a nice flight, sir."

Bronson hefted the three bags and made his way through the main terminal toward the entrance to his concourse. His arms felt like they were going to drop off. He wondered if he should have checked the two bags after all, and just kept the brief case. He was about to board the conveyor belt that went down the length of the concourse, but to his dismay it stopped working just as he stepped onto it. He looked at his watch. "Damn it to hell!" he growled loudly. It took longer than he had imagined, and by the time he arrived at his gate the aircraft was in the final boarding stage. But he had to collapse into an empty seat for a few seconds, out of breath, already feeling like he had spent the whole day traveling.

He heard the final call for boarding. He hoisted his load again with a groan and trudged over to the boarding ramp.

* * *

Mark Svenson heard the final call for boarding as he finished going through the stack of handouts he'd acquired at the Burbank air show. He drained the last of his *Americano*, tossed the styrofoam cup into a trash can, and picked up his garment bag and a cardboard box containing a new pair of climbing boots.

Most of the crowd had already boarded by the time he joined the line at the boarding ramp. He presented his ticket envelope to the gate agent and was passed through.

The airplane was another CH-12, he noticed. With a start, he recognized Miss McLain, the Irish flight attendant he'd found so attractive. As he boarded his thoughts switched to Karen and the other climbers, who must be halfway back down the mountain by now. He wondered how Karen was faring.

* * *

The cabin was a bustle of activity as Calvin Bronson entered. The flight attendant at the cabin entrance checked his ticket and pointed the way to 33-B. He found his seat and opened the overhead rack. It already contained a large carry-on bag. He lifted his suitcase up and rammed it into the compartment, followed by his briefcase. Then he stowed the garment bag in the compartment above the seat behind him. He had difficulty getting the compartment lids closed, but finally made it with a lot of grunting and heaving. He sat down, out of breath again. He ignored the complaint from the man in the window seat, whose bag he had mauled to get his own in.

* * *

An elderly lady wearing a dark brown wool coat and a small fur-trimmed hat with a veil that would have been stylish in the fifties was making her way down the aisle slowly. She was trying to manage a garment bag that was bigger than she was. She appeared to be in pain, for she had to stop several times to rest. She wasn't tall enough to reach the overhead storage compartment above her seat.

One of the flight attendants came to her rescue. "Let me help," the attendant said, taking the garment bag from her. "I'll hang this up forward for you, and I'll make sure you get it when you leave the plane."

"You're very kind," the elderly woman said. "Thank you, Miss—Miss Ryan," she said, squinting at the gold name tag on the girl's uniform.

"Yes, I'm Sally Ryan. And you are—?"

"Elsie Redfern. I'm a native of Los Angeles," she added proudly. "And you're from the South, too, aren't you?"

"Yes, from Alabama," the girl said, laughing. "The accent always gives me away."

"I guess the old saying is true."

"What's that?"

"That you can take the girl out of the South, but you can't —"

"Take the South out of the girl!" Sally laughed.

"In your case I'm glad they can't."

"Thank you! Have a pleasant flight, Elsie. And please call me if there's anything I can do for you." Sally Ryan smiled to herself. How many times had she heard that old saw? Still, coming from someone like Elsie, it was as though she was hearing it for the first time.

Sally had only gone a couple of rows forward when she encountered a flustered lady with three blond children. The woman was trying to get them all settled into the center section of row 30. Sally laid Elsie Redfern's garment bag on an empty seat. "Hello! May I help?"

The mother, whose name was Roberta Morgan, looked up and tried to smile. "I wish you'd explain to them that they have to sit down and behave on an airplane."

"Oh, you are so right!" Sally exclaimed, turning to the children. The two girls were about six and nine, she guessed, and the boy about seven. The children looked up at her, apparently fascinated by the sight of a woman in uniform. "Is this your first time in an airplane?" They nodded. "Well, let me explain, then. As soon as we take off, we'll be getting the carts out, and we have to push them up the aisles. And we couldn't do that if there was anyone standing up, because they might get hurt if the plane were to hit a bump."

"How do you hit a bump up in the sky?" the oldest of the girls asked.

Sally laughed. "I'm not sure I can explain that one, but it happens. You'll see! So it's really important that you be sitting down and keep your seat belts fastened, so you won't get hurt." She saw three pairs of bright blue eyes radiating trust. "And do you know what's in those carts?" Their heads shook in unison. "Well, we have ice cold soft drinks and chocolate milk and cookies for good little flyers. Would you like some?" They nodded excitedly and slipped quickly into their seats.

Roberta Morgan exclaimed: "Thank you so much!"

"Not at all," Sally laughed. And to the children she said: "When I return, I'll have a pair of gold pilot's wings for each of you, if you're all buckled in. Okay?"

"Yes!" they chimed.

Sally picked up Elsie Redfern's carry-on bag and continued forward, where she hung it in a closet. She stopped at the flight attendants' station to pick up three sets of plastic wings and three shiny silver toy airplanes bearing the Pacific Coastal logos.

"Are you planning on starting your own airline, Sally?"

Sally turned and grinned at Megan McLain. "Yes, I am. And I've just recruited two flight attendants and a pilot. Or maybe it's three pilots," she corrected. "They're the cutest little kids you've ever seen. Back in the center section of row 30."

"Let me take those back to them," Megan said with a laugh. "This I'd like to see." She paused for a moment. "I was just going forward to talk to the crew about lunch, Sally. Would you do that for me?"

"Sure, Megan. Glad to."

"Be careful!" Megan cautioned with a grin. "They're in a frolicky mood."

"Thanks for the warning." Megan departed for the main cabin Sally rapped on the door to the flight deck. It was opened for her and she entered.

Walter Harris craned his neck around and smiled. "Hi, Sally!" he said. "How's it going back there? Getting the sheep all bedded down?" Sally laughed and nodded. Harris set down the maintenance log he had been scanning. "It should be a fairly easy flight today," he said. "Only about two-thirds full."

"What's the final head count?" Russo asked.

"One-seventy-eight," Harris answered. "Plus the crew. Ten of us today. But Sally only counts for about half."

"I'll just ignore your smart remarks," she said with a grin. "I may be small, but I'm dynamite!" She turned to Russo. "How long, Captain?"

"We're holding for a break in the Seattle weather," he said. "LA Center promises there'll be a hole up there at about 1230. That'll put us in about fifteen minutes past our normal ETA. It doesn't look very good up there." His face showed concern. "They've had a big storm front rolling in off the ocean, and it looks like it's getting worse. We've got our fingers crossed, but we may have to settle for Spokane. All set back there?"

"Sure. They get a little antsy just sitting there, though. Especially the smokers, now that they can't try to incinerate us any more. Imagine! Two and a half long hours without a cigarette!"

"As if I could ever forget!" Russo groaned. "I still get withdrawal pains whenever I think about it."

Sally Ryan laughed. "Later!"

* * *

The ruddy-faced man in 16C was Arne Lindgren, a flight attendant supervisor with SAS. His two companions, Captain Ole Rasmussen and First Officer John Nikolaisen, were SAS pilots. All were wearing civilian clothes. They were returning from a brief vacation in Hawaii, before reporting in to the Boeing crew training center. There they would undergo a few weeks of intensive training before taking delivery of a brand-new Boeing 777. All three were in their late forties or early fifties, with the blond hair and square-jawed look of Scandinavians.

"Very nice," Lindgren remarked, looking about the cabin.

"The flight attendant? Cool it! She's much too young for you," Captain Rasmussen said, watching Glenda Abrams pass their row.

"Very astute of you to notice, Captain. But I was referring to this airplane, not the crew. Get your mind out of—"

"Watch it, or you'll be serving drinks again, Lindgren." Rasmussen gave his subordinate a withering look, then grinned at his embarrassment.

John Nikolaisen broke in. "She really is a nice ship. I like the high wing. And she's got upper surface blowing. A real STOL airplane. Somebody really knew what he was doing."

"What's STOL?" Lindgren asked.

"Short Take-Off and Landing. Where were you hiding when they taught you about airplanes?"

"I must have had something more important to do that day," Lindgren quipped, unruffled.

"They have slots along the wings to increase the lift for takeoffs and landings."

"What for?"

"To let them use shorter runways, dunderhead!"

"That's going to cost you a round," Lindgren countered, and summoned one of the flight attendants. "This gentleman—I use the term loosely—wants to buy his friends a drink, Miss. Would you mind? As soon as we get into the air, of course."

"I'll be happy to, sir," Glenda Abrams said with a polite smile.

"Watch these two," Lindgren warned with a sly grin. "They're off-duty SAS pilots, and you know what they say about airline pilots."

"Go ahead, Lindgren. Finish it. What do you flight attendants say about us behind our backs?"

"No comment!" Lindgren said, and winked at Glenda, who burst into laughter.

* * *

0948: LAX, Flight 74

Russo scanned the maintenance logs carefully, looking for potential problems. "This must be one of the first they've worked on down at San Jose," he said to Walter Harris.

"What'd they do to her? Just the B Check?"

"Yes, apart from a few minor repairs." He completed his review and returned the maintenance log to its rack.

"Hope they got everything back together right. Meanwhile, I'd better get our clearance to start engines." Harris made the call to the tower. The answer came back with surprising speed. "Coastal Seventy-four, permission to start engines. Be advised that if you can push back without delay you'll just catch a hole in the storm in Seattle. Otherwise there may be a gate hold. Can do?"

"Ground, Seventy-four. Can do."

The ground controller rattled through the formalities of their clearance to start engines and push back. "Seventy-four," Harris acknowledged. He turned to Russo: "Let's hit the road!"

Russo nodded and glanced down at the flight line mechanic waiting under the wing. He spoke into his microphone, and the mechanic answered with a thumbs up signal. Russo activated the starting sequence for number one and heard the slow buildup in pitch as the engine spooled up to idling speed. The process was repeated for the other two engines. When all three were running smoothly the tractor crew pushed the giant plane against the thrust of its three turbofans in a long arc, ending with its nose pointed down the taxiway.

"Ground Control, Seventy-Four. Ready to taxi," Russo said.

Ground Control gave them their taxi clearance. Russo moved ahead and followed the winking strobe lights of a Southwest 747. When they reached their assigned runway the Southwest jet received its clearance to take off. Russo watched it disappear into the brown haze of

California's smog. For a change there was practically no wind to push the stuff inland. He'd be glad to leave it behind.

Then it was their turn. Their clearance came through quickly. The LAX tower was fighting the heavy morning traffic congestion. Russo acknowledged the clearance and swung the huge ship onto the live runway, aligning it with the center line. The takeoff and climb-out went smoothly. Minutes later the CH-12 passed through the ten thousand foot level. Russo adjusted the autopilot settings for the more gradual ascent to their cruising altitude. "Okay, Walter, let them unbuckle."

He looked up into the clear blue of the autumn sky as they passed over the coastal mountain ranges. It should be an easy flight, he thought. He reached for the cabin PA handset. "Good afternoon, ladies and gentlemen," he intoned. "This is Captain Russo speaking. On behalf of the crew, I'd like to thank you for joining us in the exciting skies of Pacific Coastal Airlines. We have just left the LA smog behind us, and are climbing to our cruising altitude of thirty-six thousand feet. Our flight time will be two hours and thirty-four minutes. The weather is clear all the way at our cruising altitude, but the picture in Seattle is a little grim at present. An unexpected fall storm is rolling through the area. Not to worry, though: Seattle assures us that by the time we arrive there'll be a hole in the weather, just big enough for us to make it in. However, should we be unable to land at Seattle we have two alternates that will be clear, so you need have no worries. We're just coming up on Bakersfield now, and in a while we'll be passing Mount Shasta. Have a nice flight."

1011: The Mountain

Karen didn't need to do it, but she'd volunteered out of habit. She dumped the water she had used to wash their aluminum dishes and stacked them neatly to dry in the sun. They had breakfasted on the last of their rations. All they had left were a few granola bars and dried fruit. But the rest of their food supply was stashed at their last camp, which was an easy descent from here. Looking down over the blanket of white cloud tops far below she wondered how Felix was making out with the Andersons. Much better than we are, she thought with a smile.

"What are you smiling about?" Alex asked.

Karen looked up into his bearded countenance. "Felix. And our dinner together last Saturday." She rose and leaned back against a rock ledge. "I was just thinking that Felix is faring a lot better than we are right now. We're running on fumes."

"We've been through this before," Papoulis grinned. "Belt soup for lunch. We'll manage. A feast awaits us down below."

"Hold that thought," Karen said, feigning imminent collapse.

Alex gave her golden braid a playful tug as they returned to the tents, where they found Eric and Malcolm engaged in an animated discussion of Russian literature.

Karen thought of Mark, who at that moment must be speeding toward them. She wondered if he would be able to see her if she waved as he passed. But of course that was nonsense.

1027: The Main Cabin

Glenda Abrams, the youngest member of the crew, was just commencing the heaviest part of her duties with grim good humor. She and another flight attendant struggled with the heavy refreshment cart as they moved up the steep incline of the cabin's aisle. It was bad enough when they were flying level, because all aircraft had to fly with a slight upward angle to maintain lift on the wings. But while climbing it was next to impossible. Glenda noticed the blinking light above the crew telephone on the bulkhead to the rear. She went back and answered the call. It was Megan McLain.

"How's it going back there, Glenda? Still passing out the fodder?"

"What else?" Glenda replied with a chuckle.

"Captain Russo just told me he's expecting some turbulence shortly, so tell the girls to watch it."

"Tell him this would be a great time to turn on the seat belt sign! They keep going back to the lavatories, and there isn't room for a mouse to squeeze by these carts. Maybe one of these days someone will come up with a conveyor belt to pass out the goodies!"

"One of these days," Megan muttered. Her voice sounded odd and a little tired.

"Are you feeling all right, Megan?"

"Just a bit of a headache. I'll be all right."

"Call if you need anything," she said gently. Some of the flight attendants complained about Megan's aloofness. Glenda paid no notice. She really liked Megan, and couldn't see anything aloof in her manner. They just don't take the time to get to know her, she thought. As she went forward to her cart again the seat belt light winked on. Megan's lilting Irish brogue came over the PA system to warn passengers that if they weren't in their seats there could be danger. Glenda smiled.

Flights to Seattle always had a sort of carnival atmosphere. Glenda had never been able to fully understand why. She thought: maybe it's because Seattle is such a great vacation spot. The Emerald City. Seattle really was beautiful, on a sunny day. But that emerald color came from all the rain, and from the sound of it Seattle was getting more than its share today. She bent to look out one of the cabin windows. Lake Shasta and its mountain guardian were coming slowly into view a few miles ahead. She smiled at a portly, gray-haired gentleman who was aiming his camcorder out the window to catch a few seconds of the scene. She hoped the ground crew had done a decent job cleaning the windows.

Glenda made her way back to the flight attendants' station at the rear. Beth Winslow was supervising the loading of the last two carts of breakfast trays. She caught Beth's eye and drew her aside. "Megan sounds like she's not feeling too hot, Beth," Glenda said. "She might appreciate some TLC."

Beth nodded. "Thanks, Glenda. I'll go and see her."

* * *

Beth had to wait until one of the carts returned to the rear for refills, then went forward through the long aisle to the first class section. Megan was seated in one of the vacant rear seats, her fingertips massaging her temples. "Feeling tough, Megan?" she asked, bending over her superior. "Can I get you anything?"

"No thanks," Megan said, returning the smile. "I'll be fine. Just a little tired."

"A little too much late dining?"

"I guess so. I miss Sean, too. I'll be glad to be back home again."

"You're sure I can't get you an aspirin or something?"

"I'd love a nice cup of tea," Megan murmured. "That's one part of being British that I won't give up."

"Who'd want to?" Beth smiled as she rose, and returned shortly with two cups of tea. As they sat together Megan told her friend about her second evening with Frank Russo. Beth listened with interest, but refrained from commenting, then put away their cups.

"Any problems back there?" Megan asked.

"Hectic, as usual! But nothing unusual. They'll settle down after breakfast. Food always acts like a tranquilizer."

"One of the reasons airlines don't mind serving meals, Beth," Megan remarked, and turned toward the flight deck.

As Beth passed through the main cabin a middle-aged woman dressed in a jacket bearing a travel agency logo signaled. "Miss?"

"What can I do for you?" Beth asked, bending over the passenger.

"I'm Alice Princeton. I'm with a Los Angeles travel agency. I'm shepherding this group of tourists." The woman waved her arm to indicate the three rows ahead of her. "We have twenty-two seniors in the group."

"That's quite a responsibility."

"Sometimes it gets a little hectic. I'm afraid this is one of those times. One of the women is taking a prescription for a heart condition. She's run out of it, and needs to get it refilled." Alice Princeton's face reflected concern. "She's been worrying about what the captain said about the possibility of having to divert to an alternate. Her daughter is meeting the airplane in Seattle with a new bottle of pills. But if we have to go to an alternate, she'll be in trouble. Can you suggest anything?"

Beth thought for a moment. She knew they were trying to get there through a hole in the storm, but those things were often chancy. "Let me check with the captain. I'm sure we'll make it all right, but if we have to land at Spokane he could radio ahead and arrange for someone to meet the plane. Could you give us the name of her doctor and the drug she needs?"

"That'd be a great help!" Alice looked relieved.

"This isn't the first time. Quite often people get sick on board and we have to have an ambulance standing by. Pills would be no problem."

"You just saved me a lot of worry!"

"Just part of the service," Beth answered, smiling. She turned and headed back toward the flight deck.

She returned after a couple of minutes. "Captain Russo said he's ninety-five percent certain we'll make it in to Seattle on time. But just to be sure, why don't you give me the details." Beth waited while Alice Princeton conferred with one of the women in her group and returned with a slip of paper. "Thank you so much!" Alice said.

"Don't mention it, Alice. Just keep flying the Exciting Skies of Pacific Coastal."

* * *

1126: The Flight Deck

Seattle was just half an hour away. Above his oxygen mask Russo's dark eyes were fixed on the TV-like display in the center section of the instrument panel. Three vertical bars indicated the temperature of each of the plane's turbofans. They were supposed to be all green.

The right bar for the number three engine was just grazing the red zone. Trouble.

He tore his eyes from the display and looked up as Harris returned to the copilot's seat beside him. No longer alone on the flight deck, Russo removed the oxygen mask and stowed it back in the compartment by his elbow. "Hear anything serious back there, Walter?"

"It doesn't sound too healthy, Skipper." Harris resumed his seat. "There's a vibration I've never heard before."

"Keep an eye on that temperature. At the first sign of it getting worse, we'll shut it down. Oh, and better get on the horn to maintenance. They're going to love this. Jesus! The first time those sleepy Gonzaleses work on one of our planes there's trouble. What in God's name did they do to her?"

"More a question of what didn't they do," Harris muttered.

Russo watched Harris activate the private radio link to their repair station over the company's secure channel. Transmissions of this type were always encrypted to foil the attempts at eavesdropping by a multitude of media sleuths armed with radio scanners. Russo knew the reason. Reporters and TV anchors were always hoping for a chance to intercept what could become a sensational story. He grimaced. He had never understood the media's morbid fascination with news of an airliner in distress. It wasn't that they wanted to help. If anything, they just made matters worse, hampering the efforts of the people that really did have an interest in helping out in emergencies. He was jerked out of his thoughts as the airline dispatcher responded: "Coastal seventy-four, Maintenance Dispatch. Clarence Ulman speaking."

"Coastal Maintenance, Seventy-four. Hi, Clancy. Walter Harris here on Seventy-four. We're having a little trouble. Our number three is overheating and we're getting some vibrations. We're just about to start our descent into Seattle. We may have to shut it down. Advise if you wish airfax mode at this time. Over."

"Affirmative, Seventy-four. We'll take your data on channel four. Say, didn't this plane just come out of San Jose?"

"Roger that. You can guess what we're thinking. I won't comment, even on a secure channel. Data coming at you," Harris said. "See you in a bit. Seventy-four out."

Russo watched his first officer performing a bit of space-age magic that was unheard of just a few short years ago. Their onboard computer was about to share its billions of bits of data with the repair station's computer with unselfish abandon. The mechanics on the ground would be checking this information as it was received. If anything was to go wrong they would know about it as it happened. It also gave the mechanics a head start at assembling any spare parts or special equipment they might need, thus avoiding costly down time.

He glanced down to his left. The silvery thread of the Columbia River was just sliding under the port wing six miles below. Ahead he could see the white dome of Mount Rainier poking up through the solid cloud layer like a giant ice cream cone. The storm had descended to the lower slopes and valleys, where it would be causing havoc, he guessed. He motioned to Harris. "It's about that time," he said. "Let's wake up Auburn and see if we can get this bus into the station in time for lunch."

"Affirmative." Harris entered the frequency for the Auburn control center and asked for the clearance. The Auburn controller's voice came back immediately: "Pacific Coastal, Auburn Center. Please stand by."

"Seventy-four."

"Rough day for them," Russo said.

"For everyone. They're probably stacking them."

"Let's keep our fingers crossed."

After a short delay the controller came back to them. When Harris repeated his request, he added the information about their overheating engine.

"Coastal Seventy-four Heavy, Auburn Center. Do you wish to declare an emergency, sir?"

Harris glanced across at Russo, who shook his head. "Not at this time, Auburn. Will advise if the situation changes. Over."

"Seventy-four, Auburn Center, copy. Coastal Seventy-four Heavy is cleared to the Seattle area, descend and maintain five thousand. Contact Approach Control on one-two-three-point-niner. Advise tower of engine problems. Good luck, sir."

"Coastal Seventy-four, thank you. Good day," Harris acknowledged.

"Time for the fireside chat," Russo remarked, and picked up the handset that was used to talk to the passengers back in the main cabin.

"A short one would do," Harris cautioned with a respectful grin.

Russo chuckled. When he had finished talking he reached forward and entered the command for a gradual descent into the autopilot. The noise of the engines diminished slightly as Flight 74 began its long powered glide down past the gleaming white summit of Mount Rainier. "Flaps five," he ordered. Harris made the flap selection, increasing the lift of the wings as Russo further reduced the power setting to maintain a constant speed. He glanced at the engine temperature again. The reading on number three was unchanged, still up in the red. But no higher.

"Don't forget the exciting skies," Harris reminded.

"As if I could forget!" Russo made a minor adjustment to their heading to bring their flight path a little closer to the splendor of the mountaintop. It was a dazzling white as it slowly swam toward them. A great depth of fluffy new snow had obliterated the outcroppings of rock around the ancient volcano cones of Columbia Crest. Gone were all the dips and hollows. The broad double saddle shape had been transformed into a gigantic ski slope. Russo shook his head at the sight. He would never get over the awesome massiveness of Rainier, which seemed larger than ever from this close...

BANG!!

Russo's thoughts were shattered by the sharpness of the explosion. The right wing dropped, flipping them over on one side. Fighting panic, he forced his eyes to traverse the instruments. "Flameout on three!" His thumb stabbed the autopilot cutout on the control yoke, regaining manual control of the airplane. He struggled to level the wings. "Okay, we'll have to go in with two. *Damn!* Tell Megan to make sure they're all strapped in back there." He pulled the right-hand thrust lever back to the shutoff position.

Unaccountably, the red light for number three was still glaring at him, and the vertical bar of the temperature indicator was climbing ever higher. Then two new bits of information entered the picture: number three's fire warning light began blinking, and an audio alarm started to bleat with an ominous warble. "Hit the extinguisher on three!" he snapped.

Harris's fingers were already positioned over the large red button that would flood the engine nacelle with Halon gas. He depressed it. After several tense seconds the fire warning light winked off and the audio alarm cut out, indicating that whatever flames had been building under the wing were now dead. None too soon, either, Russo thought. Those near-empty wing tanks were filled with dangerously volatile fuel vapors. They had been lucky. No, that wasn't true: the system worked. Backups to backups.

After a few more seconds Harris reported: "Temperature dropping. Looks like we got it, Sir."

"Roger that," Russo agreed. His eyes were still fixed on the engine display. Although it happened rarely, shutting down an engine was not that serious, and in fact was one of the most frequently practiced cockpit emergencies. A fire was another matter entirely, but that danger appeared to be behind them now. "Is maintenance still tied in by FAX?"

"Affirmative."

"Good. Let Seattle Tower know, Walter. Tell them we're coming in on two engines."

"You've got it," Harris replied. "Do we need to tell the passengers?"

"No, but I'll let the cabin crew know," Russo decided. "With us cutting power on all three a few minutes ago, the passengers will never realize what's happened. But the flight attendants will probably have caught on. They have more sensitive ears."

* * *

Megan was so startled by the loud explosion she dropped a tray of dishes she had been about to return to the forward galley. Leaving the mess, she quickly made her way aft to the main cabin. There were loud cries of terror. All seemed fearful there was something seriously wrong. She noticed the amber light flashing over the intercom panel and picked up the handset. She recognized Russo's voice.

"Megan, we just had to shut down number three," Russo told her. "We had a flameout and very nearly a fire. Get them all strapped in tight. It may be a little rough coming in on two through this weather."

"You're a master at understatement, Captain!" She'd caught a slight tone of personal concern in his voice, but refrained from responding the way she wanted to. She switched over to the cabin PA system. "Ladies and gentlemen," she announced. "We've had a problem with the right engine. Please don't be alarmed. The captain has had to shut it down for safety, but there is absolutely no danger. These airplanes were designed to fly safely on just one engine, and we've still got two. The captain has asked that you all make sure your seat belts are securely fastened, and that you return your trays and seat backs to the fully upright position. And please place any carry-on baggage under the seats ahead of you at this time. Do *not* attempt to stand up and return them to the overhead bins. We are experiencing a lot of turbulence. Cabin attendants, prepare the cabin for arrival and cross-check."

She replaced the handset. The plane was being buffeted fiercely. It was almost impossible to stand. The brilliant flash of the Rainier snowcap caught her eye, momentarily distracting her. Suddenly, inexplicably, she felt herself falling toward the emergency exit. She had the fleeting sensation of some giant hand gripping their fragile craft and twisting it violently. The huge plane appeared to be falling sideways down toward the icy glaciers. Megan bit her lip to block the scream that tried to get out of her throat.

* * *

Sally Ryan and another attendant were moving their beverage cart back toward the aft galley. A passenger asked for a last cup of coffee. As she began to refill his cup she felt the plane suddenly lurch over onto its side. She saw what happened next as though in slow motion. The heavy cart tipped sideways toward the four center seats. Stopped by the armrest, it immediately dumped its contents. The container of scalding hot coffee went into an arc, completely missing the Morgan children. Mrs. Morgan was not so fortunate. It drenched the front of her dress. It took a full three seconds for her to realize she had been scalded. Her mouth opened in a scream as she tore at the front of her dress. Terrified at the sight, the three children started screaming in pitiful, high-pitched voices.

The cart continued to dump its contents. Beverage cans and miniature bottles arced up and over the three children, raining down upon the unlucky passengers on the downward side of the cabin. Flesh opened in ugly gashes.

Farther back, Glenda Abrams threw herself across two empty seats and held on as best she could to keep from falling across the cabin. She heard the crackling sound of tearing fiberglass and looked up over her shoulder just as a whole section of the overhead bins separated from the cabin ceiling and came crashing down. Calvin Bronson's heavy bags crashed down on Elsie Redfern. There was a sharp crack, like a dry stick of firewood being broken, and Elsie Redfern cried out in pain and clutched at her shoulder.

A shard of fiberglass hit Glenda. Its saw edge sliced through the skin of her left arm. White bone above the elbow glistened. Blood gushed from the wound. As she tried vainly to stanch the flow shock overcame her and she fainted.

At the rear of the cabin, Calvin Bronson emerged from a lavatory. Before he knew what was happening he became a human projectile, hurtling downward toward the windows on the opposite side of the cabin. He screamed in terror as his body crashed into the seats. Fortunately he didn't hit a window. Otherwise he and many of his human targets would have ended their trip on the top of Mount Rainier, sucked out by rapid decompression. But for Calvin Bronson it would not have mattered one way or the other. His neck snapped as cleanly as though he had been hanged.

* * *

Russo gasped: "What the hell?!"

"Downdraft!" Harris responded. "Can you handle it?"

"Trying!" Russo's gut went taut as he gripped the control yoke and fought to stop the violent roll. "Jesus! Jumbos aren't supposed to be able to do this!" He had a fleeting thought that this was part of a nightmare. It *was* a nightmare, but he was wide awake. That night years ago on Whidbey Island flashed through his mind as he fought to pull the right wing back up. Then things went even crazier.

BANG!!

Another loud explosion rocked the plane, this time from the left side.

"Flame-out on one!" Harris yelled. "Compressor stall?"

"Probably." Russo had been expecting it. The rapid rotation had created a wall of compressed air at the engine inlet, causing it literally to choke on too big a bite. Now there would be a flood of raw jet fuel into the hot combustion chambers, with the serious risk of another fire.

"Full shutoff on one!" Russo yelled.

Harris's hand shot to the thrust lever and yanked it all the way back.

"Going to full power on two. Flaps fifteen," Russo ordered. "Gotta increase lift or this monster's going to stall."

As Harris reached for the flap selector, Russo advanced the thrust lever of the remaining tail engine to full power. He heard it screaming as the fuel flow increased to the volume of a fire hose. The airplane shuddered as it tried to level out. They were losing altitude rapidly.

"Get on the radio. Tell Seattle!"

Harris was already on it. "Seattle, Pacific Coastal Seventy-four. Mayday! Mayday! Mayday! We're going down…"

1138:16: Sea-Tac Tower

"Say again, Seventy-Four?" Archie Crenshaw stared at the pair of radar blips representing the radar echo and the transponder signal from Flight 74. Next to the blips was a cluster of symbols giving the plane's identification and its current position, altitude, heading, speed, and a host of other vital information. The blips were merging too rapidly with the permanent radar echo from the colossus of Mount Rainier. Unless matters changed quickly, he knew he could be witnessing a disaster.

Crenshaw heard the transmission again: "Seattle, Coastal Seventy-four. Repeat, we're going down."

"Say your position, Seventy-four," Archie intoned, fighting to keep his voice calm, still unable to believe what the aircraft's transponder was telling him.

"We're going down on top of this bloody mountain! Get someone up here to help. This is—Oh, Jesus!"

The transmission broke off. Archie could still hear the sounds from the flight deck of the doomed airliner. As he strained to hear what was happening, the moving blip from the aircraft merged with the motionless radar echo from the mountain. Flight Seventy-four was down. He punched the emergency button on his control panel that summoned his shift supervisor, and alerted Darryl Washington, the approach controller up in the tower.

1138:19: The Flight Deck

"—Oh, Jesus!"

Russo heard Harris's gasp. The plane shuddered as he fought to get the nose up. The ice-clad wall of the mountain was flying directly at him in a gray blur. He and Walter would be the first to die, unless...he needed a hundred feet. Just a measly hundred feet! He hauled the control yoke back all the way to his chest and prayed that the tail engine would be enough to avoid stalling.

The nose began to lift, then falter, then tried to struggle upward again.

1138:22: SeaTac

Derek Winthrop ran his fingers through the unruly shag of his blond hair and gazed out the window. The branches of the trees that almost hid the towers of the hotel across the street were whipping wildly in the gale-force gusts. He and his cameraman had sought refuge in Denny's for an early lunch before returning to the downtown headquarters of Channel 3 News. The two had just covered a nine-car pileup on Interstate 5. Lionel Kinkaid had the whole scene on video tape, and Winthrop was busily making notes for his voice-over on a pad beside him as he drank his coffee. What he had hoped might be something spectacular had turned out to be just a gaggle of fender-benders for the insurance companies to sort out. Nothing worth their trouble.

Winthrop pushed his half-eaten lunch away from him. He wasn't hungry. He was about to say something to Kinkaid when the black-cased VHF scanner on the table beside him crackled into life. The words came through with crystal clarity: "We're going down on top of this bloody mountain! Get someone up here to help. This is—Oh, Jesus!" The transmission terminated in static at that point. A chill of fear shot through him.

"Do you believe that?"

Kinkaid was staring across the booth at him wide-eyed. "I heard it, but I'm not sure I believed it. They said they were going down on a mountain. Rainier?"

"We'd better get on the phone to the city desk. This could be dynamite!"

While Kinkaid paid the check, Derek Winthrop unfolded his pocket cell phone and called their editor at Channel 3. As he talked he wondered how fast they could get a helicopter down to pick them up. This would be the scoop of the decade if he could get on-the-scene footage. Bigger than when St. Helens blew her top back in '80.

1138:35: The Flight Deck

Russo felt the plane straining, trying to do the impossible. The wall was flying directly at them, about to crush their fragile craft. He yelled aloud to banish the panic threatening to overwhelm him: "Come on, you son-of-a-bitch, climb! Don't die on me now! That's it—just a little more—come on, baby! Come on! Don't stall!" The nose lifted. Would it be enough? Yes! Just barely! The plane was battered by a tempest of gale-force winds as they cleared the lip of the crest. Russo kicked the rudder pedals to turn into the blast. His grip on the wheel numbed his fingers. He cursed as the nose suddenly dropped. The vicious wind was driving them down. They were going to crash. No way they could clear the far edge of the summit. There would be bodies all over the snow in an instant, unless—*was it possible?* Without taking the time to think about it his hand shot out to cut power.

Harris screamed: "What are you doing?!"

"Hang on!" Russo yelled back. "Just gimme the airspeed!"

"What do you mean—?"

"Airspeed!"

"Oh!—Sorry!—One-ten."

"Come on, you sweetheart! Nice and easy now! Just ease it down." He eased the yoke back to flare the approach. Too much and he'd dig the tail in and break them in two. Too little and he'd nose it in and they'd flip.

"One hundred."

"Wind must be at least fifty knots. Thank God this baby has all those wing slots. Maybe, if we're living right—"

"Ninety. Don't stall her!"

"Another five feet. Come on! Sink!"

They seemed to float there for moments, suspended over the snowfield in the powerful wind. Then, with a sound like a thousand beer cans being crumpled, the plane's belly sank into the snow. The wing engine pods functioned like giant plows, sending plumes of snow to either side. The tail engine continued its low-pitched whine as the ship plowed its way across the broad snowfield. Then they began to rise in a sickening upward ascent toward the far edge of the summit. If they didn't stop...

With agonizing slowness the giant ship came to rest. For a few terrifying moments Russo felt the immense mass of the plane teeter on the edge of the abyss. Peering over the drooping nose, all he could see was a sea of clouds five thousand feet below them. The entire nose section seemed to be hanging over blue space. He had to avert his eyes as dizziness and nausea assailed him. After a few seconds it passed. He looked across at Harris and managed a grin. "Not a bad landing, considering," he said.

Harris just stared, eyes like saucers.

"Let Seattle know what's happened, Walter." He released his seat harness. "I'm going back to see what's happened. We'd better get them all moved back to the rear seats. God alone knows what's keeping us from hurtling down that glacier."

Harris tested his voice, found it would work, and began to speak: "Seattle tower, Pacific Coastal Seventy-four. We've just landed on top of this bloody mountain! We need help! *Fast!*"

* * *

Megan was waiting for him in the forward galley. For the first time Russo saw naked terror in her eyes. He took her gently by the shoulders. "Are you all right?" he asked.

"I—I'm not sure," she stammered. "The question is, are *we* all right? How *can* we be?" She remained immobile, her eyes searching his, trying to comprehend.

"We're down safely. We're alive. We're not burning up. That's all that matters right now. We'll make it through this. Come on!"

She still hesitated. "You're sure?"

He could feel her trembling. "I'm sure. And I really need your help now, Megan. Okay?"

She took a deep breath and let it out slowly. "I'm sorry. I'll be all right now. Thanks for understanding."

"Don't mention it, Megan. This is what our dinner the other night was all about, remember? I know you've got what it takes. I can count on you. Let's go." He released her and moved toward the cabin. Megan followed, gripping the seats for support. "What's it like back there?" he asked.

"It's a disaster! We've got some really serious injuries. I think one of the passengers is dead."

"What about the crew? Are the rest of the girls okay?"

"Not exactly," she said. He saw the strain returning to her face as she explained: "Glenda's arm is pretty bad. It's nearly severed. She's in shock. She's lost a lot of blood. But I think she'll make it. Beth's looking after her."

"Okay. We've got to try to keep the passengers calm. Panic is our worst enemy. And grab anyone who's got medical training—but I'm sure you've already thought of that. Oh—and very carefully, start moving them to the rear seats. Just a few at a time."

"Why?"

He saw terror returning to her eyes. "Just a precaution," he told her. He hoped it was the truth. He turned and made his way back up to the flight deck. Harris was just ending his conversation with the Seattle tower controller. "It's grim, Walter. We're going to need a lot of help."

* * *

1140: The Mountain

"Did you see that?!" Alex Papoulis was pointing up at the summit, where a new ribbon of white spindrift was trailing away to the northeast.

"I did, but I'm not sure I believe it," Malcolm Krouse answered. "Could it have crashed?"

"God, I hope not." Alex's head bowed momentarily.

"Maybe they didn't, Alex. Wouldn't we have seen a fireball and a lot of smoke?"

"They might have soft-landed."

"They may have gone over the side on the far edge of the summit, down the Nisqually," Malcolm suggested. "If they did, there's no helping them. But there's a chance they may have stopped in time."

Karen and Eric joined them.

"You think there's a chance there are survivors, Alex?" Karen asked, her face ghostly pale.

"It's possible," Papoulis said. "Miracle if there are."

"Dear God, please let it be so!" Karen moaned.

"Karen?" Papoulis studied her closely. She looked as if she was about to faint. "Karen, what's wrong?"

"I—Oh, God, I hope I'm wrong, Alex, but—Mark was due to return to Seattle about this time."

Papoulis's countenance fell as the thought registered in his mind. Then he snapped out of it. "The chances are pretty slim that it was his plane, Karen. There must be dozens of flights arriving. This is the busiest time of day." He wanted to believe it himself, but it was more important that Karen believe it.

"Let's go back up and see if we can help," said Eric.

"I'm thinking the same," Papoulis agreed. "But first let's get on the radio and see what information they have down below. Whoever it was must have declared an emergency. SeaTac tower would have had radar contact before they went down. *If* they went down. Hell! They could be lining up for a landing as we speak. Let's find out first."

* * *

1142: The Main Cabin

Her normally well-ordered domain looked like the aftermath of an insurrection. Megan picked up the intercom microphone. "Ladies and gentlemen," she said, relieved that her voice didn't betray the emotions lurking below the surface. "May I have your attention, please."

Some of the cries and moans stopped as the passengers looked up. She saw signs of abject terror in most of the faces. For the first time in her career she really appreciated that she would be the front line of survival for these poor souls.

"First of all, our airplane has come to a safe stop," she told them. "Captain Russo wants me to assure you that we are in no immediate danger. Unfortunately, we've had to land in a place that wouldn't normally be our first choice." She saw a couple of uncertain smiles. A good sign, she thought.

"The Captain has asked that all passengers in the forward part of the cabin move back to the rear seats. You'll be much more comfortable back there, as that's where the heat is coming from." It was a bold-faced lie, but she didn't want to start a panic. "We'll start with the first class section, and work our way aft. And please, just one row at a time. The flight attendants will tell you when to move. But if you are injured, please stay where you are until one of the crew members assists you. I assure you that everything is going to be all right. Just do as the flight attendants ask, be patient, and we'll all come through this safely." Another lie, she supposed. But what else could she say? That they were stranded up here? That it was time to get out the rosaries? As far as she was concerned it was, but she wasn't going to be the one to suggest it.

She was finding it impossible to squint into the fierce glare that was flooding in through the windows from the blinding whiteness outside. "Also," she added, "I think we might all be more comfortable if we pulled the shades down on the cabin windows. Just leave them cracked open a little at the bottom. We don't want anyone going snow blind." It might also help retain the heat in the cabin, but she kept the thought to herself.

Russo rejoined her as she finished. "I'm going to keep the tail engine running to provide heat and maintain cabin pressure," he told her. "Keep them bundled up. The temperature outside is ten degrees, and it'll be dropping below zero once the sun goes down. But it's the wind that makes it bad. I've no idea what the chill factor is, but I'll bet it's already way below zero. We've got to get them through the night."

"Then—there's no hope of a rescue before tomorrow?"

"Megan, just between the two of us, I'm not sure if they'll be able to get up to us for *days*. There's freezing rain down below, and Seattle weather is notorious for hanging around when you don't want it. I'm crossing my fingers, but we'd better do what we can for now. Just try to make everyone as comfortable as you can. Let's go and see about the injured."

Sally Ryan joined them as they made their way aft. Beth and two of the other attendants were helping the passengers move back to the rear, while others were getting out blankets and pillows. Megan marveled at the transformation among some of the passengers. *Maybe it's always this way*, she thought. *We respond to disasters with strength, not terror.*

Two men were looking after some of the seriously injured. The way they were taking charge suggested professional training. "Who are those two guys?" Russo asked.

Megan looked to where he was pointing. "They're a couple of paramedics. They were returning from a course in LA. Had their emergency kits with them. What a break!"

Russo nodded and watched for a moment as the nearest one plied his skill on Glenda Abrams's arm. She tried to smile as Russo and Megan looked down at her. The other paramedic joined them, accompanied by a somewhat rotund and balding man in his fifties, who identified himself as Doctor Kilgour, a dentist. "There's a seriously injured man we need to have a look at, Captain," Kilgour said, and led the group aft. A man in 29G was moaning from intense pain and holding his hand over a swath of gauze that had been placed over one eye.

"He needs a shot," the dentist said. "He was hit in the eye with something. He was wearing glasses. It's pretty bad. Do you guys have anything?"

"We don't have any narcotics," the paramedic answered. "But there's am emergency medical kit on every airliner." He turned to Megan. "Can you get the medical kit, Miss?"

"Only a doctor can open the kit," Megan explained. "Regulations."

"Surely that can't matter now!"

"I'm afraid it does," Megan said, her voice becoming officious, despite her efforts to sound warm and concerned. "FAA regulations. It's illegal for anyone but a doctor to open the kit because of the narcotics it contains."

"That's why we need it!"

The dentist intervened. "Wait a minute! I'm a dentist. Won't that do?"

Russo had been listening to the discussions, trying to keep out of it up to now. He held his hand up to quell the arguments. "Hold it!" he commanded. "The doctor's right. He's qualified. Would you have one of the girls get it please, Megan?"

Megan turned to Sally Ryan and nodded.

Russo summoned Megan, the dentist, and the two paramedics, and led the way to the forward galley, where they could talk without being overheard. He quickly summarized the situation. "I've already done a quick walk-through. It could be a lot worse, but it's bad enough. I won't try to kid you: we're in a real pickle. We're stuck up here. Our airplane seems stable, but our nose is hanging over the edge of a glacier. I'm sure you're aware we're above fourteen thousand feet, and that means oxygen problems. I'm keeping the tail engine running to maintain pressure and heat. Oh, by the way, there's a group of seniors back there. Rows nineteen through twenty-one, I think. Better check on them. They may be suffering from anoxia or possibly worse. We have oxygen bottles for emergencies."

"We checked already, Captain," one of the paramedics said. "One of them has a history of heart problems. She needs a prescription drug, and she's run out. We have something to get her through. The rest seem okay, but I don't know how long they'll last up here. What are our chances of a rescue?"

"There's a fierce storm down below," Russo explained. "God knows how long it'll be before help can get up to us. Severe icing conditions. No helicopter could make it without icing up and crashing."

"I guess that rules out a ground rescue party, too?"

"For some time, I'm afraid. Now, here's our situation. There's a dead man back in the rear. I'd like to have him moved outside, before—well, you know what I mean. You've already treated the flight attendant with the wounded arm. An elderly woman in row 33 has a nasty shoulder fracture. Apparently one of the overheads burst and spewed its contents down on her. A woman in 30-F was scalded when hot coffee spilled over her."

The paramedic interrupted. "I heard one for the books, Captain. There's a mother up forward with a baby. Apparently it flew out of her arms when we smacked down. It went sailing forward like a football. It would have been killed if it hadn't been for a brilliant bit of pass interception by a kid in one of the forward seats. The mother's probably suffering from shock."

"Miracles! They still *do* happen!" Russo chuckled.

"By the way, we're going to need a lot more morphine, and some antibiotics and penicillin, too. Any chance of getting an air drop?"

"An air drop? Good idea. I'll check on it. The military is pretty good at that kind of stuff. Maybe one of their cargo planes can make it up here." Russo smiled. "I guess you know how much we need you guys," he said. "That includes you, of course, Doctor."

"I wish I could be more help," the dentist apologized. "But I'll do what I can."

"Probably a lot more than you think, Doc. Quite a few passengers had unfastened their seat belts, and went ballistic when we went into that roll. I'd be surprised if there weren't a few broken teeth." He looked from face to face. "Megan, this is going to be toughest on your girls. Walter and I will pitch in with whatever we can do. Morale is our biggest concern. They have to have hope. That's *crucial*. If they start to lose hope and break into a panic, it's game over. So do whatever you can to keep their spirits up. Check to see if there are any clergymen aboard. And speaking of spirits, the drinks are on the house, as long as they last."

"I'd go a little easy on that, Captain," Dr. Kilgour cautioned. "Alcohol is only a stimulant for a few minutes. After that it can cause depression and loss of body heat. Keeping warm may be a big concern."

"You're right, Doctor. Maybe we'd better save the booze for the celebration when we get out of this mess."

"You think we will?" one of the paramedics asked uncertainly.

"I'm sure of it."

"How can you be so sure?"

"Easy! Pilots are never wrong." He winked.

Megan accompanied him back toward the flight deck. When they were alone he paused and looked into her eyes. The urge to enfold her in his arms swept over him, but he resisted it. "Are you all right now, Megan?"

"I always seem to feel all right when you're around."

"That's nice to hear!"

She laughed. "I didn't mean it the way it sounded! I meant it's a relief to have someone on top of things. To have someone we can all depend on."

"I think I liked it the first way better, but that's nice to hear, too. Hang in there."

* * *

"One of us is going to have to stay awake, Walter. Want to take the first catnap?"

Harris regarded his captain. "How are you holding up? This has to have taken a lot out of you. Wouldn't you rather take a break for a while?"

"I'm too keyed up to sleep. Why don't you get Megan to bring you something to knock yourself out for a couple of hours. Then I'll do the same."

"That's fine by me. I could use a good stiff drink, but I guess we don't want any hangovers." He rose from his seat. "You're sure you're all right?"

"As good as anyone could be with the nose of his bloody airplane hanging over an abyss. I'll manage."

After Harris left the flight deck Russo got on the radio. "SeaTac Tower, Pacific Coastal Seventy-four."

The voice of the radar controller came over the air immediately: "Coastal Seventy-four, SeaTac Tower. Can you say your condition, please?"

Russo heard the sound of concern in the controller's voice. The signal was clear and strong. At least that part was in their favor, he thought. He couldn't have picked a better place to transmit from. "Roger, Seattle. We have several injuries, some critical. One fatality. The flight crew is fully functional, but we don't expect to do much flying from here." There was a chuckle from the controller. "The airplane's hanging over the edge. We seem to be stable for now, but we could use a little help. What can you do for us? Over."

"Seventy-four, Seattle. I wish I had better news. There isn't much we can do at present. Be advised we are encountering severe storms over the entire area."

"Say the weather, Seattle."

"Roger, sir. Present conditions at SeaTac are: ceiling five hundred, visibility one-quarter mile, wind two-one-zero degrees at three-five, gusting to five-zero. Surface temperature five-four, barometer two-niner-four-five and falling. Currently rain at ground level, with freezing rain and snow from five to niner thousand, CAVU above ten thousand."

"Not a very nice day," Russo replied. "At least we have sunshine and a nice view up here. How soon do you anticipate clearing, Seattle?"

"This system is expected to remain in the area for the next two days. Perhaps longer. Say your fuel and consumption rate, Seventy-four."

"We have two-three-thousand pounds. We are using approximately one thousand pounds an hour, Seattle. That means we start freezing in twenty-three hours, if that's what you wanted to know."

"You read my mind, Seventy-four. What can we do to assist?"

"Immediate needs are for an air-drop." Russo read a list of critical supplies and drugs given him by the paramedics. "And we could use some food and blankets, if it can be arranged."

"Seventy-four, copy. We have been in touch with your company coordinator, Mrs. Gordon, who is trying to arrange some help from the

Air Force. She'd like you to call her direct on your SELCAL channel. Can you comply?"

"Affirmative, Seattle. And thanks for your help. Seventy-four out." Russo felt relieved. Janet would know what they needed. Maybe he could relax for the first time since they'd landed. He activated their secure radio link and as he waited he took out the bottle of pills his doctor had given him and took one. This was no time for vertigo.

* * *

1200: Wally's Garage

An unmarked police car pulled into Wally's parking lot at noon. A man in civilian clothes got out and came into the office where Wally was busy talking of the telephone and filling out an order form. Wally asked his customer to wait and pressed the hold button.

The policeman shoved a badge across the counter. "Detective Warren Colby," he said. "You're the one that called about the damaged Jaguar?"

Wally nodded.

"I'd like to have a look at it."

"Sure, okay. It may be nothing. We saw some stains that looked like blood. The owner claimed he'd hit a dog, but we didn't want to take a chance."

"We?" Colby looked around the shop. "Aren't you alone here?"

"I am now. But I had a tin bender here earlier looking at it." He refrained from mentioning Roger Greninger. "He'll have to haul it over to his shop. Too much to handle here."

"Where is it?"

"It's that silver job down in the last bay." Wally pointed. "Help yourself. I gotta finish taking this order." He turned back to his phone.

Colby went to examine the damaged car, and returned after a few minutes. "We'll be impounding it," he explained. He filled out a form, signed it, and gave it to Wally Knight.

After the policeman had left Wally stood behind the counter puzzling over the situation. The car owner was a good customer, one he'd hate to lose. The least he could do was to let him know his car was about to be grabbed by the cops. He consulted his Rollodex file and reached for the telephone. After a couple of rings a man's voice answered. He recognized the voice immediately. "You know who this is. There's been a problem. The police have just impounded your car." He hung up, not convinced he'd done a good thing.

1215: Downtown Seattle

Ike Gravetz, the helo pilot, looked across at Derek Winthrop in the right hand seat. "Ready?" he asked.

Winthrop turned to regard his photographer in the rear seat. "Got everything you need, Lionel? Spare tapes? Telephoto lenses?"

Kinkaid nodded and patted the nylon shoulder bag in the seat beside him. "Let's get it on!" he grinned.

Winthrop tapped the pilot on the shoulder. "Okay," he yelled over the noise of the jet turbine and the spinning rotor above their heads.

Gravetz gave him a questioning look. "You're sure you want to try this?"

"Absolutely!"

"Okay, but don't say I didn't warn you. Make sure you're strapped in tight—and secure all that damned equipment."

Winthrop nodded and passed the word to Kinkaid, who wrapped both arms about his shoulder bag. "Ready!" he yelled.

The pilot nodded, spoke briefly over his radio, and moved the power and flight controls to their takeoff settings. Suddenly the machine lurched into the air and moved away from the edge of the building. The wind was like a blast from a wind tunnel. Gravetz tilted the nose down and climbed steeply to get away from the danger of the downtown skyscrapers. The craft shuddered as it battled its way upward in the strong wind.

A hundred feet or so above the tops of the downtown skyscrapers was a forbidding ceiling of thick, churning clouds. Gravetz wanted to remain below that ceiling as long as possible so he could see other aircraft and avoid the danger of a mid-air collision. That meant flying dangerously low, but there was no alternative. He followed highway 167 down through the light industrial valleys south of Seattle. At that point he had to turn eastward and climb to avoid the foothills that were the advance guard of the Cascades.

As Gravetz ascended into the solid overcast an eerie world of dark gray cotton surrounded their tiny bubble of plastic and metal. He glanced across at Winthrop. He could see the look of fear on the reporter's face and guessed he was beginning to wonder whether the trip had been such a wise call. "We could go back," he suggested, his face unsmiling.

Winthrop gave a nervous shake of his head. "Let's press on," he urged. "This story is too big to miss."

"You could be wrong!"

They were just passing through six thousand feet when Gravetz felt the vibration. Winthrop must have felt it too. He looked across at Gravetz, his face reflecting terror. "What is it?" he asked.

"Ice!" The pilot's eyes met Winthrop's coldly. "The blades are icing up. That makes them go out of balance. I was afraid of this. It'll get worse the higher we go. We'll have to turn back."

"Keep going!" Winthrop shouted.

"No way! I'm turning back now, before we lose the rotor."

"You're being paid to fly this thing," Winthrop retorted savagely. "Just do it!"

Ike Gravetz regarded the reporter incredulously. "You're out of your mind! But I'm not out of mine. I'm not going to force Search and Rescue to have to come out and look for us in this kind of weather.

We're going back, and that's final. Next time take a bus!" He turned the craft sharply about and descended back the way they had come.

* * *

1220: PCA Headquarters

Janet held the radio microphone close to her mouth. "Frank?"
"Hi, Jan!"
"Are you all right?" she asked.
"This is not one of my better days, but we're still all in one piece."
"What on earth happened?"
"It's an unbelievable story, Jan. We lost number three as we started our descent, and on the way down past Rainier we got clipped by a downdraft and flipped over onto the right wing. Then, wouldn't you know it, we lost number one, as well—a compressor stall. It was all I could do to stay in the air. We were about to smear ourselves all over the side of the mountain. I still don't know how—I think it was a miracle!—somehow we cleared the crest and belly-landed in the snow up here on the summit."
"Anyone hurt badly?"
"One killed. Several in pretty bad shape. One of the girls may lose her arm. Walter and the rest of the crew are okay, but we're all pretty shaken up—except for me, of course. I'm indestructible. I just avoid looking down."

Janet's laugh was an explosion of released tension. At least he hadn't lost his sense of humor. "What about the airplane?"
"We haven't had a chance to go out and survey the damage yet. I don't think it's as bad as I feared, though. There was a lot of new snow to cushion our impact. All we need is a very tall crane to lower us down."

Janet suppressed a sob as the hopelessness of the situation assailed her. Frank was trying to keep his voice light, but she could read the tension in it. "At least you didn't wind up spread all over the summit. What can I do to help, Frank?"

"The tower said you were in contact with the Air Force. I know they can't get up here with a helo, but I thought they might have some ideas. Maybe they could manage an air drop for us. We need help bad."

"I'll check it out," she agreed. "We're aware of the icing. One of the news helicopters tried it and almost augered in. But the Air Force might be able to get up there with a Hercules. Give me a list of what you need."

She pulled a pad of paper toward her to take notes. The list was pretty long. The nature of some of the requests sent a shiver of fear through her. Things were a lot worse than he was letting on. At the end, he added a request for a flight surgeon. "One that's parachute qualified," Frank added.

"You want him to jump down to you? Why do you need one?"

"We've got some serious problems with a group of seniors, Jan," he explained. "We're concerned about what the lack of oxygen is going to do to them. The paramedics said something about pulmonary adema. It could effect all of us, really. I'm keeping the tail engine running to keep the cabin pressurized and warm—as long as the fuel lasts."

"How long is that?"

"Continuous idle, till about tomorrow afternoon. I'm going to try shutting it down periodically and use the APU for power. We don't dare run out of fuel before help can get to us."

Janet tried to keep her voice from betraying the fear torturing her. She knew what he meant. They would all die of exposure. And with severe icing blocking the way…"I'll get back to you as soon as I have word, Frank. Please take care of yourself. I love you!"

"I love you, too, honey," he said softly. "Try not to worry. We'll come out of this."

Janet clicked the radio off and bent over the desk for a moment. She knew what she had to do. "Please, God," she whispered, and pushed herself upright.

1230: PCA Headquarters

Carter Wycroft replaced the telephone and stared at it for a moment, unwilling to accept what he'd just been told. *So all your careful plans are down the drain. Jesus! You should have waited another two weeks!* Cold fear clutched at him. *A drink. God, I need a drink!* He went to his wet bar and splashed twelve-year-old scotch into a glass. He downed it quickly, then poured another. He returned to his desk, hardly aware of his actions.

The nightmare of that night kept forcing its way back into his consciousness, slamming into him like blows from a fist. The maddening part was that he still couldn't remember most of it. All he had to go on was what Carlos had told him. That, plus the unmistakable evidence of his damaged car, now locked away in the police impound yard.

And now, here he was, having to relive the horror of that night every time he thought about it. He had killed a pregnant woman. That meant he had killed *two* human beings. He was a monster. The kind of inhuman monster he detested with every fiber of his being. He hadn't even stopped. That's what was plaguing him. He had a feeling that had he stopped he might have saved her, or at least saved her unborn child. But he hadn't, and now he'd probably be charged with vehicular homicide. Possibly criminal negligence, too. And certainly leaving the scene.

"*Damn Santiago to hell!*" he exclaimed aloud, then glanced up at the open door to the outer office. *God! Could they hear that? What if they did?* But it was lunch hour, he remembered. Hopefully everyone had left. *And what of that stupid agreement you made with Santiago?* On top of everything else, he had been forced to elevate him to a position of responsibility he didn't deserve—probably over the objections of more than a few of his senior executives. Especially Janet Gordon, whom he had always admired and respected.

Could he trust Santiago? His reputation—perhaps his very freedom—was in Santiago's hands. And much more than *his* reputation, he realized with a sinking feeling. If word of this got out, the airline would be ruined. He had never felt so helpless, so desperately alone. He needed legal help. With a heavy heart he reached for the phone.

* * *

An hour later Wycroft rose to take the pudgy hand of his lawyer. James Thorndyke was a man in his mid-fifties, of average height, with ruddy features and a physique that advertised a taste for too much wining and dining. His stylish coiffure must have cost an hour's worth of client consultation, Wycroft thought.

"It's been too long, Carter," Thorndyke said.

"Too bad it had to be such a distressing occasion, James. Can I get you a drink? I think I need one."

"A little Bourbon would go nicely, thanks." The two men entered the adjoining conference room. Wycroft made the drinks doubles. After a couple of minutes of small talk, Thorndyke cut through to business. "Tell me what's up, Carter."

"I've just learned my car's been impounded by the police."

"How did that happen?"

"I took it in to have it repaired. They came to investigate it when the body man noticed some blood stains on it. I told the repairman I'd hit a dog, but I guess I didn't fool him."

"It wasn't a dog?"

"No. There was—there was a hit-and-run accident two weeks ago. I'm afraid it was me, but I can't remember much about it."

The lawyer's dark eyes narrowed. "Just tell me what you can remember, Carter. Take your time."

Wycroft went over as much as he could recall of the incident, which wasn't much. "I really can't remember any more," he ended. "All I have to go on is what Santiago told me the next morning."

"Santiago?"

"Carlos Santiago. He works for me."

"What's he got to do with it?"

"He was with me when it happened."

"We'd better have him join us, don't you think?"

"I guess we'd better."

Wycroft went to the door and asked his secretary to summon Santiago. He answered a few more of the lawyer's questions while they waited. When Santiago arrived Wycroft introduced him to the attorney and told him to help himself to a drink.

"Now then, Mr. Santiago," Thorndyke said, sitting forward in his chair. "I'd like you to tell me about the events of two weeks ago last Friday night." He looked at a calendar on the wall. "September fourth."

"I'm not sure I understand." Santiago glanced furtively at Wycroft. "What events?"

"Mr. Wycroft has told me about the accident. So let's save time and cut through to the details, shall we? And please, be perfectly candid."

"You can trust Mr. Thorndyke, Carlos," Wycroft said.

"Sure, okay," said Santiago. "I just wanted to be sure."

Thorndyke placed a tape recorder on the conference table and turned it on. No one commented. "Start at the beginning. You were at a party, I believe?"

"Yes. We were at a fund raiser over in the U-district. Some Democrat trying to drum up support for her run for the State Senate."

"And?"

Santiago took a deep swallow of whiskey as he glanced at Wycroft again. "We'd been talking about my ideas for the airline sales campaign. Carter was anxious to get going. Something about a party his wife had planned. I thought that was a little amusing, because he wasn't in any shape to go to another party."

"How's that?" Thorndyke asked.

"He was snockered!"

"Intoxicated?"

"That's right."

"Then—why didn't you offer to drive?"

"Are you kidding? I was in the same shape."

"You were drunk?"

"Well—I could still stand up. But I was in no condition to be driving. Neither was Carter. I had to practically carry him out to the car."

"And you let him drive home in that condition?"

"*Let* him? He *insisted!*" Carlos retorted angrily. "Hey, what the hell's going on here? You're trying to insinuate I did something wrong?"

"You might have thought about calling a taxi."

"It was my decision," Wycroft interjected.

Thorndyke ignored Wycroft's remark. "Okay. You left the party. What happened then?"

"Carter had trouble getting the car started. Then he almost took off without me—forgot I was waiting for a ride home."

"Why did you need a ride? Didn't you have your own car?"

"No. It was in the repair shop."

"Go on. What happened next?"

"Well—it's a little fuzzy, but—He was going to drop me off at Mercer Island—that's where I live. We were heading west on forty-fifth, almost at the freeway on-ramp. Carter was really flooring it. I tried to get him to slow down, but he wasn't hearing it. Anyway, all of a sudden I saw a shape move out from the curb. Before I knew what was happening there was a loud thud, and I saw something flying off toward the curb."

"Were the headlights on?"

"No."

"But you could see all this happening?"

"Sure. It wasn't very dark. About seven o'clock. Besides, the street lights were on."

"And then what?"

"I told Carter to stop—that he'd hit something."

"And?"

"He ignored me. Just hit the accelerator and took off like he was on fire. Damn near snapped my neck off!"

"He didn't try to stop, to see what he'd hit?"

"No. I begged him, but he just drove all the faster. Somehow we made it to Mercer Island. He dropped me off, and that was the last I saw of him till the next morning."

"I called him, and asked him to come over," Wycroft explained.

Thorndyke turned to face his client. "Why did you do that?"

"I didn't know what to do. I saw the damaged fender and the blood stains, and I thought I ought to go to the police. Carlos talked me out of it. Told me to say we'd hit a dog, if anyone asked. God help me, I agreed. We washed the blood stains off the car, then I locked it up in the garage."

Santiago was about to protest, but the lawyer held up his hand for silence. "And then you took it in to the repair shop this morning?"

"Yes. I thought it'd be safe by now. I don't drive the Jag very often, so I thought I'd just wait until it was off the front pages. I usually use the big Mercedes."

"Why didn't you just go to the police and admit what happened?"

"What could I tell them? I couldn't remember a thing about it. As I told you, all I had to go on was what Carlos told me. Besides, I had the airline to think of. A scandal like that would be a disaster."

"You may have made matters a lot worse, Carter."

"I know." Wycroft rose and poured himself another drink. Santiago joined him, and whispered: "I hope you didn't say anything about our agreement." Wycroft shook his head.

"What was that about?" Thorndyke demanded when the two men returned to their chairs.

"Private matter," Wycroft assured his attorney. "Nothing to do with this." But he was beginning to wonder about that. Maybe he ought to make a clean breast of everything, including the pact he'd made with Santiago.

"I hope you're telling me the truth, Carter," Thorndyke said quietly. After another ten minutes of questioning he rose to go. "I'll see what I can find out about your car. Until then, say nothing to anyone."

1230: Mercer Island

"Oh, God! Carlos!" she gasped. Her arms and calves tightened about him in the intense explosion of climax. For once she hadn't had to fake it. It was a new experience in their lovemaking. For some reason she found herself totally aroused by him today. It was several minutes before either of them could breathe normally again. Marla lay beside him, feeling the slow ebb of passion as her body returned to normal. She had almost drifted off to sleep in his arms when she was jolted awake by the telephone ringing. She reached for the instrument on the night table and passed it to Carlos.

"Hullo?" Carlos rubbed his eyes as he listened to the voice on the phone.

Marla watched his face across the pillows. Suddenly it began to twist into a mask of agony. Speechless, he passed the phone back to her and fell back into the pillows.

"Darling, what's wrong?"

"We—we've had a disaster," he stammered.

* * *

1235: McChord AFB

Captain Edna Carlson had taken an early lunch at the Officers' Club, and was returning to her office in Search and Rescue Ops when she heard the phone ringing. She scooped it up before sitting down, listened for a moment, then groped for her chair, unable to believe what she was hearing.

"On top of Rainier?" she asked incredulously. "A jumbo?…How many on board?…Any fatalities?…Serious injuries?…" She listened to the answers. Her mind raced to keep up with the unthinkable horror. At the end of the explanation she straightened in her chair. "Okay, how can we help?" She began taking notes on a pad, scribbling rapidly as her mind filled in details. "I'll have to clear this with my CO," she said at last. "But I'm sure he'll want to help. I'll be back to you A-S-A-P."

She called the Colonel in charge of SAR, explained the situation to him, and nodded enthusiastically when he told her to go ahead with her plan. She summoned her assistant from the next office. When he entered she said: "You aren't going to believe this. There's an airliner down, and they need an air drop of medical supplies. Guess where they landed?"

"You've got me."

"Would you believe the top of Mount Rainier?"

"What?! How on earth—?"

"Long story," Edna Carlson said, rising from her chair. "Come on. I'll fill in the details on the way. We've got a lot of planning to do and too little time. I hope Major Devane is on duty today."

"Devane?"

"The flight surgeon. He used to be airborne. He's chute qualified."

"God!"

"He might be a big help."

"Devane?"

"No, the other one."

* * *

1245: The Mountain

Papoulis pushed the telescopic antenna back into his radio and turned it off. "The news is not good," he told the others. "The storm's a lot worse than we thought. All the Coast Guard equipment is grounded. Everyone else's, too. It's icing like crazy down below. As far as help's concerned, I guess we're it."

"Let's do what we can," Karen insisted. Eric and Malcolm agreed.

"Okay. Let's get it together. Crampons and ice axes! And don't forget your goggles."

Half way up to the summit Alex made one more try on his radio.

*   *   *

1300: The Main Cabin

Mark Svenson heard a faint beep coming from the inside pocket of his jacket. It was a few seconds before he recognized the source. His pocket VHF scanner. He always kept it on standby. But in his pocket the antenna wasn't out. He wondered how he could be receiving a signal way up here with no antenna. Could it be one of the radios on board? He took the radio out, extended the antenna, and turned on the audio. The voice he heard sounded familiar.

"Say again, caller. This is Mark Svenson. Over."

"Mark?" The voice seemed startled, suddenly excited, momentarily forgetting the formalities of FCC regulations.

"Alex? Is that you?"

"I'll be damned! We're just below Liberty Cap. Where are you? Over."

"You'd never believe it in a thousand years. I'm right above you, here on the summit. In a big jumbo jet. We're going to need a lot of help, Alex. Can you get up to us? Over."

"I'll be damned! Sure, no problem. We're on our way already," Alex answered. "I can't see you, Mark. You must be on the other side of the saddle."

"Yes, I think so," Mark answered. "I can see the Nisqually out the window. We seem to be perched over the edge. Over."

There was a pause before Alex's voice came back. Mark could guess the excited exchanges going on between the team members. "Many injuries, Mark? Over."

"Not as many as I'd have thought. We got hit by a downdraft and went over on our side initially, so there are a lot of cuts and bruises. One guy broke his neck and died, and there're some pretty bad injuries from flying debris and luggage. And a lot of seniors that are going to get very sick if they don't get help pretty fast. We have two paramedics and a dentist on board, thank God. But we need more help. Over."

"We'll be there shortly, Mark."

"Good show! Over and—"

"Hold it, Mark. Here's a friendly voice."

"Mark?" Karen's voice trembled with excitement. "Are you all right?"

"Hi, Kitten! I'm fine. How're you? That must have been some blow you guys had to endure."

Karen's laugh was a little too loud, apparently masking deeper feelings she was trying to hide. "You know me," she said. She made an attempt at laughter, but it wasn't quite making it. "I'm indestructible", she said. "My Teutonic blood, I guess. We'll see you in a bit. Save us a few seats. Over."

"First class or economy?"

"You nut! Over and out!"

* * *

1330: CPA Operations

Janet had set up a temporary command post in CPA's flight operations center, where she was coordinating a series of calls to the Air Force, various rescue units, and her own maintenance people. She looked up to see Carlos Santiago looking down at her.

"What do you want?" she asked.

"Just observing how the great lady-executive is coping with something serious for a change."

"You'll read about it in the papers tomorrow, Carlos. So why don't you go back home and leave the business of running this airline to those who know how."

"Ah, the newspapers. But that's the point, isn't it? Public Relations *is* my business. That's what I'm here for."

"What are you talking about?"

"There are several members of the press—and radio and TV—out there waiting for a story. I'll bet you haven't even thought about what you're going to tell them."

Santiago had a point, much as she hated to admit it. Someone had to handle the media. This was a sensational story, and she didn't want them putting the wrong spin on it. Pacific Coastal's financial future would depend on the public's reaction to what had happened up on the mountain. Letting Santiago handle the PR would free her to look after coordinating rescue activities on the mountain. The question was how far she could trust him.

"Okay, Carlos," she said at last. "But I want one thing clear. You're not to mention anything about that deal you made with Costa Rica. *Not a word!* Frank told me all about the crash. There's no doubt in his mind that those grease monkeys did something wrong. Engines don't catch on fire for no reason. As far as the public is concerned, I want you to tell them that it was the storm that caused the accident, and that it was due to the skill and presence of mind of the pilots that a disaster has been averted. All but one of the passengers are still alive up there, and we intend to get them all down safely. And that's *all* you're to tell them."

Santiago glared at her for a moment. "Carter may have something to say about that."

"Don't even think about going to him, Carlos," Janet said, glowering. "I don't know what's going on between you two, but don't think you can jeopardize the reputation of this airline. If it comes to that, I'll take you both on. And I'll win. The board won't stand behind you. And remember: your own future depends on Pacific Coastal's success. If this airline folds, you go down with it.

Santiago turned and left her office without a word.

1340: The Main Cabin

Mark Svenson was working on the article he intended to file with the *Seattle Globe*. His attention was drawn to the window by a riptide of excitement running through the cabin. Several passengers were pointing and talking in excited voices. When he looked out he caught sight of a man with a red stocking cap and a shaggy black beard coming toward them across the blinding white snowfield. Three other figures followed him.

He heard Megan McLain trying to restrain the passengers from surging over to the left side and disturbing the airplane's precarious balance. The first officer came striding down the aisle past him. Svenson rose to his feet and followed him to the rear exit door, which two of the men passengers were attempting to open. "Better let me look after that," Harris said firmly. He placed himself in their way before they could do any serious harm. Svenson helped Harris to release the lock, allowing the large door to pop inward, then swing open. They were met with a blast of icy wind. He looked down into Alex Papoulis's beaming face.

"Hi, Mark!" Papoulis shouted from below. "Some runway you guys picked!

Svenson chuckled. "Best we could find!"

"Do you guys have a ladder?"

"Sure do," Harris answered. He disappeared into the aft storage area and returned with a telescoping ladder. He extended it and passed it down to the waiting team, securing the upper end into holes in the door sill. Papoulis ascended the ladder, followed by the other three climbers.

"Alex Papoulis at your service, sir," Alex said, grinning broadly. "I expect you could use a little help."

"You're a godsend!" Harris said, taking the powerful hand and pumping it vigorously. Russo came back and joined the group. Harris made the introductions.

"We'd better get the door closed quickly and save cabin heat," Russo urged. "Let's go forward and talk. Guess you could use a hot cup of coffee. Or something a little stronger? You don't know how glad we are to see you here."

"Excuse me!" Karen said, squeezing past the group. Her eyes shone as she greeted Mark. The rest of the group continued forward, leaving them to themselves.

"Hi, Kitten!" Svenson broke into his first smile since they had crashed on the summit. He opened his arms and drew Karen close.

"Hi yourself," she murmured happily, looking up into his eyes. "I've missed you. We all did."

He searched her eyes for signs of tiredness, but all he saw was a happy sparkle he'd never seen before. Her body felt strong, vibrantly alive against him as he continued to hold her. "I can't tell you how glad I am to see you! And I'm really proud of you. I guess I don't need to worry about you any more. This trip proves it."

"You never did!" she laughed happily.

He took her forward and they sat down together. "Tell me all about the climb," he urged, taking her hand in his. And as they talked the snow began to fall again, closing off their world in a sea of solid white.

* * *

1400: Seattle Police Headquarters

A red-haired man wearing a windbreaker and a faded Seattle Mariners baseball cap entered the door marked "Detectives". A woman receptionist looked up. "Yes? May I help you?"

"Name's Ingram," the man said, removing his cap. "I'm to see—" He took out a slip of paper from his shirt pocket and glanced at it. "Detective Steele."

"What's it about?"

"An accident. I was a witness."

"You spoke to Detective Steele about it?"

"Yes—He said I should come in."

"Just a moment, please." The woman pressed one of the buttons on her telephone. "Mr. Ingram to see you," she said. She listened for a moment and replaced the phone. "He'll be right out."

Detective Steele emerged from one of the offices along the wall. He was a stocky man in his early forties with dark brown hair, a ruddy face, and bushy eyebrows that softened the cold gray of his eyes. He smiled broadly and held out a beefy hand, causing Ingram to nearly drop his cap. "Harold Steele," the detective said. "Come on back to my office. Would you like some coffee?"

"That'd be good," Ingram said. "Black."

"Megan, would you, please? Make it two."

The receptionist scowled as she got up from her desk. Steele ignored the look. She'd been making noisy protests lately about being used as a waitress. He had serious doubts Megan would be able to cut the mustard in that job, either. He led the way to his office and waved Ingram to a seat. He looked across the desk at the man for a moment as he mentally reviewed what he knew about the hit-and-run case so far. Not very much, as it turned out. His efforts to find any witnesses had drawn a blank until this man had called in out of the blue. This could be the break he'd been hoping for.

"Your name is Myron Ingram?" Steele began.

"Yes." Ingram hunched forward on the edge of the chair, fidgeting nervously with the bill of his cap.

Steele asked for and wrote down the man's address and a few other particulars. The receptionist entered the office and put two heavy white mugs down without a word. "Thanks, Megan," Steele said, smiling. The smile went unnoticed. "Civil servants with tenure are sent to test us," he commented with a grin. He returned his attention to the man before him. "Now then: You said you witnessed an accident."

"Right."

"When was that?"

"Two weeks ago last Friday."

"What took you so long coming forward about it?"

"Conscience finally got the better of me, I guess. I didn't want to get involved. But when I read about it in the papers—you know how it is."

"We're glad of any help, Mr. Ingram. Were there any other witnesses?"

"A few standing at the bus stop, but they took off when the police showed up. So did I."

"What time did it happen?"

"About seven or so. I'm not that sure. Still daylight."

Steele nodded. Something about this eyewitness convinced him that he was an honest man. He'd already run a check on him, and found he'd never been in trouble with the law.

"Tell me what you saw." Steele switched on a miniature tape recorder as he spoke.

"What's that for?" Ingram asked, visibly alarmed.

Steele laughed. "Don't pay any attention to it. We used to have a steno to take notes. Then downsizing hit us. A tape recorder is a lot cheaper. It's not legal as evidence. If we find we need it, we'll get you to make a formal statement. This is just for the record."

"Just for the record?"

Steele smiled, trying to put his witness at ease. "You aren't in any trouble, Mr. Ingram. Much the contrary. If you can help us catch the person who killed Tracy Wingate we'll be extremely grateful. As will everyone else involved. Especially her family. Did you know she was pregnant?"

Ingram nodded. He seemed relieved by the detective's words. "I read about that."

"Where were you when it happened, Mr. Ingram?"

"I'd just come out of my apartment building."

"The Carleton Arms, you said?"

"That's right." Ingram fumbled in his shirt pocket for his cigarettes. "Okay to smoke in here?"

"Afraid not. The triumph of political correctness. Sorry."

"I guess I'll live."

"Okay. What can you tell me about the car?"

"Not a helluva lot. I didn't catch the license number. It all happened too fast."

"Was it a Washington license?"

"Yeah, I think so, but—there was something else—one of those European license plates, too—you know—a long, rectangular deal—but I couldn't read that one, either. He blew out of there before I knew what happened."

"It was a man driving?"

"I'm not sure. Why?"

"You said 'He blew out of there'. The mind works in funny ways. You may have had enough of a glimpse of the driver to tell you it was a man, even though you couldn't describe him. Could that be?"

"Funny," Ingram said slowly. "You may be right. I do have a vague recollection that it looked like a man. But that's about all."

"Okay. Don't worry about it. What about the car?"

"It was one of those foreign sports jobs. Silver colored."

"Did you recognize the make? How old?"

"No, I was watching the woman lying there. All I caught was the color and that it looked sleek, foreign. Real expensive. Probably new."

"Anyone else in the car?"

"Yeah, another man, in the passenger's seat. I got a pretty good look at him."

Steele's attention suddenly sharpened. "Can you describe the passenger?"

"I think so. Dark hair, kinda foreign looking. Dark complexion, I think. But not black."

"European? Asian? Latin?"

"Latin, maybe," Ingram nodded. "Either Spanish or Mexican, but not an Indian, if you know what I mean. Fine features."

"Tell you what, Mr. Ingram. I'd like you to sit down with our artist, and see if you can help her put together a sketch of the passenger. Would you mind doing that?"

"Sure, if I can. Anything I can do to help. I sure hope you nail this guy."

"Oh, no doubt about that, Mr. Ingram. You can't hide that kind of thing very long. If it's an expensive foreign car that's got to be repaired, there are just so many places he can take it. Sooner or later we'll get him. But if we can find the passenger, that'll be a help."

"What do you want him for?"

"Just for questioning at this point."

Steele watched the red-haired witness depart. He wondered: What was it that made Ingram come forward? His first instinct had been to see Ingram as a possible suspect. Sometimes a perpetrator would pretended to be a witness to deflect suspicion. But Ingram clearly wasn't affluent enough to own such a car. He thought about that for a moment. Was the hit-and-run car *really* an expensive foreign sports job? Or was that just another clever way of deflecting attention away from the truth? He didn't think so, but it was a possibility. One more lead he'd have to check out.

* * *

1500: The Flight Deck

Papoulis peered out through the windscreen and drew in a sharp breath as he realized how precarious was the perch of the huge plane. "God! What's keeping you from tipping over?" he asked.

"Physics—and maybe lots of prayer," Russo said. "I've moved all the passengers back to the rear. It's just the nose section that's hanging over the edge. I hope we're all right."

"As long as the snow holds," Papoulis observed slowly. "Let's hope it'll continue to hold until help can get up here. And speaking of help, I'm afraid we aren't going to be much use to you, Captain."

"Why?"

"We only came up to see if there was anything we could do to help with your injured. We were stranded up here, just like you are, until the storm clears. I'm afraid—"

"You mean you can't help us get down?"

"Get down?! You surely didn't think—I'm sorry, Captain," Papoulis said. "I'm afraid that's out of the question. Until this storm clears and they can get up here with rescue helicopters—I'm afraid there's no way down."

Russo was silent. "We had hoped—but you're right, of course. We're out of just about everything. I've been trying to arrange an air drop." He looked out the front windscreen. He tried to fight the dizziness as he looked down the glacier slope. He noticed a dark ridge of exposed rocks about three quarters of a mile downhill from their perch, just visible through the driving snow. "What's that ridge down there?"

Papoulis looked where the captain was pointing. "That's the Nisqually Cleaver," he said.

"Cleaver?"

"Mountaineers' language. I guess it's because it looks like a giant meat cleaver stood on edge."

"We seem to be aimed straight at it. Not a very pleasant thought."

Mark Svenson had joined the group in the cockpit. "Did I hear you say something about an air drop?" he asked. Russo nodded. "We can help you there," Mark said. "We can organize a drop zone and lay out some signals. Who've you contacted?"

"McChord." Russo to evacuate the injured. But they're going to fly over with a Hercules and make an air drop tomorrow morning."

"How come they can make it, if the helicopters can't? Won't they ice up too?"

"The C-130s have better de-icing equipment than the helos, and they can get up through the ice layer faster."

"Then our worries should be over. At least for food and supplies. Those C-130s can carry a whole store."

Russo looked out the windows. The snowstorm outside had steadily increased in fury. By now he was barely able to see the nose of the aircraft. "God, that's some storm," he said.

"Typical," Svenson observed. "It's a white-out. No telling how long it'll last."

"I hope it'll clear by morning. I guess there isn't much we can do—except to pray for help from below." He thought about what he had just said and broke into laughter. "That's a good one! Imagine praying for help from below!"

No one else was laughing.

1540: Seattle Police Headquarters

Harold Steele sat at his desk with a cup of coffee. There was nothing else on the hit-and-run car, but he believed he was closing the gap. He had the eyewitness's testimony. All he needed was the driver's identity. Probably the owner. Find the car and he'd know that—unless someone else was driving it, which was always what they always claimed anyway. The eyewitness report might help. They knew what the passenger looked like. If they just had some way of ID-ing him, he might tell them who was driving. He'd need more than guesswork to arrest someone for vehicular homicide or whatever else the prosecutor would go for. But sooner or later he would have him. It was just a matter of time. Time, and a lot of boring bull-work.

He smiled to himself when he thought of the Hollywood image of police work. Only cops knew that it was mostly boring routine and dogged attention to detail, with a little luck thrown in. If he got lucky someone might call in with a tip. With the publicity the accident had received in the media, he thought it could happen soon.

Opinion polls indicated that most of the citizens were outraged about this accident. MADD members, suspecting another drunk driving atrocity, were demanding the death penalty. Steele smiled. In today's legal system, getting a jury to impose the death penalty was about as likely as it would have been in the O.J. trial. He'd be lucky to get this perp behind bars for a few years. He'd do what he could.

There was one hitch. The owner of an expensive sports job probably would be someone of substance in the community. Someone with powerful friends. What he needed was some bit of hard evidence that would clearly point to the identity of the driver, without violating rights or running afoul of any of the endless roadblocks the courts had placed in the path of criminal investigators. Especially high-priced lawyers.

He examined the sketch made by his artist, with the help of Myron Ingram. It showed a finely featured face, straight black hair, dark eyes and skin. Not much to go on. It could match thousands of Hispanics. Ingram said this guy was the passenger. How to find him was the problem.

As he finished his coffee his secretary came in with a file folder. He opened it and quickly scanned the first page. It was an investigation report filled out by Warren Colby. His pulse quickened as he read the details. "Hot damn! We've got the car!" he chuckled. He read the rest of the report rapidly. Colby's a damn sharp cop, he thought. Wouldn't go for the "hit a dog" story. He riffled through the forms. Among them were several eight-by-ten glossies of the car, showing the damaged front right fender, and a report from the lab on the blood stains. Definitely human, and they matched

Tracy Wingate's exactly. No doubt about it: this was the car that did her in. It looked convincing enough to stand up in court. And the car had been impounded legally, following up a report from the repair garage. No snags so far.

The car was registered to Carter Wycroft, a sixty-three-year-old white male, with a Hunt's Point address. President of Pacific Coastal Airlines. Just the kind of well-heeled owner he'd figured on. Lots of influential friends—and a two-hundred-dollar-an-hour downtown Bellevue lawyer, no doubt. The big clanger was: who was driving the car that night? Was it Wycroft? They'd lifted the driver's prints from the steering wheel, but they didn't match any prints on file anywhere. Whoever the driver was, apparently he'd never been in trouble with the law. He'd already run a check on Wycroft. He'd never been in trouble. But so what? Neither have I.

He returned his attention to the pictures of the car. Nice, he thought, and tried to imagine sitting behind the wheel with that much horsepower under him. Suddenly he tensed, looked closely at one of the photos, then snatched up the phone. He dialed Warren Colby's number.

"Colby?...Steele here. Hey, nice job on that Jag, Warren. Are you busy right now?...Never mind, give that to Roberts. I need to talk. I just noticed something in these photos...Okay. Soon as you can."

It took Colby three minutes.

"Have a look at this," Steele said, passing the photo to Colby.

"What about it?"

"Am I looking at the real thing, or did those guys in the photo lab get the print reversed?"

"What do you mean?"

"It happens sometimes. They put the negative into the machine backwards." Steele pointed at the steering wheel. "It's on the wrong side."

"No, it's the right side. It's an English car. Right-hand drive."

"*Jesus Christ*! You just earned your pay for the month—maybe the whole fucking year! This guy in the sketch is our hit-and-run driver. The eyewitness definitely identified him as the guy in the right-hand seat. He thought it was the passenger side. Didn't realize—Damn! All we need is this guy's prints, and it's game over."

"If he was driving, who was the passenger? Wycroft?"

"Probably. The question is: Why?"

"Could be half a dozen reasons. Too tired? Too drunk? Too—"

"Too drunk, maybe. We need to have a talk with Wycroft. Get him in here, Warren. We're going to have to handle this one like eggs. Set it up as soon as you can."

"You've got it. Do we tell him why?"

"No. Just tell him it's about his car—and he might want to bring his lawyer."

1700: Hunt's Point

Carter Wycroft parked the big sedan in the garage. Lots of room now, with the Jaguar still in the impound yard. He'd just returned from the post office to post the registered letter he had written immediately after getting the call from the police. He knew what they wanted him for. No question about that. They'd put it together, after finding his car. Of course they would. He'd been a fool to hope he might get away with it. In a way he was glad it was over. Finally over.

The house was quiet. Paula, his wife, was in Bellevue, shopping, and it was the maid's day off. He went directly to his study and sat down in the large leather swivel chair behind his massive mahogany desk. From his jacket pocket he took out a copy of the letter and reread it one more time. Then he carefully refolded it, put it into an envelope, and laid it on the desk before him. The envelope bore the single name: Paula.

There's really no other way, he thought. *You have killed. You deserve whatever comes. You've killed a woman. A pregnant woman! Snuffed out the life of a woman and her unborn baby as quickly as though you'd mowed her down with a machine gun. By all the rules of civilized society you're a monster. You ought to be put away.*

But do you really? Couldn't you just fight it? There'd be a long, drawn-out trial. You'd have a good chance of winning. You've got the right lawyer. You might get off with a light sentence. A year or two in one of those country club jails. A glimmer of hope surged within him. Maybe he should— But then he saw in his mind the newspaper photo of the dying woman lying in the street in a pool of blood, and he knew he could never go through with it. *The trial,* he thought. *The notoriety. The terrible cost to your family. And to the airline. PCA would be destroyed by the scandal.* He knew he couldn't let that happen.

Carlos Santiago's face formed in his thoughts. The letter he had mailed would fix Santiago permanently, irrevocably. The thought brought the hint of a smile. He despised blackmail and any person that would resort to it. *Let Carlos try to wriggle his way out of this.*

He put his hand into the desk drawer. It was there, smooth, cold to the touch. He took it out with care and looked down at it, turning it this way and that. Cold, efficient, deadly. The perfect solution. The *only* solution.

There's really no other way.

He closed his fingers around the shiny black pistol and lifted it. Its weight in his hand felt lighter than normal. There was only one bullet. One was all he needed. Careful to the end, he would not leave a loaded pistol where someone could be hurt by it. He stared down into the black hole of its muzzle. *No other way.*

He felt sorry about not being able to say good-bye to Paula. But she'd just cry and try to talk him out of it, the way women always did, and he would not be able to stand that now.

He opened his mouth and brought the muzzle up. It pressed up against his palate. Cold, impersonal. Something solid in a world suddenly become a vapor. *No other way.*

The first squeeze of his finger had no effect. He tightened his grip and squeezed a little harder. It was awkward. He'd never tried to fire a pistol this wa—

Thursday

◆

Thursday, 0600: The Summit

By daylight the next morning the sky was crystal-clear above the mountain summit, but the heavy layer of clouds below continued to obliterate the valleys. Russo was sitting in the first class section of the cabin talking to Mark Svenson when he noticed the intercom panel light blinking. He picked up the handset.

"They're coming!" It was Walter Harris's excited voice.

"Great!" Russo listened to the details, then replaced the handset and turned to Svenson. "The Air Force will have a C-130 overhead at about O-seven-hundred, Mark. What do we need to do?"

"Not much. Just lay out a drop zone. I'm sure they'll have no trouble spotting us. We'll take care of it."

Svenson went back and summoned the climbing team to a forward row of seats, out of earshot of the passengers. "We've got a Hercules coming in," he told them. He glanced at his watch. "It'll be overhead in about fifty-five minutes. They'll probably want us to lay out a target and some sort of wind indicator. I'll come out and—"

Papoulis broke in. "How can you, Mark? You haven't any gear!"

"I'll see if I can borrow a heavy jacket from someone. And I just picked up a new pair of boots. I'll be okay." He looked outside. "This wind has packed the snow down pretty well overnight. That's the good part. But the wind will also make it imperative that we grab the stuff as it comes down. So be ready to grab the chutes and collapse them as soon as they hit."

"Okay," Papoulis agreed. "You want a big X, I imagine?"

Svenson nodded. "Let's see if we can use some of the stuff from the cabin to make it easier to see from the air. With this glare, it's hard to see anything. I'll check with the captain while you guys get ready."

Svenson summoned Russo back to join them in the cabin and explained what they needed.

"Take whatever can be moved," Russo agreed. "The red blankets should work. Use some of the luggage from the overheads to weight them down."

Svenson grinned. "It won't be the first time an airline lost luggage. It just never happened this way before." He passed the word to the other four, who were already dressed and ready to go. "Get all the stuff ready by the door, then chuck it out as fast as you can. Try to avoid losing too much heat."

Outside the sun was well up in the sky and creating a blinding glare on the broad snowfield. There was still a brisk wind. The temperature was about ten degrees, well below freezing, but the sun on their backs as they worked was warm enough to prevent excessive heat loss. Svenson, wearing a borrowed parka and Papoulis's spare snow goggles, joined the others, who were stamping their feet along two intersecting lines in the snow to mark out a large X, the standard distress signal, which meant "Unable to proceed". It was certainly true in this case.

In half an hour everything was ready. They had positioned the drop zone as far away from the edges of the summit as possible. Finally satisfied, Papoulis herded the team back into the warmth of the cabin.

"You guys go ahead," Papoulis said. "I want to have a look around before I come in."

"What are you looking for?" Svenson asked, joining him.

"I didn't want to alarm the rest. Come with me." Papoulis led the way around under the wing. The fuselage was buried up to a height of four or five feet, as best he could estimate. He kicked at the snow along the side of the fuselage with the toe of his boot. "This is pretty solid," he said.

"The wind and cold." Svenson stamped his feet on the hard-packed surface. "The wind packs it down. The cold produces a coating of rhyme frost on the metal skin, and that binds to the snow like glue. As long as it doesn't get too warm, it should hold."

Papoulis shrugged. "Maybe. But come on up forward and have a look at something." He led the way under the wing to the nose section, which was thrust out over the edge of the broad, gently sloping expanse of new snow.

"Look at that." He pointed to a fresh shear surface where the snow had broken away from under the nose.

"Uh-oh! What's causing it?"

"Vibration and noise, I'd say. It's from keeping that tail engine running."

"That could cause—"

"I know."

"Good God! We'd better get him to shut it down. There'd be no way of stopping this brute if it ever started moving."

"What's she weigh, anyway?"

"About three hundred thousand pounds." Svenson shook his head. "There's probably nothing we can do. He has to keep the engine running. Elderly, young children, mothers with babies—and the injured, of course. Shut down and they all start to die."

"Keep it running and it may happen a lot faster," said Papoulis.

"Damned if you do, damned if you don't. Let's get back into the sunshine. It's cold here in the shadows." Svenson looked at his watch. "They should be over us in a few minutes. I hope they managed to fill our shopping list!"

* * *

0655: PCA Headquarters

Janet Gordon looked down at the jumble of vehicles and crisscrossed audio and video cables. Despite the early hour the scene in the parking lot was chaotic. All the spare parking spaces had been grabbed by a hodgepodge of vans and station wagons bearing the familiar logos of local TV and radio stations. The TV vans had erected their satellite dishes, ready to tie in to their networks at a moment's notice if anything exciting were to break in the unfolding drama on Mount Rainier.

A gaggle of people clustered around a converted bus where an enterprising individual was doing a brisk business dispensing lattes and croissants to the hungry news cadre. Janet turned from the window to regard Carlos Santiago, who was draped across one of her office chairs, his back propped against one arm and his legs dangling over the other. "Why aren't you down there shepherding that mob?" she asked.

"I never try to tell the media how to conduct their business. Why does it bother you?"

"You said you'd handle the media. What have you been doing about it?"

He straightened in his chair, suddenly petulant. "Why is it you always try to shift the blame to me? That crowd down there isn't my fault!"

"Carlos, you're supposed to be the vice president in charge of PR. If you aren't doing your job, then it certainly *is* your fault. Now, I suggest that you get up off your duff and get down there and handle that crowd before they start to invent news, the way they always do. Have you told them about our getting the Air Force to make a supply drop?"

"Are we releasing that?"

"Of *course* we're releasing it! I want them to know we're doing everything in our power to help those people. I want you to get with our operations people and put together a news release. Make sure they're aware of everything we're doing. *Cooperate* with them. Get them pictures and backgrounds on all the crew members—pilots *and* flight attendants. And don't forget the airplane. It's a new type the public knows very little about."

"Okay, okay! I don't know why you're so steamed up about it."

"Good Lord! We've managed to make a safe forced landing in the worst storm of the decade with two engines out on top of a mountain—with only *one fatality*. That's got to be the biggest news story of the century. Frank could have hit the side of that mountain and killed everyone on board—a hundred and eighty-eight people. Let's get some credit for the survivability of our airplanes and the incredible skill of our pilots, instead of letting the press spin a story that makes it look like we're a bunch of uncaring incompetents."

"Who the hell wound you up this morning?!" Santiago growled. "Okay. I just resent your implicating that I'm to blame for anything. None of this was my doing."

"Carlos, I thought I made that clear. This accident *was* mostly your doing, as I told you yesterday."

"How do you figure that?"

The nervous look he gave her told her he had already guessed her thoughts. She said, in barely controlled fury: "They had an engine catch fire, Carlos. On an airplane just out of San Jose. *Your* setup. I think you get the implication."

"Lots of planes land with an engine out with no problem. Your brother just wasn't exercising due caution. Pilot error, as usual. That's what got us into this mess."

"Nice try, but it won't do. The thing that complicated it was your Exciting Skies bullshit. Frank was trying to follow your idiotic directive when he had the flameout. Coming in too close caused him to lose the other engine. So we have two things to thank you for."

"Oh, no you don't!" he cried, rising to his feet. "You're not going to lay this on me!

Janet struggled to keep her voice calm. "When an airline issues a directive, pilots know it's to be complied with unless it clearly conflicts with safety. The weather up there was clear, and there was no apparent danger, so your directive took precedence. You've just identified what was wrong with it in the first place—a point I tried to make last Friday at the board meeting. It is *never* safe to fly close to mountains, even in clear weather. You were forcing our pilots to fly in an unsafe way. They did, and then got into trouble after your friends down in San Jose screwed up the works. So don't try to weasel out of it now."

Santiago glared at her for a moment. "We'll see about that," he muttered. "Carter may have a few things to say to you."

"That remains to be seen, but I sincerely doubt it. He wouldn't go that far. In the meantime, I expect you to do your job with the media. Is that perfectly clear?"

Santiago turned and left her office without answering.

Janet was left with a disturbing thought: Carter Wycroft was bound to support Santiago. She was no closer to understanding the hold Carlos had over the airline's president. Something had to be done about these internal politics, before it was too late. The life of Pacific Coastal depended on it.

* * *

0658: The Summit

Svenson looked out across the drop zone. Karen, Malcolm, and Eric were positioned downwind, and Alex Papoulis had taken smoke flares from the airplane's emergency kit, and was standing upwind of the large X, ready to ignite them. Svenson walked over to Karen. "Nice job, Kitten," he said, smiling at her rosy countenance.

"I could do with a little more Oh-two!" she exclaimed. "I've never had to work so hard."

"You'd never make a good mountain sheep."

"You'd rather I was a mountain sheep?"

"Nut!"

"Look at those two kids!" Karen pointed toward Malcolm and Eric, who were firing snowballs at each other with increasing fury.

"Hey, you guys!" Mark yelled. "Better save your energy. You're going to need it." They had to duck as a volley of snowballs came their way. The frolic was interrupted when Svenson heard the sound of a multi-engined turboprop approaching from downwind. "Here they come!" he called. Papoulis activated one of his flares, producing a streamer of brilliant orange smoke.

Russo poked his head out the cockpit window and shouted: "They'll make one pass over to test the wind! They'll start dropping on the second pass!" Svenson, just able to hear above the whine of the tail engine, gave him a thumbs-up.

The big plane lowered its flaps and undercarriage and made a slow pass over the summit. Svenson, at the center of the X, raised his arms. The Hercules wagged its wings in answer and banked around for its second pass. As it came back in Svenson saw the huge clamshell doors opening. The plane dropped a cluster of canisters, which floated down on colored parachutes. By the time the plane had completed two more passes the summit was littered with containers. Some were large canvas bags about the size of an oil drum, and others were stacks of boxes loaded on wooden pallets. The last one out, with a red-and-white striped chute, was smaller, and marked clearly with a white circle and a red cross. It was lighter than the rest, and its chute was immediately caught by the wind and dragged across the summit. Before anyone could react it slid down the slope of the saddle and disappeared over the lip of the Sunset Amphitheater.

Svenson called to Papoulis: "That was probably the medical supplies, Alex. Better see if it can be retrieved. We may have to ask for another drop. We really need that stuff."

Papoulis nodded and went over to the edge to look down into the shadows. He returned in a few minutes. "I can see the chute," he said. "It's a couple of hundred feet down, caught on a ledge. There's no wind down there, so it should stay put. Good thing it didn't go all the way. But it may be tough getting down to it." He beat his arms across his chest vigorously. "It isn't getting any warmer."

"I know. Better bring the team back into the plane to get warmed up before you start."

Back inside the plane Alex looked around at the other team members as they sipped hot chocolate. He saw resolution in their faces. "We'll make it," he said.

"All but Karen," Svenson said. "Three should be enough."

Karen stiffened. "I'm part of the team…"

Papoulis interrupted her protest. "Mark's right, Karen. You're not experienced enough for this."

"Stow that!" Karen stormed. "I made it up here! You need me, damn it!"

Mark intruded. "No, Kitten. I'll go in your place."

Karen was silent for a moment. Then she said, "Mark, you're just trying to be the white knight, as usual. I don't need saving. Without proper climbing gear you could be killed. I'm perfectly able to do this. I'm not letting you put yourself in jeopardy just to prove a point." She turned to Papoulis. "You know I'm right, Alex. I can do this."

Papoulis grinned at Svenson. "I have to admit she did okay on the way up, Mark. Besides, we could use someone light like her, in case we have to lower her down to make the grab."

"I guess I'm beaten," Svenson said, grinning. "That's what I get for training you!" He turned to Papoulis again. "Be careful, Alex. The snow's good up here, where the wind's packed it down. But over there on the leeward side you may find soft spots. Don't take any chances."

"It should go," Papoulis said. He looked around at the others. "Ready?" The three climbers nodded. "So," he grunted, and moved back to the cabin door. Karen was about to join him when Svenson said, "You watch yourself, Kitten. I wouldn't be able to replace you."

"I like that," she said, smiling happily. "And quit worrying. I'll be fine. Sorry about our argument. I like you being my white knight. Save me a sandwich."

"You've got it."

He watched her join the others at the door. They climbed down onto the snow and made their way single-file across the snowfield, careful of their footing with the wind in their backs. A well-trained team, he thought.

Returning to the plane, Svenson was surprised to hear the Hercules engines approaching again, this time a little higher. It appeared to be getting ready for another pass. As the airplane slowed one more parachute, a full-sized rectangular para-wing, billowed above them and turned into the wind as it descended. In seconds a man alighted precisely in the center of the drop zone, gathered his chute up quickly, and strode over to the downed aircraft. Svenson met him at the entrance. The newcomer was quite tall, black, and wore the uniform of an army major, with the medical corps insignia on the shoulder of his parka.

The man smiled and extended his hand. "Major Gus Devane," he said. "I'm the flight surgeon."

* * *

0730: The Main Cabin

Buck Warren was a big man, six-four, about two-thirty, heavily muscled from hard work outdoors. He had a close-cropped head of rusty-brown hair and a sinister, unsmiling face. The man in the middle seat next to him was of medium height, just as powerfully built, clearly an outdoorsman like Warren. His name was Gill Stone. And next to Stone was the third member of the party, Oscar Wilson, a little older than the other two, but equally rugged looking. All three were wearing parkas, heavy pants and work boots. They were construction hands working for an oil exploration company.

Warren was becoming angry. All through the disaster he'd had to sit there and watch things deteriorate without a fight. To him it looked like a scene straight out of a pulp novel. Grown people weeping and wringing their hands like a bunch of old women, unwilling to do anything on their own, sitting here waiting for…*what? Jesus Christ Almighty!* Rainier's no monster mountain! Climbing this mole-hill's just a Sunday stroll. Child's play! He'd heard some of the guys talking about it. Compared to other mountains, this one was for cream puffs.

"We oughta be doin' somethin', Gill," Buck said in a low voice. "I can't stand this sittin' around waitin' for somethin' to happen. The only way we're gonna get outa this is on our own. What d'ya think?"

"I hear you, Buck. I can't believe somebody hasn't had guts enough to get us organized yet. Hell, we could be half way down by now. Maybe we could help get them organized down below to come up here and get the rest down. The weather's cleared up this morning. What's a little cold? We're dressed for it."

"Exac'ly what I was just thinkin'. Why should we all rot up here, just because of a few cripples and old coots that aren't gonna to make it anyway?"

The third member of the group joined in: "You guys thinkin' what I'm thinkin'?"

"You up for it, Oscar?" Buck Warren asked.

"Why not? Hell, we've seen worse country'n this! We've got our sleeping bags and heavy clothes."

Bill Stone intervened: "They're just breaking open those care packages now. We'll need some food. It'll take us 'till tomorrow night to get down, prob'ly."

"All right!" Buck Warren exclaimed in a low chuckle. "Let's get it on! Oscar, you go first. We'll have to do this so's not to arouse any interest. We don't wanna start no exodus." One by one, the three moved to the rear where their packs were stacked, along with a lot of other baggage from the forward section of the cabin. No one seemed to notice or care what they were doing. Everyone was too excited about the food and hot coffee being passed out by the flight attendants.

Back in the aft galley Gill Stone pilfered some food supplies from one of the open boxes and stowed it into their packs. The exit door was still slightly ajar from the loading of the supplies minutes earlier.

Amid the excitement no one noticed as the three men dropped their packs out the door and departed. They made a dash past the tail and headed around the back of Columbia Crest in the direction of the Winthrop Glacier. In minutes they were over the edge of the saddle and out of sight.

* * *

Megan made her way back to the aft galley to get another load of sandwiches. On the way she noticed the open door and closed it. She reached for the intercom handset and buzzed the flight deck. Russo answered. "Someone left the door open," she said. "Why don't you fire up the tail engine again. Let's get the heat back on and bring the cabin pressure back to normal after all that prancing about."

* * *

Russo turned to Walter Harris as he replaced the intercom handset. "Wind up number two again, Walter. Megan says it's getting cold back there, and wants to get it back to normal."

Harris's eyebrows raised. "Normal?"

Russo chuckled. "As close as we can get to it."

Harris nodded and went through the start sequence, then shut down the auxiliary power unit that had been providing power temporarily.

* * *

0758: The Amphitheater

Karen heard Alex call to her from fifty feet above: "Can you reach it yet?" Alex was standing on a ledge with Malcolm and Eric, belaying the rope through a steel piton he had hammered into a crack in the wall. Karen was hanging from the rope, unable to find any hand or foot holds in the smooth wall.

She looked up and waved from her end of the rope. "Down another five feet!" The rope moved down slowly. She reached down into a fissure in the gray rock where the dark green canvas pack rested, its red cross proclaiming its contents. Her fingers closed over the cold metal ring on its top. "Got it!" she called. She unsnapped the D-ring that released the small parachute, which went floating off in the swirling eddies of the wind, and brought the pack up against her chest and clipped it securely to her safety harness.

"Okay, take me up!" she called. For most of the way all she could do was hang from the rope and let the others haul her up as a dead weight. Once she was back up on the ledge they all took a breather.

"See?! You guys *did* need me after all!" she chided.

Papoulis laughed. "I have to admit you're right. I'd hate to have to lower one of these guys down there and haul him back up. You're just the right size." He looked at the others. "Ready?"

"Ready," they both responded.

"And so…"

Half an hour later they were banging on the exit door of the aircraft. Svenson was waiting for them, flanked by Major Devane and the two paramedics. Devane took the medical pack from Karen quickly and took it forward to the center galley, which was set up as a medical station, while Svenson took Karen's hand and led her forward to his row. "Sit down, Kitten. I'll get you a sandwich and some hot chocolate. Sound good?"

"Mmmmm!" She grinned in anticipation.

* * *

0815: The Winthrop Glacier

"We shouldn't'a' come this way!" Buck Warren complained. He was clinging with nearly frozen toes and fingers to the cracks in the old, weathered ice of the glacier. He craned his neck sideways and down to get a better look at the snowfield below, where the glacier leveled out again. The three men were connected together with a hundred-foot length of half-inch braided nylon rope from Warren's pack. It was the only useful item any of them had been able to find. There were no crampons, no snow goggles, no ice axes, or a host of other things they hadn't thought about back in the comfort of the airplane cabin. The mountain seemed anything but gentle this morning.

"Let's go back," Oscar Wilson entreated.

"Easier to keep goin'," Warren said hopefully. But he was beginning to have doubts. He feared it might be much harder descending than climbing. But he wasn't about to voice his fears to the others. "We'll make it all right," he said.

"We'd better," said Gill Stone.

Buck Warren kicked and stepped his way down the steep surface another twenty feet toward the level spot below them. The rope moved slowly downward, urging the other two to follow. Toward what, he could only hope.

* * *

0820: The Main Cabin

Mark Svenson smiled at Karen as she perched on the seat beside him, her feet tucked up under her, watching him assemble his equipment. "What are you up to?" she asked.

"I'm about to deliver the scoop of the year—and maybe win myself a Pulitzer in the bargain."

"You think you have a chance?"

"I was just kidding. I have no delusions about my winning a prize. There's a lot of competition out there."

"You're a fine writer, Mark!"

"How would you know? You're a biologist, not an English major."

"I've read some of your articles," she insisted. "I don't pretend to understand a lot of that aerospace jargon, but you have a nice way with words. But this really *is* a break for you, isn't it. No one else is getting this kind of chance."

"I know. This story is dynamite—as long as it has a happy ending. Think about it! A whole planeload of people marooned on top of a frozen mountain. The human interest angle alone is the kind of material most journalists never get close to. But that's just the surface story. Underneath is where my real objective lies: the reason this mess happened in the first place. Some of our airlines—this one, too, apparently—have been playing little games with cost cutting and crazy promotional schemes. You can see what happens. I aim to force these guys to look at what they're doing and what can result from it.

It's really crucial that it get slanted in the right direction, though. I'm not going to give it the sensationalist spin the news media always put on aviation accidents."

"Aren't you worried someone else will steal your story while you're up here?"

"Sure," Svenson said. "That's what all this equipment is for. It'll prevent anyone from stealing my stuff."

"Tell me all how it works. I want to know everything."

"You really want to?" He regarded her with surprise. He could see the interest in her face as she nodded, and realized she wasn't fooling. "The key to it all is an encryption algorithm in this." He pointed to the laptop computer, which was connected by a cable to a small box the size of a package of cigarettes, and thence to his VHF radio. "The computer transforms what I've typed into random strings of characters that look like gibberish to anyone trying to read it. Then it goes to this little box, which translates those strings of random letters into Morse code—dots and dashes—and passes them on to the radio, which transmits them down to my editor in Seattle."

"Where did you get the coding algorithm?"

"Alex helped me design it. Having a friend that's a math wizard has its spin-offs."

"Alex is a genius," Karen agreed. "And where'd you get the little box?"

"I built that myself. I've always liked fooling around with electronics. I have a friend that's a Ham radio operator, and he showed me what to do. The whole thing is pretty simple, really."

"And no one will be able to decipher your message?"

"Not without a lot of work on a large computer. No code is completely foolproof. But it'd take an expert several days to work out the algorithms. By then the story would be old news."

"And you thought this all up yourself?" Her eyes were shining as she looked up at him.

"I had a lot of help. But the idea was mine. And of course the story is mine."

"My hero!" she murmured. She slipped her arms up about his neck and planted a warm kiss on his cheek.

"You'd better watch that, little Heidi! I might just—"

"What?"

"Kiss you right back."

She smiled broadly. "I might like that."

He smiled back at her. "Maybe I might, too," he said. "But not now! You're too much of a distraction. So you have to just sit there quietly until I've finished filing this story. I'm beginning to think that only single guys can ever win Pulitzers."

"I promise not to bother you," she said softly.

"You have to go away!" he protested, looking into her eyes.

"What's wrong, Mark?" she asked innocently. A smile played about the corners of her mouth.

"You know damn well what's wrong! Now get out of here and let me do my job!"

"Some day you'll appreciate having me around." She got up from her seat and smiled at him. "Later!"

Mark watched her depart and shook his head to clear it of thoughts that had nothing to do with his story.

He spent another hour composing his story, then pressed the sequence of keys that would prepare it for transmission to his editor at the *Seattle Globe*. When he had finished the screen displayed a long series of five-character strings of random letters. He turned on the radio and called Cecil Burns, his editor.

"Mark Svenson here," he said. "Is that you, Cecil?"

"Who else?" Burns challenged in his usual gruff voice.

"This is Mark. You know where I am. I don't want to give anything away over the air. I have a story for you."

"In code?"

"Encoded and ready to go," Svenson acknowledged. "Ready to copy?"

"Stand by." There was a pause. "Okay, ready to copy. Let 'er rip, Mark."

"You're going to like this," Mark commented. "Here comes." He flipped a switch on the radio and set it down, then typed in the transmit sequence into his laptop keyboard and hit the enter key. There was no noise to indicate anything was happening, but the screen of his laptop was a whirl of scrolling lines as his laptop dumped its memory contents to its big brother down in the city below.

"Did you get all that?" Svenson asked as his screen went blank.

"I got something," Burns acknowledged. "I'll call you back when I've had a chance to decipher it and look it over." Burns signed off.

When Burns called back ten minutes later Svenson could almost feel the excitement coming up through the air waves. "Mark, this is dynamite!" Burns exclaimed.

Svenson chuckled. "For once I find myself in complete agreement with my editor. And that's about all we ought to say about it over the air. I'll have more later. This story is far from over, unfortunately."

"Is there anything we can do down here, Mark?" Burns's voice was filled with concern.

"I'm not sure, Jeff. One thing you might look into, though: I'm sure there's a media circus going on over at Pacific Coastal headquarters at SeaTac. They could probably use a friendly voice at court. I've met all the crew, and they're really fine people."

"I'll see what I can do, Mark."

As Mark signed off he became aware of the noise from the tail engine. He frowned as he put away his radio and computer. He got up and made his way forward to the flight deck. "Forgive the intrusion, Captain, but is it necessary to keep that engine running? I'm concerned about the vibration. This snow isn't exactly like sitting on solid ground. It's undoubtedly very deep, and I've no idea what's going on under us. Snow is highly unpredictable."

"I'm afraid we have to, Mark," Russo replied. "We're keeping it down to idle speed, but we really need the cabin pressure. Without it, some of my passengers wouldn't have lasted the night."

"I see your point. Let's just keep our fingers crossed." Mark turned to go.

"What's so dangerous, Mark?" Russo queried. "I thought we were stuck pretty solid."

"Snow isn't nearly as solid as you might like to believe."

The two pilots exchanged nervous glances but said nothing.

* * *

0900: CPA Headquarters

Janet looked up from the report she'd been reading. It was her executive assistant. She was standing in the open doorway, and the look on her face betrayed a gravity that had nothing to do with running an airline. "Janet, I'm sorry to break in on you. You have a visitor."

"Who is it, Ethyl?"

"It's a detective from the police."

"Did he say what it was about?"

Ethyl shook her head. "He said it was personal."

"Please show him in."

Ethyl departed and in a moment returned, followed by a stocky man with ruddy features and thick, bushy eyebrows. "Mrs. Gordon, this is Detective Steele."

"Thank you, Ethyl." Janet rose and extended her hand across the desk as Ethyl closed the door on them. "Please sit down, Detective Steele. What can I do for you?"

Steele waited for Janet to sit down before taking one of the chairs clustered around her desk. "I'm sorry to be bringing bad news, Mrs. Gordon. Had you heard anything regarding Mr. Wycroft?"

Janet shook her head, puzzled.

"He's dead, Mrs. Gordon. Apparently he took his own life." He sat silently for a moment as Janet tried to get her mind to accept the news. "Would you like to be alone for a few minutes?" the detective asked gently. "I don't mind waiting, if you need a little time. I know it must be a shock."

Janet sat there looking at the detective for a moment, waiting for her brain to stop whirling. At last she felt calm enough to speak. "No. I'm all right, Mr. Steele. Thank you for your consideration. Yes, it is a shock. Where was he?" She remembered she had not seen him this morning.

"He was found at home, in his study."

"How—?"

"He shot himself."

"Does Mrs. Wycroft know?"

"I'm sorry to say it was Mrs. Wycroft who found him. I wish it could have been otherwise."

Steele's eyes told her what he meant better than any words. Janet tried not to think about it. "The poor woman!" she murmured. "Is—do you know if anyone's with her now?"

"She's been taken to Overlake Hospital, Mrs. Gordon. She looked like she was going into shock. She's in good hands." The detective produced an envelope, extracted a single sheet of paper, and handed it to Janet. "I think you'd better read this. He left it on his desk."

Janet read it in silence:

> *"To whom it may concern:*
> *I have decided to take my own life. I can no longer live with the guilt hanging over my head. On Friday evening, September fourth, I was intoxicated, driving home from a cocktail party with Carlos Santiago, when I struck a woman who was crossing the street in front of me. I*

learned later that she was pregnant, and that she died of her injuries.

Carlos Santiago urged me to leave the scene of the accident, and to hide the evidence from the police, which I did.

I would have come forward to confess my guilt before this, but Santiago threatened to make a public statement if I did, which would have brought disgrace upon my family and ruin upon Pacific Coastal Airlines.

I make this confession now, at the time of my death, and ask God, my beloved wife, Paula, and the family of the victim for forgiveness. May God have mercy on me.

Carter M. Wycroft"

When Janet had finished reading the letter she lifted her hand to her forehead. "Dear Lord!" she said in a barely audible voice. "Oh, dear Lord!" She looked up at Harold Steele. "Have you seen Santiago?"

Steele nodded, his eyes suddenly grim. "He's being arrested as we speak."

"Arrested? What for? As an accessory?"

"No. We've learned that it wasn't Mr. Wycroft that was driving that night, although apparently he thought he was. Mr. Santiago must have told him he was the guilty one who was behind the wheel, to cover up his own guilt."

"Dear Lord God! Then—Carter—Mr. Wycroft—killed himself—needlessly?"

"I'm afraid that's true, Mrs. Gordon. I wish we'd been able to find out the truth in time. But unfortunately..."

Janet was unable to speak. The calamity of it all was too much to digest at once. She was in a state of shock bordering on collapse. She had to talk to someone. Whom? Frank was her first choice, but of course he was stranded up on the mountain. Roger would have to do.

But she must talk to someone in the company, too. Who was next in line to Wycroft? With a start she realized it would be herself. The weight and the loneliness of responsibility settled over her like a heavy blanket, adding to her dismay.

"Are you all right, Mrs. Gordon? May I call someone for you?"

"No—thank you I—I'll be all right. It's just such a shock—" She looked up, drawing on what reserves she could. "Is there anything else I can do for you, Detective?"

Steele rose. "No, I think not, Mrs. Gordon. Again, I'm terribly sorry. I know how you must be feeling. You had no hint of what was going on, I gather?"

"No, except—their relationship had seemed strange lately. We had suspected Santiago had some sort of hold over him—but never anything like this." Tears came suddenly. "Please excuse me," she said, dabbing at her eyes with a tissue.

"I understand. We'll be in touch." Steele left quietly. Janet returned to her chair. After resting for a moment she buzzed her assistant again. Over the phone she told her: "Ethyl, Mr. Wycroft is dead. He's taken his own life. Please call Roger Greninger for me. And tell the staff that the office is closed for the rest of the day. They may all go home. You may go too, after you've delivered a statement to the staff and another for the news people. I'll have them for you in a few minutes."

Janet put her elbows on the desk and tried to think. A confusion of thoughts whirled like dry leaves in her mind. Why hadn't Carter simply gone to the police about it? Even if he thought it had been his fault, clearly it had been an accident. Why would he let Carlos talk him into hiding? But of course Carlos was trying to protect himself, and Carter was made to order for his purpose. If Carlos had been blackmailing him, he undoubtedly hadn't been thinking that clearly. Suddenly she realized how very little she knew about the man that had headed the airline these past years.

Her thoughts were interrupted by the telephone. It was Roger.

"Can you come over, Roger? There's been a terrible tragedy." She told him briefly what had happened.

"I'll be right with you," he told her.

Janet thought for a moment. "Let's meet somewhere." she said. "I need to get out of here."

"The Doubletree Suites?"

"Okay. Make it half an hour."

"I'll be there."

After hanging up she wrote a statement for the news media and a shorter note for the staff. She gave them both to Ethyl.

She regarded the scene outside her windows absently. Along the highway below tree branches were still whipping wildly. Highway signs were threatening to break loose and crash down on passing automobiles. Rain was driving down in dense, gray sheets. Beyond the hotels and restaurants bordering the airport she saw a Boeing 767 fighting its way in to a bone-jarring landing. What next? she thought. It seemed as though her whole world had suddenly turned upside down. Once again she felt the need for Richard's help. But maybe Roger would do.

* * *

0945: The Winthrop Glacier

Buck Warren felt his spirits lifting. He and his two companions had made it down over the steep, icy section of the glacier, and were now moving easily over the less rigorous slope of the glacier. It was buried under a good six feet of new, hard-packed snow that made it child's play to traverse. It was almost like descending a concrete staircase, he thought, as he brought his heels down into the crust, kicking steps in the gentle incline. A line of scrub firs was just emerging from the mists at the edge of the snowfield. Unfortunately, the storm down at this altitude appeared to be returning, threatening to bring another white-out. They must keep moving, Warren thought grimly. For safety's sake they were still roped up.

"Time out?" called Oscar Wilson from the rear end of the rope.

"Okay," Warren agreed. "Make sure you kick a couple of holes to dig your feet into before you sit down. This crust is pretty slippery. Damn! We could really use some ice axes…"

"…and a hot meal, a snug cabin, three hot broads, and a bottle of Jack Daniels!" quipped Gill Stone.

"I'll settle for the hot meal and the bed," said Oscar Wilson. "What d'ya think, Buck? We make camp down there in the trees?"

"Sure. No sweat. At the rate we've been going we oughta be there in another hour. Maybe we can pick off some game before we make camp. I've got some wire for a snare in my pack." He twisted around to look at the other two. "Anybody got any smokes? I'm fresh out."

Oscar Wilson took a pack of cigarettes from his pack and tossed it over. "I've got a whole carton. We can smoke, at least." As they sat and talked the snow line continued to move slowly up the slope. Warren rose reluctantly. "We'd better git our asses movin'," he said. "Easy does it from here on. Let's not take any chances."

The other two rose with him, rechecked the knots of their rope, and started down the glacier. Warren took the lead again, kicking and stepping, kicking and stepping, in a monotonous rhythm. They had gone a mere hundred yards or so when, completely without warning, the crusted snow under their feet cracked and disintegrated into powder.

Buck Warren was the first to scream: "Jesus Christ! There's no bottom to it!"

* * *

1000: Doubletree Suites Hotel, Seattle

Roger Greninger was deeply concerned. Janet's voice had sounded strained to the breaking point. His first thought had been that a disaster had happened up on the mountain. Thankfully, it wasn't that, although the situation up there was still grim. But the suicide of the firm's president was a terrible tragedy. It could have a dreadful impact on the airline's financial picture. It had been bad enough at the last board meeting, when the rise in fuel prices was announced. Then came the media frenzy over the crash of Flight 74, which was going to be devastating. Wycroft's suicide, coming on top of the other two shocks, might prove to be a worse tragedy than Janet had imagined. But it wasn't the airline, or his stock in it, that worried him. It was Janet. What would this do to her? And what could he do to help?

He drove through the driving rain to the Doubletree Suites Hotel. Janet was waiting for him in a booth back in the corner of the spacious atrium.

"Been waiting long?" he asked, joining her.

"No. I just got here."

Roger signaled to a waitress and ordered coffee. After the waitress had left he looked into her red-rimmed eyes. "Can you talk about it?" he asked gently.

"Read this," she said. She took Carter Wycroft's suicide note from her handbag and passed it to him. He read it quickly, then again more slowly. He handed the letter back to her. "This is dreadful," he said. "I'm so sorry, Janet."

Janet nodded. "Strangely, I've discovered a deeper, more personal feeling of loss. He was a very troubled man. I'm just beginning to realize how sincerely he believed in the airline—how much he cared about it. I feel like I've let him down. It was all Carlos Santiago's doing."

"What's happened to Santiago?"

"He's been arrested. I have no idea what they'll charge him with."

"It doesn't matter much. He won't be bothering you any more."

Janet nodded again. "He's history at PCA." Her voice took on a hard edge.

"Will you be calling a board meeting?"

"I guess we'll have to. We need a new president and chairman."

"That'll fall on you now, right?"

"It could be. I was next in line to Carter. But it's up to the board, of course."

"When will it be?"

"Not till next week. There'll be the funeral, of course. Probably on Friday. I must go to Paula Wycroft. She's resting in Overlake."

"Mind if I go with you?"

"I was hoping you would." She rose to leave. "Remember your offer of help at the party last Saturday? I think I'll take you up on it now."

* * *

1130: The Seattle Globe

No one save a select few knew what the story was about, but word of something really big shot through the *Globe* building like an electric current, charging everyone with a sense of urgency. Finally, the thunderous roar of the presses down in the basement signaled the end of another monumental race with time.

Burns returned to his desk at eleven-thirty. The noise of the presses down in the basement had become a physical vibration throughout the building. He dialed Mark Svenson's cell phone number. In a moment Mark's voice came on clearly. "Mark, I don't know whether you can hear it, but the noon edition is just rolling now, and your story is the front page banner. Congratulations! And Abe said to tell you you'll be hearing from him when you get back."

The words he heard next sent a shudder of fear through him. "God be with you all, Mark," he said quietly, and hung up.

1205: The Summit

Papoulis drew Mark Svenson aside. "Is there anything else we can do up here, Mark? Eric and Malcolm are eager to get back down. So am I."

Svenson considered the question. "No, nothing. I think it's a good idea, Alex. If I had my gear I'd be with you. I have a nervous feeling about staying. Anyway, I'd like to see Karen safely out of it." Svenson lowered his voice. "You and I know the situation up here, Alex. Our only hope is a helicopter, and that doesn't seem likely for the next day or two. By the time the mountain rescue guys can get up here it may be too late for a lot of them."

"I hear that." Papoulis and Svenson returned to the others.

Papoulis explained the situation to them. But Karen objected loudly. "I'm not leaving Mark!" she exclaimed. She went to him and looped her arm though his possessively. "I *mean* that! I'm staying here."

"Karen," Mark said gently, "I want you to go."

"I'm staying!" she insisted. "You guys don't need me. The three of you can make it down easily. I'd rather stay here and take my chances."

Mark could see there was no use arguing. In the end he had to relent.

"We'll get help for you," Alex said. "We'll get the Mountaineers organized, once this storm clears a little. Then we can start getting these people down." Mark Svenson nodded without comment. He knew what Alex wasn't saying. *Those that are able to make it.* It was one of the primary rules of mountaineering. If you couldn't save everyone you saved the ones that had the best chance of surviving. Many of them simply wouldn't stand the strain.

Mark and Karen went back to the exit door with Papoulis. Eric and Malcolm were already dressed and waiting. "Karen wants to stay," Papoulis told them. "We'd better be on our way." With that the three exited and made their way single file across the summit. Mark watched until he could no longer see Alex's red stocking cap. He turned to regard Karen with a worried smile. "I wish you'd gone with them," he murmured. "But I'm glad you wanted to stay."

* * *

1345: The Flight Deck

Russo cried out in alarm and grabbed for the arm rests to avoid falling over as the ground shook under them. The plane gave a sickening lurch, causing the nose to tip downward. He could feel it teetering in slow, sickening oscillations, poised precariously over the abyss. One more lurch could send it careening downward. He stared wide-eyed down the endless chute of the glacier, which disappeared into the clouds five thousand feet below. In his mind he was back on the wall again, terrified, unable to move. He averted his eyes, trying to shut out the vision.

"What the hell was that?" Harris gasped.

Russo shook his head, speechless.

Svenson, crouched behind the two pilots, said: "It could be the start of an avalanche. Or maybe an earthquake."

"Anything we can do?" Russo asked.

"You might tell them to get strapped in." There was a note of urgency in Svenson's voice.

Russo turned and met Svenson's eyes with undisguised terror. "You think—it might—again?"

"I'd bet on it. For the moment we seem to have stabilized. But God knows for how long. All that's holding us is the grip of the snow on the metal skin, and that can't be much."

"Shouldn't we think about evacuating?" Harris asked.

"And then what?" said Russo.

Svenson grunted. "It's a rock and a hard place, isn't it."

"I'd say so," Russo muttered. "In fact, I wish we had a good, solid rock under us right now. Whatever happens, it's fairly certain it will be quick."

* * *

Megan's forehead smarted where she had hit it on the edge of the galley counter when she fell. She touched it and looked at her fingers. No blood. She pulled herself back to her feet. Screams of terror came from the cabin. She looked back to see if the crew were all right. She was about to go aft when she noticed the intercom light blinking. It was Captain Russo. She tried to make her voice sound calm. "What happened? Are we all right?"

"I wish I could say yes, Megan," he said. "I don't know what it was. It may have been the start of an avalanche." There was a pause. He seemed to be searching for words. "Better get them strapped in. You girls, too, Megan."

"Roger." Then she added softly: "Please take care of yourself."

She made her way back into the cabin with difficulty. The cabin floor was tilted enough to make progress difficult. Beth Winslow and a few of the other girls were on their feet, already getting the passengers to strap in. Megan picked up the cabin mike. With an effort she managed to keep her voice calm as she spoke: "Ladies and gentlemen, we've had a little earth tremor. The captain has requested that you all fasten your seat belts as tightly as possible, and return your seat backs and trays to their upright position. And please, try to remain calm. This airplane has been built to withstand a lot of abuse. We've never lost one yet."

Some of the passengers were attempting to smile. She did her best to do the same. She wished she knew as little about things as the passengers. That was the problem with being part of the crew. She knew too much.

* * *

Harris looked across at Russo in undisguised terror. "What the hell do we do now?"

"For once I don't have an answer, Walter. Beyond the obvious, which I've been doing ever since the first slip."

"I trust he has big hands!" Harris attempted a laugh, but it sounded more like a gasp.

Russo summarized: "Let's look at the possibilities, before we have no choice. We could evacuate the airplane. But that would mean trying to get all the wounded and sick down the chutes. Not easy, and probably not fast enough. And out there in the snow they'd just start dying on us. We'd all start dying. We'd never survive the night. So staying with the plane seems to be our only choice."

"Right," Harris agreed. "But—what if it happens again?"

"We could try thrust reversal, assuming it isn't frozen up like everything else, but that would run us out of fuel really fast. Besides, I'm not convinced it'd do any good," Russo said. He frowned. "The vibration might just shake us loose from whatever is still holding us."

Russo noticed Svenson still looking over their shoulders. "You should be back there strapped in, Mark. It could get pretty hairy if we slip again."

"I was listening to what you were just saying. I might have an idea," Svenson said. When he had finished explaining the two pilots looked at him in naked terror. Svenson shrugged and left the flight deck.

* * *

Svenson sat down beside Karen. She tried to smile, but he could tell she was frightened. "Will we be all right?" she asked. "Please, tell me the truth."

"I think so." He cursed himself again for not insisting that she go down with Alex and the others. Now it was too late. "We're in trouble, all right. I won't try to kid you." He took her hand and squeezed it. "I've no idea how long we can sit here. It's that damned tail engine that's causing the problem. If they'd just shut it down, I'm sure we'd stay here till hell freezes over. We're hanging over the edge of the Nisqually, but the snow under us is almost solid by now." He knew this was far from certain, but it was better for her to believe there was a chance. He knew that one more jolt could break the fragile hold of the frozen snow on their hull. After that, a quick plunge down the glacier into the rocks of the Cleaver. Then one massive fireball. At least it would be quick.

"Can't they shut it down?"

"Not for very long. Those old folks are on the ragged edge now. They'd start dying. And there are a few mothers with infants on board, too."

"But—if we slip again, we may all die anyway!"

He could see the unashamed fear in her eyes. He nodded slowly. "It's possible, Kitten." He brushed the tears from her cheeks. "We've faced it before."

"Mark—Mark, there's something I want you to know."

"What?"

She tried to smile. "I love you, Mark!"

He looked into her eyes, fighting back his own emotions. "I love you, too, Kitten. I guess I've always felt that way. I thought it was just my way of being protective, but—"

Suddenly she was in his arms. Her lips sought his, and he could taste the salt of her tears as his arms tightened and drew her close. And somewhere along the long interlude of beating hearts and whispered endearments it happened again. But this time it was different. A lot different.

* * *

1413: The Flight Deck

"We're sliding!" Harris yelled.

Russo stared down the incline in abject terror. "Mother of God!" he gasped. There was no doubt about it. Their fragile craft was moving—and it was accelerating. Icy tendrils of fear probed deep into his viscera. His fingers slipped as he tried to grip the control yoke, not sure why he was trying. His vertigo assailed him. He breathed deeply, fighting waves of nausea.

Harris looked across at him. "What do we do? Svenson's alternative?"

Russo thought feverishly, his mind racing down half a dozen paths, but without success. He was out of time. "There *is* no alternative!" he gasped. His right hand shot to the thrust lever for the tail engine. He rammed it all the way to emergency power.

"God help us!" Harris moaned.

Russo's eyes were fixed on the downward slope before them, an unbroken slope of white that ended in the dark rocks of the Nisqually Cleaver. "Amen!" he moaned.

* * *

"What the hell?" Back in the main cabin Arne Lindgren turned to stare at his two SAS companions.

"Our pilot has gone mad!" Ole Rasmussen gasped.

"Has he?" asked John Nikolaisen. "What would you do?"

"You mean…?"

"Shut up and pray!"

* * *

Megan was thrown off her feet as the floor suddenly tilted sharply downward. She tried to focus her whirling thoughts. We're moving.

Sliding! But—why the roar of the engine? Thrust reversal? Yes, of course! He's trying to brake our slide. Is it possible? She couldn't tell from where she lay sprawled on the floor. The deafening roar was drowning out all other sensations.

She reached up for the edge of the galley counter and pulled herself to her feet. *Must see to the passengers,* she thought. She almost lost her footing again as she reached for the cabin mike. Panic could become a rampaging monster in seconds unless she did the right thing, and quickly. "Attention please!" she cried. "All passengers immediately tighten your seat belts. As tight as you can get them. Remove all eyeglasses, pens, and other loose items and stow them. Lean forward, cross your hands on the top of the seat in front of you, and rest your head on your arms." She saw the crew responding, double-checking seat belts, showing them how to assume the crash position. Good! she thought. The training was paying off.

She made her way aft, climbing hand-over-hand, clinging to seat backs to keep from falling. A quick glance out a cabin window sent a stab of fear through her. They weren't slowing. The thrust reverser wasn't working. She caught the searching glance of one of the paramedics. "I think we'd better sit down and strap in!"

"Roger that!"

All around them, terrified passengers were yielding to their worst fears: some crying out in terror, some silent, faces ashen with fear, some with heads bowed in prayer. All seemed to sense that death was near.

* * *

Mark Svenson held Karen close. "It's going to be all right, Kitten. Trust me," he soothed. He saw terror in her eyes as she looked up at him. But as his words penetrated, her terror faded. In its place was the beginning of acceptance. She closed her eyes and raised her lips to his, warm, tender, and just for one brief, private moment it was beautiful. And then the terror returned.

* * *

Up forward, Frank Russo was too busy to notice his fear. If they were to survive it was crucial that he do exactly the right thing at the right moment. He must win this desperate gamble. No second throw of the dice. His airplane was rocketing down a concave chute of snow. What lay underneath the snow was anyone's guess. Rocks, crevasses a mile deep, things too horrible to contemplate. He had no control over the direction of their rocketing run. Their giant winged toboggan was subject only to the whims of gravity as it shot down the glacier, propelled ever faster by the raging inferno at their tail.

"Thank God for the new snow! We'd be hamburger without it!" he gasped. His knuckles were white on the control yoke as he stared down at the rapidly approaching clouds. What lay under them he knew only too well. Nine thousand feet of more ice, boulders, and then trees. "Read off the air speed!" he shouted to Harris.

"*Fifty!*" Harris yelled above the engine's shriek.

"We need rudder control! We've got to get to the right of that bloody meat-cleaver!" He kicked the rudder pedals. Nothing yet.

"*Sixty!*"

He could feel the gradual lessening of the jolts as the wings began to respond to the torrent of air flowing over them. They'd been covered with snow. Would the slots clear? If they didn't, his gamble wouldn't matter.

"*Seventy-five!*"

He risked a quick look back through his side window. A gale of white powder was flying up from the wing. Bare metal showed along the leading edge. Were the flaps down? Yes. He remembered putting them down before they landed. Not all the way, but better than nothing. They were high enough to avoid being torn off. God bless the designers that put in a high wing!

"*Ninety!*"

Russo tried kicking the rudder pedals again. There was a response. Would it be enough? The Cleaver was dead in their path. He rotated the wheel but couldn't feel the ailerons. Hydraulic failure? Probably. Everything's frozen solid. But gradually he felt something. A slight rocking. He risked another quick glance. They appeared to be riding the crest of a white wave. *Avalanche!* Could he keep on top of it? The roar of the tail engine was like an angry dragon. If it faltered, they would be buried under tons of snow. The feel of the controls was stiffening. *Maybe. Just maybe!*

"*One hundred!* What's our rotation speed?"

"God knows!" Russo tried to chuckle. His throat was too dry. "If we have frozen snow on the wings, it won't matter. I've got to try. Jesus! Those rocks—right in our path!" The Cleaver was a scant two hundred yards ahead. The name was fitting. It would slice their left wing off, and that would finish them. The first spark would ignite a fireball. But gradually—incredibly—he felt the ride smoothing. The fuselage seemed to be rising up, trying to shake itself free of the white wave. The more they lifted, the less the drag. But the faster they went, the less time left. *Good news, bad news.* It'd be quick, if they hit it.

"*One-fifteen!*"

"All or nothing! Help me!"

Harris gripped the control yoke. Together they hauled back. The force on the yoke was tremendous.

"Come on, baby! You can do it!" Icy perspiration trickled down Russo's sides. "I think—she's coming unstuck!" Suddenly the jolting and the noise of the snow under the belly ceased. The nose jerked upward. "*We're off! Hard right turn, NOW!*" Together they depressed the right rudder pedals and rotated the wheel. The jagged line of rocks flashed by their left wing. "We missed it!" His breath came out in a long shudder.

"Thank God!" Harris cried.

"Don't thank him yet!" Russo eased the wheel back to neutral and tried to get the wings level. "We may have just guaranteed a crash landing. Get Megan up here, then get on the horn to Seattle. Our own people, too. We're going to need to talk to our mechanics."

"I'm on it!" As Harris summoned Megan Russo glanced at the clock on the instrument panel. Just twenty seconds had elapsed since the start of their plunge. It seemed like hours.

"Seattle tower, Pacific Coastal Seventy-four Heavy..."

As Russo listened to the exchange he was hit by a sudden wave of exhaustion. All through the nightmarish takeoff he had been too busy to notice the tremendous stress. But now that it was behind him he felt himself succumbing to shock. He had faced the unthinkable horror of crashing into the merciless rocks. But he *had* gotten through it. From somewhere he had found reserves he hadn't realized he possessed. All that was left was a dim memory of something conquered, now safely behind him. That, and the lingering feeling of nausea. But he could deal with that.

* * *

1413:25: The Mountain

"Hold it up!" Malcolm Krouse cried. He looked up over his shoulder and cupped his hand to his ear. "Can you hear it? It sounds like they've gone to full power. Why would they...?"

The other two stopped and raised their eyes to scan the sky but could see nothing.

Alex Papoulis listened intently. "I must be hearing things," he muttered. "Surely it's not moving!"

"God, I hope not!" Eric exclaimed.

"The snow had been shearing away under them yesterday," Papoulis said. "Keep your eyes peeled. Meanwhile, we'd better keep moving."

The three climbers began moving down the snow-covered surface again. Alex, in the lead, carefully probed the snow with his ice ax before each step. They were roped up, but as an extra precaution Alex insisted that only one should move at a time. The other two served as belays, digging in with their crampons and axes to prevent a fall into an unseen crevasse. Unaccountably, the noise of the plane's engine seemed to be growing as they descended.

* * *

1413:35: SeaTac RAPCON

"Coastal Seventy-four? Say again, please." Archie Crenshaw's attention was riveted to the radar display before him. There it was, where nothing had been before: The clear double image of the radar skin paint and transponder signal from an aircraft. Clearly, both were separating from the permanent radar echo from Mount Rainier. Close by the transponder return was the cluster of letters and numbers that identified the signal—but it couldn't be! *Pacific Coastal 74!* Yet there it was, squawking "7700", the emergency code. He couldn't believe what he was seeing, but the radar and transponder couldn't lie. It must be real.

The anxious voice came through again: "Seattle, Coastal Seventy-Four. We need help!"

"Seventy-four, Seattle. We have you on radar and read your squawk. Your present position is five-zero miles from the airport at one-two-thousand. Say your condition, over." As he spoke he motioned to the shift supervisor. "I don't know how they did it, but it's Coastal 74. *They're airborne!* Better alert the emergency units. God knows where they'll be setting down. Or *if!*"

"Seattle, Seventy-four. We just made the wildest takeoff you've ever heard of. I still can't believe it. We have very limited control. Everything's frozen. We're running on just number two. We're able to maintain speed and altitude for now, trying to check on damage. Can you get someone to come up and have a look at our underside? Over."

"Coastal Seventy-four, Seattle. We'll try to get an observer up to look you over. Will advise. Maintain present altitude if possible. Report otherwise. Turn right to heading three-five-zero. Reduce speed to two-five-zero knots. The sky is yours, and welcome back, Seventy-four!"

"Seattle, Seventy-four confirms."

Crenshaw looked at his supervisor. "Who can we get to scramble and have a look?"

"I'll get through to McChord. They have fighters on standby. Whether they can make it up through the icing is anybody's guess." He motioned to an assistant.

* * *

1415: The Flight Deck

Russo turned in his seat as Megan entered the flight deck. "Megan, I want to ask how things are back there, but I think I can guess." She nodded. Her grim expression told him everything. "I've got a serious problem." He looked at her and chuckled. "A few serious problems. One is that I need someone that has a little experience with airplanes to go down into the baggage bay and have a look at the damage to the wheel well doors. I can't spare Walter. Would you see if you can find somebody?"

"Okay," Megan agreed. "Are you two all right, Captain?"

Russo saw concern in her eyes that went beyond the professional. He smiled. "We're all right, Megan. Not having one of our better days, but I think we've got a fighting chance. Just pray that number two holds out."

"I'll find some help," she said. "There's the Air Force flight surgeon, but I don't think he's a pilot. Maybe there's someone dead-heading back there. I'll check the passenger manifest." She turned to go.

"Morale is our biggest factor, Megan."

"Oh, is that it? I could have sworn it was two superb pilots." She grinned and waived as she left the flight deck.

"That's a gutsy lady," Harris remarked.

"Oh, you noticed that, did you?" Russo grinned. His eyes flitted over the flight instruments. They were flying straight and level. Everything appeared all right, which surprised him. He tried the autopilot control: it seemed to be working. He entered an altitude and speed hold. He could hear the noise gradually diminish as the computer cut back on the power, easing the strain on their one good engine. "How's our fuel, Walter?"

"Down to thirteen thousand, if we can trust the instruments."

"It should be enough for just one engine. What's our max thrust at twelve thousand?"

Harris consulted the operations manual. "Forty-one thousand pounds available, but I wouldn't recommend pushing it," he reported.

"Thank God the builders decided to put in three big fans! If we'd been flying a two-holer we'd be dead now." He looked at the thick cloud layer below. "We have to get down through all that freezing rain next. When we do I'm going to come down pretty fast, to prevent an ice buildup. We've been damned lucky so far. Whatever's left on the wings apparently isn't enough to stall us. But the wheels are probably frozen up like blocks of ice. Let's get through to maintenance and see what they recommend, in case they refuse to come down."

"You read my mind." Harris reached for the radio panel to activate their secure channel to the airline's repair station.

* * *

1416: Pacific Coastal Repair Station

"Seventy four? Say again your position!" Clarence Ulman stared at his monitor, unable to believe what he was seeing.

Walter Harris's voice came over the speaker above him again. "We're at twelve thousand, about fifty miles south, holding at two-fifty knots. All we've got is the tail engine. We got off by sheer luck. The tower's trying to get an Air Force jet up here to check the damage to our underside. The undercarriage is the most critical problem. If we can't get the wheels down we may have to ditch. We're trying to get a look at them through the mouse holes down in the baggage bay. We'll let you know what we find. Meanwhile, we could use some advice about how to get them down if they're hung up. Over."

"Roger your request. By the way, you might give Mrs. Gordon a call. She's standing by at operations." He grinned to himself. Standing by was an understatement. Janet Gordon wasn't the type to just stand by and wait. She'd probably been going crazy with worry, as had everyone else.

Ulman signed off and called the lead mechanic on duty. He tried to imagine the damage a snow landing would do to the wheel well doors, and possibly to the airplane structure itself. He shook his head slowly. Flight 74 had a lot of hurdles to get over. They might be better to try for a ditching. Could a jumbo ditch? He wasn't sure. As far as he knew no one had ever tried before. Certainly not in a raging storm. Still, this was a CH-12. With its high wing it just might make it without digging a wingtip into a wave.

1417: The Cargo Hold

The two SAS pilots had been wondering what they could do to help when Megan McLain found them and enlisted their aid. Glad to help, they followed her forward and down into the lower deck of the fuselage that served as the baggage bay. "You'll find the inspection ports out at the ends of the cross-aisle just forward," Megan explained. She left the two pilots and returned to the upper level.

Captain Rasmussen was amazed to learn how little damage the airplane had sustained. He could see wrinkling in the outer hull's skin, and he could feel the icy draft from dozens of cracks. But the hull bottom was still there. It hadn't been caved in, as he'd expected. This hull must be as tough as the old Gooney Bird, he thought. The C-47s were the only airplanes he knew of that could take this kind of pounding and survive.

He made his way out through the narrow passageway that led to the port side, where there was a pie-sized observation port. Through it he could view the underside of the wing and engine pod. A pair of long, hinged panels under the pod covered the cavity where the port main undercarriage was stowed. When they functioned properly the panels swung down and out, allowing the tandem dual wheels to drop down and lock into position. Should these doors fail to open, the undercarriage could not extend.

Rasmussen scanned the surface of the doors. There was no serious damage that he could see. Fortunately the engines were slung well above the fuselage bottom, so the impact of the landing had been absorbed by the belly.

"This one isn't too bad," he called across to his first officer on the other side. "How's yours?"

"Marginal," Nikolaisen reported. "Anyone's guess. There's a section about three feet long where the two doors have been jammed together. They may be stuck."

Rasmussen joined his companion and took a look out the starboard side. "Not too promising," he grunted. "We'd better get back up and report. We don't have much time."

"What would you do?" Nikolaisen asked as they made their way back to the ladder and hatch leading up to the flight deck.

"Try like hell to get the wheels down. There's a chance they might. Of course there'd be no guarantee they'd be locked down. The indicators may be malfunctioning, too."

"Could they foam the runway for a belly landing?"

"Not for a jumbo. You can't belly land these big brutes."

"So, what are you saying?"

"We're close to the water."

"A ditching?"

"It may be the only way." Rasmussen shrugged his shoulders. "If he brings it down carefully, and the waves aren't too high, we might have a chance. It'd be a lot tougher than that landing on smooth snow. But at least there'd be little chance of a fire."

"But—the injured?"

"Yes. The injured."

1418: PCA Operations

Janet Gordon heard the electronic chimes of the SELCAL system. She switched on the speakerphone. "PCA Operations, Janet Gordon."

"Janet, this is Frank. Are you sitting down?"

"Yes." Janet closed her eyes for a moment, and tried to keep her voice calm. "Thank God you're still alive. Are you all right up there? Is there anything else I can—?"

"Janet, you're not going to believe this, but we're airborne!"

"You're—you're *what?!* Say that again?"

"You heard right. We're airborne. We got caught in an avalanche. Rode it down. There was nothing else to do, so I just took the only chance we had. Poured on full power with the tail engine. With the downhill slope it was enough. It's one for the books. I wouldn't have believed it. But we're flying, so I guess I have to."

For the first time since yesterday she felt the terrible tension beginning to ease. She took a deep breath, held it, then let it out. She knew she wouldn't be able to relax fully until Flight 74 was safely on the ground. As a pilot, she knew how impossible that could be, even given their miraculous takeoff. "How can I help, Frank?"

"Nothing for the moment," he told her. "We're in touch with the tower. They've alerted the rescue units. We haven't tried the gear yet. They may be frozen, so we might wind up having to swim for it."

"You might have to ditch?" A sudden shock went through her as she forced herself to consider the possibility. She had listened to the weather report on the way in from home this morning. It was so bad they'd canceled most of the ferry runs across the Sound. "Please, Frank, try to get the wheels down. You don't want to try a water landing today."

"Bad?"

"It's a maelstrom."

"I was afraid of that. Okay, we're in contact with Clancy over in maintenance. He's going to see what can be done about the wheels. I've got a couple of SAS pilots down in the belly eyeballing it through the mouse holes, and SeaTac is getting an Air Force jet to come up and look us over. We'll manage."

"I know," Janet said softly. "I've been wearing calluses on my knees. I'm sure you'll make it, dear. I'm going to the field now. I'll talk to you when I get there. Safe landing!"

Everything would depend on getting those wheels down. She knew what he was thinking. With no wheels, ditching was their only hope. But it would be a very slim hope today. The waves were running over five feet, but not the long rollers of the ocean. These were the short, choppy kind typical of inland waters. But even if they did survive the landing, she feared no one would survive more than a few minutes in that frigid water. It's the runway or nothing, she thought, pulling on her raincoat.

1419: The Mountain

"Look! Up there!" Eric Whitely was pointing excitedly. "It's got to be them!" The other two paused, digging in with their ice axes, and looked up.

"I don't believe it!" Papoulis gasped, his eyes widening. "It simply isn't possible!"

"Possible or not, there they go!" Eric's eyes followed the path of the huge plane as it labored northward.

"Seeing is believing." Papoulis broke into a huge grin. "Mark has finally got his big story! Meanwhile, we'd better be on our way." He looked down at the boiling tops of the clouds, now less than a thousand feet below them. What lay beneath them he could only guess. Probably freezing rain or more snow. Or both. They might have to wait another day before they could make it down. But at least they had plenty of food now. He could see the bottom of the ridge through the mist. They would be there in another hour or so.

* * *

1420: The Flight Deck

"Pacific Coastal Flight Seventy-Four, Air Force one-niner-three-five-six. Over."

Russo glanced across at Harris and grinned. "The cavalry!" He thumbed his transmit button: "Air Force three-five-six, Coastal Seventy-four. Glad to hear you! Over."

"Pleased to be of help. Captain Ike Gudansky here. Watch for the F-16 on your port side. Say your problem, Seventy-four."

"We need you to check for damage as we try to lower our gear, Captain."

"Understood. Hope I can slow this baby down enough. Over."

"Sorry 'bout that. We're humping along as fast as we can." He turned back to Harris. "Take over, Walter. I'll watch for him."

It wasn't long before he spotted the F-16 converging on them. Gudansky wagged his wings as he lowered his flaps and speed brakes.

"Air Force three-five-six, we have you in sight."

"Copy, Seventy-four. Are you able to hold attitude?"

"Affirmative."

"Okay. I'll make a pass under you from left to right, then back again. Stand by."

In fifteen seconds the sleek silver fighter had traversed their underside and taken up his station again. "You're going to need a little Tango-Lima-Charlie when you land, Seventy-four."

"Tango-Lima-Charlie?" Harris asked, puzzled.

"TLC", Russo chuckled. "Roger that, three-five-six. How about the wheel doors?"

"The nose doors are completely sheared away. Your main doors don't look too bad, but I can't tell for sure. Are you ready to try to lower them?"

"Trying now, Air Force." Russo reached for the selector. "Here goes everything," he muttered, and moved the lever to the down selection. There was a loud cracking noise below them. The nose gear indicated green: down and locked. The other two remained red. "We indicate nose gear down and locked. No main gear. Over."

"Stand by," Captain Gudansky answered. The F-16 disappeared under them again. He came back on the radio quickly: "Not too good, Seventy-four. Confirm your nose wheel is down. The left doors are partly open, but the wheel is hung up. The right-hand doors appear jammed."

Russo's fears were confirmed. "Okay, Air Force. We'll have to do some head scratching here. Please stand by." He turned to Harris. "I'll take it again, Walter. See what the manuals recommend. But I think I know already. The gear is probably unlatched, just hung up by the doors.

They're designed to come down just with gravity, as a safety backup. See what they recommend if that doesn't work."

Harris nodded. After a few seconds of searching he found something. "There's one possibility," he announced. "Page 322 of the manual gives the procedure."

"What's that?"

Harris chuckled. "The Stuka maneuver! It ought to shake up the passengers."

"It may snap our wings off, too," Russo thought out loud. "What's the gee-limit of the CH-12, anyway?"

"The manual says it can take three Gs. It's a pretty strong airplane. Most jumbos can't take more than about two-and-a-half without breaking something."

"We'll probably need it," Russo commented. "Okay. Alert the tower to our situation. We'll wait to make our final decision until after we try lowering the wheels again."

"Roger."

"We need a break here," Russo said grimly.

"No way to belly-land?"

"Not a chance! We'd have a broken airplane and a fireball."

"You're thinking about ditching, then?"

"It's the only alternative, without wheels," Russo said.

"Not a hell of a lot better, is it?"

"Not much. Janet said the Sound's a nightmare. I'm sure she's right. One wingtip catches a wave and we cartwheel, and that's all she wrote. A broken airplane and bodies all over the water, most of them drowning, the rest dying of hypothermia before rescuers can get to them."

"Let's keep our fingers crossed," Harris murmured.

Russo assessed the situation. Normal procedures were useless. They had a badly damaged airplane, possibly with structural damage, probably with frozen flaps and jammed undercarriage, flying on one engine. This was one they'd never programmed into the simulators. But what about that hairy takeoff down the side of the mountain? He'd survived that. He'd just have to rely on professional skill and intuition. No manual. No procedures. No checklists. Just raw piloting skill—and guts. Lots of guts. First he had to find out what he had left of his airplane.

He turned off the autopilot and checked his controls. The response was barely adequate. "Let's check the flaps and slats, Walter." Harris manipulated the control, but there was no movement. They remained frozen at the fifteen degree position.

"Maybe they'll thaw as we descend," Harris said.

Russo nodded. "Decision time," he grunted. "I'm going to try the sharp pull-up. Better let Gudansky know what we're up to, and have Megan warn them in the back that we haven't gone completely wacko."

Harris chuckled and made the calls.

"Okay: Hang on. Here goes!" Russo pushed the control yoke forward, tipping their nose down to pick up momentum. When he was satisfied with their speed he pulled back on the yoke. "Wheels down!" he yelled, and jerked the nose up into the kind of climb the designers had never intended the airplane to perform. There was a loud bang from under the left wing. "We got something!" he grunted.

Russo thumbed his transmit button. "Air Force Three-five-six, what's our undercarriage state now? Over."

"Coastal Seventy-four, stand by."

Russo saw the air force jet drop down under them again, then come up on the other side. "Seventy-four, your port main wheel is down. I can't tell whether it's locked. The starboard is still hung up by the jammed doors. Over."

"We'll try once more, Air Force. Stand by."

"Roger."

Russo put the nose down again, and this time he rammed the thrust lever for the tail engine to full power. Again he hauled the yoke back, harder than he had ever done before. The maneuver brought back memories of that night on Whidbey Island. He felt the same feeling of high gee force he had experienced that night as the airplane shot up out of the dive.

"Watch the G-loading!" Harris shouted over the noise.

Russo nodded and eased back on the yoke pressure. There was another loud bang, this time under the right wing. "Another check please, Air Force."

"Roger, stand by."

The fighter swung down under them again. This time it stayed down there for several seconds before reappearing.

"Coastal Seventy-four, you have three wheels down," Gudansky reported. "No way I can tell they're locked. But it's looking better. Over."

"Air Force, Coastal Seventy-four. Thanks for your help. We still have two red lights, but we're going to try it, and hope for the best. Seventy-four out."

"Good luck, Seventy-four. See you on the ground. Air Force Three-five-six returning to base. Out."

Russo turned to Harris. "I'm still not committing one way or the other, Walter. I want to keep our options open till the last minute. I'll try to grease it onto the runway. If the gear starts to fold, we'll try to abort and go for a swim. If the engine dies during the abort—I guess that's the chance we have to take. Do you agree?"

Harris nodded. "We think alike, FDR."

Russo grinned nervously. "Okay, notify the tower we're on our way in. Tell them we'd like to come down fast, to avoid icing up, then try a normal approach. Ask for sixteen left. I'd like to keep as far away from the buildings as possible, but sixteen right is too short. We're going to need all the runway we can get. And have them alert the Coast Guard for a possible ditching, if we have to abort."

Harris relayed Russo's requests to the control tower. The tower responded almost immediately with their clearance to descend.

"They're going to want fuel and souls, Walter," Russo said.

Harris consulted the fuel display panel. "Down to eleven thousand pounds, skipper."

"And souls on board?"

"You'd better get that from Megan. I'm not sure what the status is back there after that takeoff. I hope they all made it."

Russo nodded and called Megan. Her voice came on almost immediately. She sounded confident, but he knew her well enough to detect an edge of concern. "I hope we didn't shake things up too badly back there," he said. "Are you all right?"

"Better, now that I can hear a friendly voice."

"Megan, what's our head count back there now? SeaTac is going to need to know."

"No further fatalities," she reported. "But we have three missing."

"Missing?!"

"Apparently three guys took off on their own, before anyone could stop them. I just found out about it. So make it one-seventy-four passengers, plus ten in the crew."

"Damn!"

"Don't blame yourself, Captain. No one could have stopped them. Maybe they'll make it."

"Let's hope so," he breathed. "Okay, here's the situation. We're going to try a landing, Megan," he explained. "We're pretty sure our wheels are locked, but just in case, better get them to practice the crash position. Have the girls ready to evacuate fast when we come to a stop. If the wheels don't hold, we'll have to abort and go for a water landing, so dole out the life jackets, too. One way or the other, I think we'll be all right."

"I wish I could be with you."

"So do I, Megan," he responded. "We'll make up for it later. That's a promise."

"I'm going to hold you to it!" she said, and hung up.

A surge of feeling went through him as the warmth of her words got through to him. That's something to focus on, he thought.

Another reason to make it, if he needed one. He switched to the main cabin P.A. system and began to speak: "Folks, This is Captain Russo. I'm not going to try to fool you: we're in a bit of a bind here. But they're all ready for us on the ground, and your cabin crew is well-experienced in emergency procedures. We have our wheels down, and we'll be landing at the airport. Should anything go wrong, we may have to make a water landing. The Coast Guard air-sea rescue units are standing by, and they know what to do. Either way, I'm sure we'll come through this. Now, I want you to assume the crash position, which the crew will demonstrate, and to remain in that position until we come to a complete stop. Then I want you to follow the crew's instructions as we evacuate the airplane. Please do everything you can to cooperate, and we'll all come out of this safely. God be with us all!"

He turned to Walter Harris. "Here goes." Harris nodded. Russo peered out at the featureless white stratum of clouds below and pushed the nose downward for their plunge. After a minute or so the dense clouds engulfed them. He had to rely on the instruments. Almost immediately the turbulence became violent. He pushed the nose down a little more to increase their speed through the wall of snow that was flying at them in a blinding fury. At seven thousand feet the snow gave way to driving sheets of hail that threatened to smash the windshield. At five thousand the hail turned to rain. He fought his way down to three thousand, then eased the control yoke back to lessen the dive angle. The outside temperature had risen sharply as they descended.

"Controls should be starting to thaw," he said.

Harris checked the instruments. "Fifty degrees outside."

"Good. I can feel a little more give to the ailerons, and we've got full elevator and rudder control." That was the good part. But the airplane was jerking like a puppet on strings manipulated by some invisible giant. "Rough ride," he grunted. He leveled out at two thousand feet and reduced his power setting in the denser air.

The tower controller's voice broke in. "Seventy-four Heavy, Seattle."

"Hello, Seattle. Seventy-four Heavy. Lousy weather you're having. It was much nicer up on top. Over."

"Welcome back, Seventy-four. We have you on radar at two thousand feet. Distance one-five miles, speed two-five-zero. The airport is at your ten o'clock position, sir. You may commence a gradual left turn onto final. You are cleared to land, runway sixteen left. The wind is one-eight-zero at three-zero, gusting to four-five. Barometer two-niner-four-three. Good luck, sir."

"Seattle, Seventy-four Heavy. Copy. We are still unable to see the ground. We'll have to trust you that it's still there."

There was a burst of laughter over the air, then Darryl Washington's smooth voice continued: "We'll bring you in, Seventy-four. Say fuel and souls on board, please."

Russo turned to Harris. "How's the fuel now, Walter?"

"Make it ten thousand."

"Seattle, Seventy-four Heavy. Fuel is one-zero thousand. There are two in the cockpit, and one-eight-two in the cabin, total of one-eighty-four souls on board. We've lost four passengers. One dead, and three escaped to try to climb down on their own. We have no idea what happened to them." Russo grimaced. It was a part of the emergency procedures he never liked, but it was essential that the rescue crews have an accurate count of the number of humans aboard when they began sorting out bodies, if it were to come to that. Had there been any live pets traveling down in the cargo hold, he'd have included them, too.

* * *

1430: SeaTac Tower

"Seventy-four Heavy, copy one-zero thousand pounds of fuel, one-eight-four souls." Washington turned to his supervisor, who was looking over his shoulder at the scope display. "Want to take it, Ralph?"

"You're doing fine, Darryl," Ralph Whittaker said, and grinned reassuringly. Whittaker picked up his portable mike and began speaking to the ground rescue team again. "Seattle Tower to all rescue units, we are declaring an Alert Charlie, I say again, Alert Charlie. We have a CH-12 on emergency approach with two engines out, landing on tail engine only. One-eighty-four souls on board, one-zero thousand pounds of fuel, current position eight miles southwest. They'll attempt a landing on runway sixteen left. Be advised aircraft reports all three wheels are down but they have red lights on both main gear. They should be lining up on final in four minutes. If they have to abort they will try for a ditching in the Sound. Air-sea units please copy."

The answers came back immediately. Whittaker patted his controller on the shoulder. "I'm glad you were here for this one, Darryl," he said.

Washington was too busy to respond, but he felt his eyes go misty. He spoke into his boom mike again with a low, steady voice: "All traffic in the Sea-Tac area, be advised that SeaTac runway sixteen left is now closed for an emergency landing."

* * *

1433: The Flight Deck

Russo completed a slow, gradual turn, bringing the airplane around to a south-westerly heading. He felt the wind buffeting the wings as they turned into it, and fought off the mental image of that night on Whidbey Island years ago. He thumbed his mike switch:

"Seattle, Seventy-four Heavy, ready to start final descent. Say the runway condition, please. Over."

"Seventy-four Heavy, Seattle. Runways are clear and wet," Darryl Washington replied. "Sixteen left is eleven thousand nine hundred feet in length. Is there any change in the status of your undercarriage?"

"Our nose gear indicates green, but both main gear are still showing red. The Air Force observer confirms they are both down, but cannot tell if they're locked. Request clearance for a touch-and-go. If they hold, we'll land. If we have to abort, request immediate diversion for a ditching in the Sound."

"Copy, Seventy-four. You are cleared for touch-and-go, land at pilot's discretion, runway sixteen left. The Coast Guard has been alerted, and units are now on station off Seattle. They recommend that if a ditch is attempted it should be made from the northeast, approaching to the east of Bainbridge. The waves are less severe in that region."

"Seventy-four, copy." Russo turned to Harris. "The only trouble with that is that nobody's ever ditched a CH-12. I'd rather not be the first." He tested the controls. They seemed much freer. He depressed the transmit button again. "Okay, Seattle. We've got good control now. But we aren't trying any aerobatics."

"Coastal Seventy-four Heavy, understand. Turn left to one six zero."

"Roger, Seattle. Turning left to one-six-zero."

Russo now had to prepare for a part of his duties that he didn't relish. He picked up the cabin mike, gathered his thoughts for a moment, and began to speak.

* * *

1434: The Main Cabin

In the main cabin, Megan was helping the other flight attendants to make sure the passengers were all strapped into their seats firmly and were wearing their life vests. They had moved them to the forward seats again for landing. The one problem they didn't want, she thought, was a tail-heavy airplane that might make it impossible to get the nose down in the heavy gusts. The Captain's voice broke into her thoughts over the cabin speakers.

"Okay folks, this is the captain again. We've just been cleared on final approach, and we expect to be on the ground in a few minutes. I'm not going to try to pretend there aren't any problems. We're going to try what we call a touch-and-go to make sure everything is working before we commit, so don't be alarmed if we don't land the first time. If necessary we'll go around again and come in for a landing on the second approach. I want you to listen carefully to everything your flight attendants tell you. We'll have to evacuate the aircraft after touchdown, but please *remain in your seats with your belts done up tight* until you're told to move. The flight attendants have passed out life jackets, in the event that we are unable to set down on the runway. Please don't be alarmed about this. These airplanes are designed to survive water landings just like a seaplane. But we're counting on a normal runway landing. We hope to have you back at the gate shortly. Please brace yourselves now and follow the cabin crew's instructions. Good luck!"

* * *

Russo turned to Walter Harris. "Luck!" he snorted. "We're going to need all of that we can get. Keeping this bird on the runway long enough to bring it to a stop is going to be the big problem."

"Maybe we ought to reconsider ditching," Harris suggested.

"No. That's still our second choice. Too much risk of drowning a lot of lousy swimmers—or freezing them. Our best bet is the runway. It's plenty long enough. But with only one engine we can't expect much help from thrust reversal. The brakes are going to have to carry the load—*if* the wheels don't fold up, and *if* we have brakes. That's two too many ifs, to my liking. It's time to see if we're living right, Walter. Let's try the flaps now."

"Here goes." Harris reached down for the lever that would extend the flaps and leading edge slats. He flipped it to the full down position and both pilots waited to hear the whine of the motors that would announce a successful extension. *Silence.* "No dice," Harris said grimly.

"Still stuck. Not surprising," Russo muttered. "Try recycling it again."

Harris brought the lever back to the up position and repeated the down selection. Still no sound. On the third try there was a cracking noise, and the motors began to emit a stuttering whine. Harris looked up at the leading edge of the wing. "The slats are extending," he reported. He craned his neck to look back. "Flaps coming down full. Looks like we're in business."

"Part of the way," Russo corrected. "There's still the little matter of the wheels and brakes."

* * *

1437: SeaTac Airport

They had decided to trust Lionel Waid's aging Volkswagen bus for the race to the airport. Despite its vintage, Waid insisted that he kept the bus in excellent mechanical condition, for it was essential to his work. Derek Winthrop shook his head as his eyes swept the interior of the vehicle. There were two VHF scanners mounted under the dash—one for the police and fire bands and one for the aircraft frequencies used by the control tower. Tucked out of sight behind the visor was a police radar detector. He didn't know whether the former was legal in Washington. He knew damn well the jammer wasn't—*anywhere*. The back seats were littered with several bags containing 35 millimeter cameras and lenses, TV minicams, and boxes of film and mag tape. There were two large boxes on the floor. One contained Waid's stash of junk food. The other overflowed with outer clothing for just about every weather condition imaginable.

"You're pretty well equipped," Winthrop remarked.

Waid grinned as he pulled out to pass a slow-moving truck. "Have to be. You never know where you'll be or what you'll be doing on assignments. Sometimes I'm away from home for days at a stretch."

They were heading south on the little-used Highway 509, which bypassed the impossible snarl of the southbound lanes of I-5. Even this early, "flex-hours" at Boeing and a lot of other major industries had turned Seattle's arterials into nightmares by this time in the afternoon.

As they reached the end of 509, Winthrop pointed to a large building just at the edge of the airport property. "Pull in there."

"That's the Pacific Coastal repair hangar. We can't get in there."

"Trust me!" Winthrop insisted. As they stopped an elderly guard came out to intercept them. Winthrop reached inside his jacket and produced an envelope, which he passed to the guard. The guard opened the envelope, looked inside, then grinned and waved them on.

"What was in the envelope?" Waid asked as he parked at the rear of the parking lot.

"What do you think?"

The two exchanged grins.

Across the broad expanse of tarmac to the west of the huge hangar the airfield was a beehive of activity. SeaTac's full complement of gargantuan, gaudily colored crash trucks, foam trucks, ladder trucks, and assorted command vehicles was converging on runway sixteen left, which was the runway closest to the long row of terminal buildings. Silver-suited figures rode each truck, ready to combat the flames and smoke that were always expected in crash landings. Assorted ambulances and aid units from all the surrounding communities were arriving in a continuous stream. The fire chief, wearing a brilliant red suit, jumped out of a bright yellow sedan, talking into a hand-held radio to the troops under his command, organizing what could be the first line of defense for the arriving jumbo. Under his direction the trucks raced out to take up positions at intervals down each side of the asphalt.

Along the tarmac in front of the main terminal were several police and hospital helicopters, rotors turning, ready to evacuate the injured to the major area hospitals, where teams of surgeons, EMTs, nurses, and a host of other specialists were waiting with grim resolve.

"Can you get a good shot from here?" Winthrop asked, as Waid set up his equipment. "We could go up to the hangar roof."

"No. This'll be better. If there's a fireball it's more dramatic from a low angle."

"You're a real ghoul, aren't you!"

"I know what the public likes," Waid said. "Lots of close-ups. *They're* the ghouls. We just feed their hunger."

"And I write about it. We're a great bunch, aren't we."

* * *

1439:40: Flight 74

"...You are now six miles from touchdown, on center line, above glide path. Adjust rate of descent."

Russo nudged the control column forward slightly to bring the lumbering giant down at a slightly steeper angle. They were descending through the dense clouds at the standard instrument-landing rate of 300 feet per minute. Walter Harris, his eyes fixed on the airspeed indicator, continued to jockey the power setting on the tail engine, doing his best to counter the gusty blasts of wind were frustrating their descent down through the dense clouds.

"How's the brake pressure?" Russo asked.

"Primary's lost it all," Harris answered. He flicked a switch. "Backup's marginal. Barely enough now, but there's probably a leak. That landing on the mountain—we're lucky to be alive at all, I guess. Brakes are like frosting on the cake at this point."

"Pretty important frosting, if we get down to a runway."

They had tried to work their way through the landing checklist, but several of the items had to be bypassed because of damage sustained up on the mountain. The brake pressure was one of those items.

"Read off the altitude and speed from here on, Walter," Russo commanded. "I'm going to cut it short and try to touch down close to the button. We need every foot of runway we can get."

"Roger. We're at six hundred feet now, speed one-eighty-five."

The tower came through with another routine transmission: "Five miles from touchdown. On centerline, on glide slope. Current conditions: wind one-eight-five at three-zero, gusting to four-zero. Barometer two-niner-four-three. Ceiling three hundred. Visibility one quarter mile in heavy rain."

"Five hundred feet, one-eighty knots," Harris intoned.

Russo activated the cabin intercom. Megan answered the call almost immediately. "We're five miles out, Megan. Have them assume the crash position, and you girls get strapped in tight. Shoot anyone that tries to move before I give the signal to evacuate!" He heard her attempt at laughter. an intense desire to be with her swept over him. He wondered if she shared his feeling.

"Four hundred, one-ninety." Harris eased the thrust lever back a trifle to slow their descent.

"In this wind I'd like to slam it down on the runway and hit the reverser, Walter. But I'm afraid it might collapse the gear. So I'm going to ease her down as gently as possible. Be ready with emergency power if I have to overshoot. Let's hope we don't have to. It's really not a very nice day for a swim." Another problem, which he was sure was running through Walter's mind too, was whether a single engine would be enough to do a successful abort and stagger back into the air. He had serious doubts. This wasn't like taking off down the glacier. They could end in a fireball in the midst of a dense residential area. He tried to close his mind to the horror.

"Four miles from touchdown. On centerline, on glide slope. You're looking good, sir, and be advised all emergency equipment is in place if you elect to land."

"Roger, Seattle."

"Three hundred, one-eighty-five."

* * *

1440: Gate S-24

Janet Gordon looked anxiously out over the airport at the waiting crash equipment. The airport was like a ghost town. No aircraft activity of any kind. The storm had either diverted or canceled all flights in or out. She could barely see the end of the runway through the broad plate glass windows of the gate area. Heavy rain and mist shrouded the airport. Despite the poor visibility she continued to stare north for the first sign of the approaching jumbo. She'd give anything to be riding in the right-hand seat beside her brother right now.

"He's going to make it," she murmured.

"He's the right man for the job," Josh Edwards affirmed. "There's no finer pilot."

"Waiting is always tougher than piloting," Roger Greninger said.

Janet nodded. "I still can't believe they've made it this far."

"It's one for the books," Edwards agreed. "I was thinking—I'd like to try it in the simulator. I wonder if they could set it up for us?"

"I doubt that!" Janet said, breaking into a nervous grin. "Where would they start? They'd have no data base." She shook her head. "Frank will certainly be able to provide one—if he makes it."

* * *

1440:15: The Tarmac

"Any sign of them?" Derek Winthrop watched his cameraman squinting through the viewfinder of his minicam. Winthrop was wearing a raincoat and a broad-brimmed felt hat to ward off the driving rain, which was thankfully at their backs. Waid had donned rain pants and a hooded jacket from his stash in the back of his bus.

"Nothing yet," Waid yelled, his voice barely audible over the roar of the crash truck motor just fifty feet away.

"The tower had them four miles out a few seconds ago."

"Yeah, but they're probably still in the clouds. They've won't break through till they're almost over the runway. Better check our data link with the studio. This weather could play hell with the connections up on the roof of my bus."

"We're on the air," Winthrop said. "I've been in touch. So is everybody else in the world. Everybody and his dog is on the field waiting."

"Yeah, but nobody has a position like ours. We're going to be close enough to see his wheels hit the pavement. If anything goes wrong, we'll be the first to know about it. And so will everyone watching Channel 3."

"As usual." Winthrop supposed that was a good reason for watching Channel 3. There weren't many others, he was learning.

* * *

1440:35: Flight 74

"Three miles from touchdown, slightly left of centerline, on glide slope. Adjust heading to one-six-five."

Russo fought with the controls to bring the left wing up into the vicious crosswind. They were too far to the left, on a path that would put them dangerously close to the hangars and terminal buildings, which were still hidden from view. "Any sign of the ground, Walter? We ought to be over the south end of Boeing Field by now."

"Not a sign yet," Harris reported. "Can you handle the controls all right?"

"Yes, but I'll need help with the rudder."

"You've got it."

* * *

Megan had finished her walk-through inspection of the cabin. Now, satisfied she'd done everything in her power to see to the safety of her passengers, she sat in one of the rearward-facing jump seats next to Beth Winslow. "We'll be all right, Beth," Megan said, amazed at the strength of her voice. She squeezed Beth's hand. Actually, Megan believed it. She had nothing but confidence in the piloting skill of Frank Russo, and of Walter Harris, too. No one else could have managed that feat coming down off the mountain.

Once again she went over the sequence of actions that she and her crew would have to execute once they landed. *If* they landed, she corrected. The crew had already shown the passengers how to inflate the yellow life jackets. But Megan was well aware of what a water landing could mean. She had lived by the seaside as a girl, and had seen the wrecks of ships caught in the fierce gales that raged across the Irish Sea. While the Puget Sound was not nearly that rough, it was bad enough—and every bit as cold. The elderly and the very young would have no chance for survival. For the rest, it would be very, very chancy. One out of ten, she estimated. So a successful runway landing was crucial.

She wondered about the undercarriage. She knew what the brutal pull-ups had been for, even though she'd had to lie to the passengers about them. And she knew there still was no guarantee the wheels were safely locked down. If one of them folded on landing their chances were even less than they would be in the water, unless they could evacuate quickly. If a fire should develop before they could start evacuating—she shuddered at the thought. She had seen the film of the DC-10 crash landing at Sioux City, Iowa.

"We'll be all right, Beth," she repeated, and told herself once more that she believed it. And then she thought of Sean and the tears came.

* * *

Harris leaned forward and peered through the thinning mists ahead. "I can see the ground!" he cried.

Russo nodded. "I see it." He thumbed his transmit button again. "Seattle, Coastal Seventy-four. Ground in sight. We can take it from here. Reconfirm landing instructions."

"Roger, Seventy-four." The controller repeated their instructions. The wind and rain were worse, if anything. "Good luck, Sir," the controller said sympathetically.

"Seventy-four, thanks for your help. See you in a bit." He turned to Walter. "Damn! I was hoping for a break on the crosswind. It's worse! It's really going to be rough. Okay, give them the signal back there. Make sure they're braced for impact."

Harris made the announcement over the cabin intercom as Russo strained to get the first glimpse of the runway in the mists ahead. Below he caught a glimpse of a highway as they continued their slow, battered descent. There were a lot of vehicles stopped on the shoulder, their occupants standing outside, peering up at them. We must be quite an item of interest, he thought absently, then refocussed his attention on the scene straight ahead.

* * *

1441:40: The Tarmac

"I hear it!" Winthrop yelled.

Waid peered through the telescopic lens of his viewfinder. "No sign of it yet, but I can hear it too. It must have broken out of the clouds. It won't be long now."

"Hell of a wind," Winthrop said. He could feel the force of the gusts and the pelting rain on his back. "God, I hope they make it all right." For the first time since the disaster had unfolded he found himself empathizing with the poor souls strapped into their seats inside their bucking cylinder of metal and plastic. He knew what it was like. He'd experienced enough landings in Detroit and Chicago during thunderstorms to know the fear that would be gripping the unfortunates aboard Flight 74 right now. "Poor bastards," he murmured.

Lionel Waid hadn't heard what his partner had said. He was too busy adjusting his lens. This was a situation where it had to be done right the first time. There would be no second chance. That there would be no second chance for the passengers and crew of the stricken airplane never occurred to him.

* * *

1441:50: Gate S-24

Janet Gordon slipped her arm through Roger's and clung to him tightly as she fought to control her desperate fears. Still no sight of Frank's plane, but she knew it had to be close now. She looked up at

Roger. He smiled. "They're going to make it, Jan," he said softly. "I'm buying the drinks when they come in."

She broke into a smile, the first for the past hour. "And dinner's on me!" she answered.

Suddenly there was a stir among the other people watching with them in the gate area. Some were pointing excitedly. She looked in the direction they were pointing. "There they are!" she cried. "They're almost down!"

* * *

1441:55: The Flight Deck

"Seattle, Coastal Seventy-four. Runway in sight." Russo turned to Walter Harris. "Ready on the rudder pedals, Walter?"

Harris nodded. "All set. Good luck, FDR."

"To all of us!" Russo said. "I have a good feeling about this. I'm going to try to touch the main wheels down just past the threshold. If they hold, I'll say *FULL STOP* and bring the nose down. Be ready to hit the speed brakes and reverser immediately. But if it doesn't feel solid, I'll hold the nose off and say *ABORT*. In that case be ready to go to emergency thrust for a lift-off."

"Copy." Harris moved one hand to the speed brake selector. The other was poised over the thrust lever, prepared to go forward or back.

"Okay, here goes everything," Russo murmured. The understatement of the year, he thought grimly. With just one engine and a damaged airplane he had no illusions about being able to abort. He'd have to try to get the wheels up and hope for the best. If they failed to retract, it would be over quickly. The threshold lights flashed by under the nose. He eased the plane down over the black asphalt surface. He held his breath as the plane sank the last few feet. A sudden gust caught them, driving the left wingtip down dangerously close to the ground that was streaking by at over 100 miles an hour. Thoughts of Whidbey Island numbed his brain as he fought with the wheel. He willed the ship back level again. He forced the plane down a little lower, bleeding another few knots of airspeed. At last he heard the screech of the eight main tires as they accelerated to match their speed over the black asphalt. He held his breath, waiting for the aircraft to begin sinking toward the runway. It didn't.

"I think—I think they're holding!" Russo exclaimed.

"I think you're right!" He brought the nose down and felt the shock of the nose gear hitting the surface. "*FULL STOP!*" he barked.

Harris chopped the power and activated the speed brakes. Wing panels sprang up to break the airflow over the wing. "*REVERSE!*" Russo commanded. Harris's hand moved almost before the word came out. The tail engine once again roared to life. The airplane shuddered to the sudden rearward thrust. Both pilots fought with the rudder pedals, trying to resist the yawing motion of the nose as the wind tried to skid them to the left, into the waiting line of crash trucks.

"*EMERGENCY BRAKES!*" Russo yelled over the roar of the thrust reverser. Harris's hand shot forward. Eight sets of brake pads rammed down onto the searing hot wheel discs to slow their frantic dash down the runway. They could hear the sudden protest as the tires tried to grip the wet surface. *Still too fast!* A row of white and red lights flashed by. *Just three thousand feet of runway left.* Russo could hear the pounding of his own heart. Would the brake pressure hold? A row of amber lights. *Two thousand feet.* The brakes continued to shriek. His glance darted to the brake temperature gauge. *Dangerously hot!* A final row of red lights flashed by. *One thousand feet.*

"Ground speed?"

"Thirty-five knots!" Harris yelled.

Too fast! Russo's eyes were fixed on the rapidly approaching threshold lights at the end of the runway. He had nothing left to throw into the battle. The runway's southern extension was a bridge over an arterial. No way to veer off. Beyond the runway the terrain dropped off sharply into a cluster of trees and buildings. "We need an anchor!" he muttered between clenched teeth. The speed was down to twenty knots. A hundred feet left. Brake temperature way into the red. Fifteen knots. Ten…He smelled smoke…Five…

Zero! They had stopped. Flight Seventy-four was down. Harris cut the power. The single engine died. Silence.

The next sound Russo was aware of was the thundering noise of the foam truck's engine. The smell of smoke was growing. He activated the cabin intercom immediately. *"Evacuate! Evacuate! Evacuate!"* Both pilots released their seat harnesses, jumped to their feet and dashed aft.

The scene in the main cabin was amazingly orderly. Emergency exits and doors popped open and evacuation slides quickly inflated into sausage-like yellow chutes. Megan was using the emergency bull horn to give instructions to the other members of the crew as they herded the passengers toward the eight gaping exits. The two paramedics, the dentist, and Major Devane, assisted now by several crash truck crew members that had climbed aboard, were helping the injured and the elderly to evacuate. Russo and Harris helped the cabin crew to manage the rest of the passengers amid the din of roaring foam and CO_2 nozzles.

The whole evacuation took less time than Russo could have believed. At last he and Harris made a final check of the cabin. "All clear!" Russo yelled. "Let's get the hell out of here!" They jumped down the inflated slide to safety.

* * *

1444: The Runway

Outside the scene was anything but calm. The foam pumper had inundated the main wheels with mountains of white foam, which were still steaming from the red-hot heat of the wheel discs. Russo joined the fire chief. "Nice job," the chief told him, extending his hand in a firm grip.

"You're the guys who did the nice job," Russo insisted. "We'd have been barbecued without your fast response."

"We had plenty of time to get ready. This is just routine to us. No, the nice job was entirely yours, Captain. My congratulations. That was some landing."

"Well—thanks. For everything!"

Russo turned to Harris, and just as they were about to rejoin the rest of the crew a car sped up and stopped. Out jumped Janet, followed by Roger Greninger and Josh Edwards. "Thank God you're safe!" Janet cried, and flung her arms about his neck. "I think I died a dozen times!"

He held her close for long seconds and kissed her cheek. Finally, as he drew away from Janet's embrace he sensed the presence of Megan at his side. He turned to face her. Her eyes glistened. He slipped his arm about her waist and drew her close. "You haven't met my sister," he said. Janet, this is Megan McLain, our cabin crew supervisor, and the one that managed to bring all of our passengers safely through all this."

"I'm so glad to meet you, Megan," Janet murmured.

Russo saw the look on Janet's face as she noticed his arm, which was still around Megan's waist. He grinned broadly. He was past worrying about appearances.

1435: The Tarmac

"Did you get it all?"

"Sure! There wasn't a hell of a lot to get. Hardly worth the trip," Lionel Waid said, disgusted. "We should have been down at the other end. At least we could have filmed the evac. I think there might have been some kind of fire, but I couldn't get a shot. Too much mist. Ready to head back?"

Winthrop pulled his coat tighter about him. He could feel a trickle of cold water making its way down the back of his neck. "Yeah, we might as well. No way to get down there and interview anyone. They'd be gone by the time we got there."

Just as he was turning to leave an airport police cruiser came up beside the two men and stopped. A uniformed black man got out of the car. "What are you two doing out here?" he challenged. His right hand moved behind his back ominously.

"We're with Channel Three News," Winthrop said, careful to keep his voice pleasant as he sized up the situation.

"So let's see some passes."

Winthrop had anticipated the demand. Slowly, he moved his hand to his inside pocket.

"Hold it!" the black man ordered. "Make it nice and slow."

Winthrop complied. His hand went inside with extreme caution and emerged with another envelope like the one he had given the PCA guard. He extended it to the policeman.

The official took the envelope cautiously. He looked down at it. "What's this?"

"Open it," Winthrop said evenly, meeting the black man's angered stare.

"This had better not be what I think it is." Keeping his eyes on the two newsmen the officer opened the envelope and felt inside with his fingers. What he felt brought a grim, determined look to his face. "Okay, you two. Into the car." He opened the car's rear door and held it for them.

"What the hell does this mean?" Winthrop demanded furiously.

"We're going to have a little talk at my office, while we wait for the Sheriff's guys to come and join us. You two are under arrest for trespass and for attempting to bribe an airport security cop. If you're smart you'll just get in the car and keep quiet." The shiny black of the unholstered Beretta ended any arguments.

As they sped off toward one of the terminal buildings Winthrop caught sight of the guard they had bribed on the way in. The old man was grinning. That dirty bastard, Winthrop thought.

* * *

1455: PCA Hangar

Glen McDougall squatted under the belly of Flight 74 with Darryl Washington, who had come down from the control tower after his shift to see the damaged airplane.

"This is what saved them," McDougall remarked, patting the side of the fuselage as he rose from the wrinkled underside. "The belly is a big baggage bay. All the fuel tanks are way up there in the wings, so there was nothing down here to rupture and spill fuel all over the place. This is one of the few jumbos that could tolerate that kind of landing. But only on snow."

"Having the engines up high was a help," Washington said, pointing up at the relatively undamaged engine pod.

"Yeah. That's how they were able to get the wheels down. No other plane would be able to do what this baby did. Most of them have main wheels along the center line. And center fuel tanks down in the belly." He led the way aft to the high tee-tail. "But the real hero of this story is that tail engine," he said, pointing. "It kept them safe up there. The other two engines are still frozen solid, full of snow. But with this one up high, they were all right, as long as they didn't run out of fuel."

"How much did they have left?" Washington asked.

"They had another ten minutes in the air."

"Close!"

"I'll say. You did a great job bringing them in, Darryl."

Washington shrugged and grinned. "All in a day's work. What's to become of this airplane now?"

"She'll go into the repair hangar for a complete rebuild. There's no structural damage that I can see, so it'll be mostly skin replacement. The wings and all the control surfaces are undamaged. Tail, too. The wing engines and pods'll have to be replaced. And they'll rebuild the fuselage bottom. I think they'll probably decide to do it here in Seattle. I imagine they've had enough of Costa Rica. She'll fly again.

"Quite an airplane," Washington said.

"Just like the old Gooney Bird, Darryl. Indestructible."

* * *

Elsie Redfern had Roberta Morgan by the arm and was leading her and her three children over to the waiting area. Elsie's coat was draped over her shoulders. Her left shoulder was held out from her body in the temporary splint the paramedics had used to treat her shattered shoulder. "You should let them take you in to the hospital, too, Roberta," Elsie insisted.

"Oh, that's just a lot of needless bother. I've had burns before. I know how to look after it. Those nice paramedics on the plane gave me some salve. I'll be fine."

"You're sure?"

"Absolutely! Aren't we, children?" The three children nodded happily. "We just want to get home for a nice warm bath and a sleep in our own beds."

"Oh, dear! Yes, indeed!" Elsie said, smiling. "It's the little things you miss." She rose to leave. The two women embraced. "It was so nice meeting you, Roberta—even under the worst of circumstances. Good luck to you all," she said.

"Thank you, Elsie. Where are they taking you?"

"I'll be going to Swedish to have my shoulder reset." She felt a momentary stab of pain. There would be plenty more of that before her day was over. "I'll be in good hands."

"Let's stay in touch," Roberta Morgan said. "I'd like to come and visit you, once you're well again."

"I'd like that." Elsie waived to the three children with her good arm and returned to the wheelchair where an ambulance driver waited for her. "One more little task," she said, looking up. "Do you mind? I must see the nice southern girl—one of the stewardesses—What was her name? Sally—Oh, yes! Sally Ryan. She was so kind to me."

"No problem, Mrs. Redfern," the driver said, smiling.

"I think I saw her heading for the PCA counter over there a few minutes ago." As she rode over in her wheelchair she wondered if they would ever find her garment bag. Sally would know.

* * *

Sally Ryan was busy talking to Alice Pendleton, the travel agent in charge of the seniors group. "All of them were taken in to Valley General?" Sally asked. Alice Pendleton nodded. "Most of them were fine," she said. "They just wanted to take them in for observation. I think they'll all come through it all right. What stories they're going to have for their grandkids!"

"I'll say!" Sally agreed. "But I'd much rather have seen them do without the experience. You're sure there's nothing else we can do to help?"

"You've been wonderful, Miss Ryan. Thank you so much. I must be on my way now. I've got to stop in at the hospital and see them."

As Mrs. Pendleton left Sally noticed a frail woman in a wheelchair with one arm protruding wing-like in splints. She recognized the fur-trimmed coat and hat: it was Mrs. Redfern. "Hello, Elsie. I'm so glad to see you've survived our adventure. Are they taking you to the hospital now?"

Elsie nodded. "I'm afraid I'll have to go. It's not going to be one of my better days. But I wanted to thank you for all your kindness while we were stranded up there. And all the other girls, too. By the way, how is that young girl doing? The one with the nasty cut on her arm?"

"Glenda Abrams. She's going to be all right, Elsie. The paramedics were a big help. They gave her penicillin, and she's gone to Harborview. They'll be able to save her arm."

I'm so glad. She was such a dear!"

"You're the kind of passenger that makes our job easy, Elsie. Is there anything else I can do for you?"

"Just one little thing. Remember my garment bag? I think you were going to stow it somewhere."

Oh, yes! I do remember. I'll get one of the baggage people to look after it for you. Just wait here, Elsie. I remember it. It was a pretty red plaid bag, wasn't it?"

Elsie nodded, smiling. "Thank you so much. I hope we meet again."

"That's easy, Elsie. Just keep flying with Pacific Coastal." As she left the elderly woman sitting in her wheel chair Sally chuckled. For a moment she had been about to say "The Exciting Skies." She had a feeling that nonsense was gone forever.

* * *

Arne Lindgren, the SAS Flight Attendant Supervisor, let out a soft whistle as Sally Ryan passed their group. "I'm going to make sure we fly PCA again," he remarked. "These American girls are stunning!"

Captain Ole Rasmussen's eyes followed Sally Ryan briefly, then turned to Nikolaisen, his first officer. "I think Lindgren needs to get back home," he snorted. "SAS has lots of pretty stewies."

"I think we all need a drink," Nikolaisen said.

"Now you're talking!" Lindgren chuckled. The trio moved off in the direction of the South Satellite lounge.

Friday

1000: Seattle Courthouse

Marla Russo picked up the telephone. A heavy plate-glass barrier separated her from the prisoners on the other side. She waited for Carlos to pick his up. She studied his face for a moment. He was pale and tired looking, a shadow of the handsome figure she had known. The prison coveralls he was wearing were several sizes too large, making him look even frailer. For the first time since she had met him she saw defeat in his dark eyes.

"You shouldn't have come," Carlos said despondently.

"I had to!" Tears suddenly filled her eyes. "Oh, Carlos! What are we to do?" She tried to keep the despair out of her voice, but knew it was failing.

"It's hopeless," he said flatly.

"You have an attorney?"

Carlos nodded. "He can't do anything. They've got me. They're considering vehicular manslaughter as well as leaving the scene. I have no defense. It's utterly hopeless. Damn Wycroft to hell!" There was a sudden look of intense hatred in his eyes, then it faded. "His confession skewered me."

"Can't your lawyer do anything?"

"Impossible. There was an eyewitness. He saw the whole accident, and he's identified me as the driver. I've had it."

"What am *I* to do?" Marla wailed, suddenly losing control. "I called Frank, and he won't even talk to me! He—"

"You called *Frank?* What ever for?"

"I thought—he might reconsider—"

"But it was you that asked for the divorce," Carlos countered, suddenly animated. "I can't imagine he'd be willing to listen to your pleas now."

"He won't! He's so Italian!"

Carlos broke into a smile. "You may have to learn to like Seattle, Marla. We all have our problems." He was about to put down the phone and get up.

"Carlos! Wait! Tell me—tell me you still love me!"

He looked at her through the thick glass. Emotions flitted across his face. "Yes, I still love you," he murmured. "Not that it'll do you any good. But I do." Slowly he rose and looked down at her despondent face. "Have a nice life, Marla."

Marla sat there for a few moments, crying miserably. At last she took a tissue from her handbag and did her best to repair the damage to her eyes. As she rose a thought entered her mind. The man she'd met at the art show. What was his name? Warren something. She searched in her handbag. She found the card he had given her and took it out. Warren Roth. She smiled at his use of "Smith" as a cover, and his admission of his real identity after their night together. She wondered if he would still be in the city. He had spoken of a trip to Florida to research his book.

She found a telephone in the entrance lobby of the courthouse building and dialed the number. A man answered.

"Warren?"

The man said, "Yes?"

"Warren, this is Marla. Remember? We met at the art show last Sunday?"

"Oh, Marla!" he said, his voice suddenly excited. "I'm so glad you decided to call."

"Warren, I was wondering—I'm free tonight. Could we get together?"

"That'd be wonderful!" he said. She could almost see the smile on his face. "Same place?"

"I'll be in the lobby. About six?"

"Wonderful," Warren said. "I'll be looking forward to it."

"Me, too!" Marla hung up and looked at her watch. She had plenty of time to get back to her hotel and shower, then maybe a visit to the hotel beauty parlor. And maybe a new dress. She felt her spirits lifting. Miami wasn't that bad…

Sunday

◆

1130: Sommerset

"We're in real trouble, Frank," Janet said. She sat across the table in the breakfast nook, holding a mug of coffee in both hands, as though she needed its warmth. "For the first time since Richard died, I'm completely at a loss. I don't know what to do."

"What's the problem? I thought after we made a safe landing the media would have backed off."

"It's not just the media," Janet said. "They're part of it, but our main problem is our stock."

"Down a lot?"

"We were down to sixteen on Friday. A week ago we were selling for twenty-eight."

"That *is* bad."

Janet nodded miserably. She looked up into Frank's eyes. She could see pain there. "It's not your fault, Frank," she insisted. "We'd have survived the mountain escapade easily. After all, you brought them back alive. No one holds you responsible for the market drop. If anyone's to blame, it's Carlos. He really did a number on us. The hit-and-run. Carter's suicide. The Costa Rican fiasco."

"Sure, but he's behind bars now, isn't he?"

She nodded.

"And you've canceled the Costa Rican contract?"

She nodded again.

"What else, then?"

"It's something a lot more sinister. We've been hit by a barrage of attack ads from some of our competitors. The bastards have been paying for full-page ads in the newspapers suggesting that we've been operating unsafely."

"How could they make a case like that?"

"That's what's so maddening about it. They don't *have* to! All they have to do is hint that there might be a problem. They picked up on Carlos's Exciting Skies idea, found the obvious flaws in it, and now they're all posturing and doing a lot of arm-waiving, boasting about their own safety records. They haven't really said anything that can be countered. But the flying public reads it and suddenly we find ourselves with a lot of canceled reservations. *That's* what the market is reacting to—coming on top of everything else. There've been rumors that the NTSB is about to start crawling through our safety procedures."

"We really owe Carlos a lot, don't we," Russo said grimly. "I'd like to take him up and drop him out over Rainier."

"So would Josh Edwards!" She laughed in spite of her depression. "But nevertheless, we're facing really serious financial problems, Frank. I don't know how we can avoid bankruptcy."

"That bad?"

She nodded. "It isn't known yet, but we're going to have to start laying off, and even then I'm not sure we can meet our payrolls. I'm going to have to ask our flight crews to take a temporary reduction in salary. We'll promise to pay it back later, once we've climbed out of this hole. But if we have to go bankrupt—I guess you know what that means."

"I wish I had something concrete to offer, Jan," Frank said sympathetically. "Why not let the board wrestle with the problem? What does Mike Shea, our CFO, say about it?"

"He isn't very optimistic," Janet sighed.

"Yeah, but he isn't a pilot. Airlines ought to be run by pilots. Bean counters know nothing about how to operate a modern airline. You should be the new president, Jan."

"Thanks, Frank. I've thought about it, of course. And I know how to make it work, too. But only after we solve our financial problems, and I don't have a clue how to do that. It would take an act of God, and I doubt that he's really interested in the problems of businessmen. He has enough to do keeping people from freezing to death up on mountain tops."

"Amen to that," Frank murmured.

* * *

1400: Bridle Trails

"Sean!" Megan looked out the back door to see if her son was out in the small yard.

She heard stirring behind her. Her son appeared at the top of the stairs to the upper level, holding a copy of *SAIL*.

"Yes, Mom?"

"Are you cleaned up?"

"I haven't done anything to get dirty!"

Teenagers always had an answer, she thought. How would Rodney handle this? "We have company coming. I need a shining face, combed hair, clean clothes. Now, into the shower. *Scoot!*"

"What's the big deal?" Sean protested. "Who's coming?"

"A friend of mine," she explained. Then she realized that the question needed a little less vague an answer. "He's a very special friend, Sean. An airline pilot. The captain of my crew. You'll like him. He's the pilot that saved us all up on the mountain."

"Oh." The voice sounded a little more interested, but wasn't exactly projecting enthusiasm. That would be Frank's problem, she decided.

She wasn't going to try to sell Sean on the idea. If it developed, fine. But it had to be a natural thing, between the two of them. She was beginning to appreciate how close the relationship between Sean and Rodney had been, and how difficult it was going to be to rekindle that with a total stranger—if she decided that was where she was heading, which was not at all certain this afternoon.

As Sean caved and headed for his room she glanced at the kitchen clock. Frank would be here soon. She needed a little time to think before he arrived. She put on a pot of coffee and looked outside as she waited for it to brew. After ravaging the Puget Sound region for over a week, at last the storm had moved inland. It looked like Indian Summer had returned. She thought of their unbelievable adventure up on the mountain and shuddered.

She took her coffee out onto the deck overlooking her tiny yard. She eased into one of the new rattan chairs and relaxed. Her mind had been wrestling with a problem the past couple of days, and so far it had not yielded to a solution. Would it ever? The problem, of course, centered on Frank. More accurately, Frank, Sean, and herself. A very complicated human triangle. When she'd gone to dinner with Frank in Honolulu everything had seemed straightforward and simple. She needed a husband. Sean needed a father. Solution: find a good man and get married. Along came Frank Russo, and suddenly her problem seemed solved. But was it? Would a new husband really solve anything? What did she need one for? She was earning a very good living from her job, and of course she had her widow's pension. She didn't like being away from home so often, now that Sean was into his teen years. But he was a good boy, and wasn't showing any of the usual signs of teenage rebelliousness. So, apart from underlying sexual drives that had been surfacing with more intensity lately, she really had no need of a husband.

Sean, of course, did need a father. She was finding it all but impossible to take Rodney's place in her son's life. She wasn't well enough up on the myriad of things boys were doing these days to begin to satisfy

Sean's needs, and as time passed she'd been feeling more and more inadequate. For example, Sean was keen about sailing these days. Last weekend with Frank and Walter had shown her how hopelessly unskilled she was in that sport. Lots of women could hold their own handling a sailboat, but she wasn't one of them. And what if Sean wanted to take up shooting? Or mountain climbing? Or any of dozens of other typically male activities that didn't interest her much. She loved being a wife and a mother. Gallivanting around the skies in the glamorous role of flight attendant had been exciting, and certainly profitable. But that was the extent of her wishes to depart from traditional domestic roles. She'd always been a thoroughly feminine woman, happy with that role, and didn't want to change it.

Sean's needs seemed to be beyond her, she thought. But wasn't that natural? Wasn't that why God created both Adam and Eve? Each had his or her unique roles, and they were complimentary. Her femininity and Rodney's masculinity had made a happy combination. Could she find that combination with another man? That's really the problem, she decided.

Apart from the father role, would Frank be desirable? She'd felt a strong physical attraction toward him from the first encounter. No doubt about that. That night in Honolulu, she'd wanted him to kiss her. And many times up on the mountain she'd wanted the comfort of his arms about her. She wanted that now. She wanted to take him to bed with her, to submit to him, to—Yes, of course! She missed the fun in bed with a loving husband.

There was another dimension to it: she still wanted more children. She and Rodney had always planned to have three or four. Those plans had come to a sudden stop when Rodney died, but her desires in that direction were now alive and growing again. Perhaps these were the factors that would bring all three of them together. She needed a lover. She wanted more children. She knew Frank had always wanted children. And Sean, as well as needing a father, needed siblings. She didn't want him growing up an only child, fatherless, possibly growing effeminate from over-association with a very feminine mother.

What about the practicalities of such a union? She'd heard Frank was having his marriage to Marla annulled. It would be as though it had never happened, she knew, leaving him free to marry in the Catholic Church. As a widow, of course, she was equally free. They would have no religious hang-ups. Frank appeared to be a devout Catholic, as was she. And they would never want for material things. If she chose to, she could give up flying and become a full-time mother, a role she really preferred.

The bottom line, of course, was whether Frank would want to share this dream with her, and with Sean. And whether Sean would warm to the idea of Frank as a surrogate father.

She'd invited him over for dinner today with the hope of getting to a solution to this many-sided dilemma. She knew it couldn't be completed in one magic afternoon. But it might be a good start. She felt hopeful as she rose and went back into the house.

* * *

Russo experienced a feeling of panic as he rang the doorbell. The feeling emanated from two unexpected sources. First, he was meeting a single woman for the first time since his twenties. Dinner in Honolulu to get acquainted with a new crew member was not at all like going to her home on a weekend. And on top of that, the woman was the mother of a teenage boy. Childless, he had no idea how to handle such a situation. He'd heard enough horror stories about unruly modern teens to be apprehensive.

The door was opened by a youth with dark brown hair and blue eyes. Russo was unprepared for the shock of the boy's resemblance to Megan. "I'm Frank Russo," he said. "And unless I'm way off the mark, you must be Sean." He offered his hand to the youth, who took it firmly and met his eyes steadily.

"I'm pleased to meet you, Captain," the boy said. "Yes, I'm Sean. Won't you come in? My mother asked me to look after you while she's going through the final countdown."

"Final countdown?!" Russo let out a loud laugh. He followed Sean into the living room, feeling the generation gap shrinking. The teens he had read about didn't have Sean's manners and *savoir faire*. Of course, they didn't have mothers like Megan, either. He glanced at the boy. "Did she use that expression?"

"No way! She'd probably kill me!" Sean's face reddened visibly.

"Don't worry. It'll be our secret." He smiled conspiratorially. As he followed Sean into the living room he noticed a beautifully finished plastic model airplane sitting on an end table. He recognized it as a Hawker Harrier. "Say, that's a beauty!" he said, looking closer. "Did you build it?"

Sean smiled with evident pride. "Yeah," he said.

"You have real talent." Russo looked closely at the paint job. "You used an air brush?"

Sean nodded. "You can't do a decent job with a regular brush." He looked up at Frank. "You know about model airplanes?"

"A little. I built a lot of airplanes when I was younger. I've thought about trying my hand at it again, if I can ever squeeze it in. Where'd you learn? A club?"

"My father got me interested when I was little. Before he died."

"Oh." Frank remembered Megan's reminiscences in Hawaii. "I'm sorry, Sean. He was a fighter pilot with the RAF, wasn't he?"

Sean nodded. "This is the kind of plane he was flying."

"I see." He detected a lot more in Sean's expression. Lingering pain, of course. But mostly intense pride. "I never flew fighters," he said. "I used to fly P-3Cs for the Navy, out of Whidbey Island."

"Orions? You were in ASW?"

Russo nodded and smiled. "You're pretty well up on airplanes. Maybe you'll be a pilot one day?"

"Could be," Sean said. "I like flying. And sailing, too. Mom said you're a sailor."

Russo nodded and chuckled. "I'm afraid we gave her a pretty bad time over in Hawaii! She told you about it?"

"A little."

"Four of us took a rented sailboat out for the afternoon. I'm afraid the girls were pretty tired when we got back in, after cranking winches all afternoon."

Sean broke into laughter. "That's one I'd like to have seen!"

"Oh, you would, would you?" It was Megan's voice from the doorway. Russo rose to greet her. "What have you been telling my son?" she demanded with a knowing smile.

"How Walter and I made slaves of you girls out on the ocean last Sunday," he said, smiling back at her. She was dressed casually in a cashmere sweater and skirt. She'd let her hair down. The effect was glamorous, a sharp contrast with the professional image he knew so well. He watched Sean's face as his mother entered the room. He read undisguised admiration, and a lot more. Twelve was a transitional age, he thought. To Megan, he said, "I didn't tell him *all* the details."

"I'll bet you didn't!" Megan laughed good naturedly. "Did Sean tell you he's been crewing on the Lake Washington races?"

"No! Really?" He looked over at Sean. "What class, Sean?"

"Lasers," said Sean, apparently glad to be included in the conversation.

"They're incredibly fast. Almost as fast as the cats."

"Really! Some day I'd like to own one."

"It might be fun to try building one," Russo observed, and saw another spark of excitement in the youth's eyes. He wondered if there was any limit to the boy's interests. "Maybe you'd like to come and crew for me once in a while. I have a San Juan."

"Wow! They're really cool boats! You mean it?"

"Absolutely," Russo affirmed. "I'm always in need of crew. He glanced at Megan, who was smiling happily. Her expression reflected what he took to be a mother's love, perhaps tinged with a great deal of pride. "We could make it a threesome," he suggested. "I've already shown you the basics. Maybe now that we're getting some decent weather again we'll have a chance to give it a try."

"That'd be lovely," Megan said. Then she shook her head and laughed. "I've a feeling I'd be spending most of my time down in the galley, though, with two ravenous sailors to feed. Speaking of which, I'd better get with the program, or we may go hungry. Sean, why don't you go and start setting the buffet?"

Sean protested mildly, but did as he was asked, leaving them to themselves for a few minutes.

* * *

Megan took Frank out to the kitchen. "A glass of Chablis?" she offered.

"Sounds good." He sat in one of the kitchen chairs as she took a tall bottle from the refrigerator. "I hope I didn't embarrass, talking about our weekend in front of Sean, Megan," he said.

"It's perfectly all right," she said, smiling. "I'm still not used to the idea of seeing men. You're the first since Rodney died, actually. Or did I tell you that? It's very difficult with a teenager hanging around your skirts."

"He's hardly hanging from your skirts any more!" he said, laughing. "Not for a long time. But I do know what you mean. I think I'd be terrified if I were in your shoes." She took out two glasses and let Frank pour. He handed her one.

"Thanks for understanding, Frank. Sailing would be a terrific idea. A chance for all of us to get acquainted." She tasted her wine, then set it down. "I'm really glad you two hit it off. I could tell he really likes you. And that's a lot, for Sean. He doesn't make friends easily."

"I know what it's like," he said. "My parents moved around a lot when I was little."

"Mine lived in the same little village all their lives. Sometimes I wondered what it would be like to move around a little. Village life isn't very exciting for a teenage girl. That's one of the reasons I was so eager to get into flying."

"I'm glad you did! I don't know what I'd have done without your cool head up on the mountain."

She laughed. "Not as cool as you may have thought at times," she admitted. "There were times I was terrified out of my wits. I just couldn't show it around the other girls." She watched him refill their glasses. "How are things with you and Marla, Frank? Any change?"

She saw his face cloud over at the question. "She moved out," he said. "She left last weekend, while we were down in Hawaii. Carlos Santiago helped her."

"Santiago? But—I heard he'd been arrested. Something about a hit-and-run accident?" She concentrated on keeping emotion from her face. This was the first time she'd heard Santiago's name coupled with Marla's. A mystery cleared up.

Frank chuckled after a moment. "Poetic justice, maybe. She thought he was going to be her passport to the future. Now he's in jail, and she's left high and dry." He sighed heavily. "I'll be having the marriage annulled. We had no children, so it won't be difficult."

"I'm so sorry," she murmured. "I know how lonely you must be. But any time you'd like to share Sean with me, I'm sure he'd be delighted. He really likes you. And so do I," she added.

"That means a lot, Megan. Because I really like you, too. Both of you."

"Thank you, Frank."

* * *

They ate on a deck outside overlooking a little stream that wended down through the back of Megan's tiny yard. After dinner Sean went off to visit a friend for a backyard basketball session, leaving the two of them alone. Megan suggested they take their coffee inside in the breakfast nook.

"I've really enjoyed this, Megan," Frank told her. She saw his eyes lingering for a moment and smiled at him. "Families are lucky," he said. "Marla and I never had that."

"You're living alone now?"

"Yes."

She saw pain in his face. She got up and went over to sit beside him and put her arm up about his shoulders.

Their eyes met. "Megan, I—"

"You don't have to say anything, Frank," she murmured. On a sudden impulse she raised her lips to his. It was warm and gentle, and as he responded she kissed him with a tenderness she'd all but forgotten. When he released her she could see the flush of emotion in his face.

Their eyes met again and lingered. "I'd better be going," he said at last.

"You don't have to," she said. "Sean won't be back for a couple of hours."

He was looking at her. She sensed he was struggling with emotions that were suddenly overpowering. His voice was calm when he finally spoke. "You have no idea how much I want to stay here with you, Megan. I think you know I want you that way. Perhaps more than you could ever imagine. But I'm going to go home. Because I want the rest of it. Not just the here and now, but all the days and nights that will follow. Perhaps by the time I get home I'll accept that, though God knows I don't right now! But I'd never be able to look Sean in the eye if I went to bed with you now. When we do—well, then it will be right."

"Frank, are you proposing to me?"

"I have no right to yet, Megan." He smiled at her. "If I had, what would you have answered?"

Suddenly it was her turn to feel flustered. She didn't know what to say. She wondered if her eyes were giving her away, the way they often did when her emotions surfaced. "Frank—I can't answer that now," she stammered.

"I think you just did," he murmured, and smiled.

"Perhaps." Her eyes filled with tears of happiness. She felt his hands encircle her waist. She let out a soft whimper and kissed him again, and this time it was strong and filled with desire, and when they parted she was trembling. She felt him pushing her away.

"God, I want you!" he said.

"So do I, Frank!"

"So, I must do this!" He released her.

She walked to the door with him. "Call me when you get home?" she asked softly.

"I'd like that."

"Me, too."

She waived from the doorway as he drove off. This is going to be difficult, she thought, as she tried to still the beating of her heart. Or is it? Maybe it's going to be all too easy.

Tuesday

Tuesday, 1100: PCA Headquarters

Janet looked up from a copy of *The Wall Street Journal*. PCA's stock had dropped even farther by Monday's close. "Come on in, Frank," she said, smiling despite her dark mood. "Join the wake. We might as well have had a double funeral last Friday. It looks like we're finished."

"I wouldn't count yourself out yet," Russo said, dropping into a chair beside Janet's desk. "We're down on the exchange, true enough. But it's what you and the board do about it from here on that makes the difference. You've got to regain the public's confidence, that's all."

"That's all! That's more than enough!" she exclaimed. "We've had cancellations all over the system. As I told you, it isn't just the accident and the scandals. Our ticket agents report the public is afraid we're unsafe. There are rumors the NTSB is thinking of investigating us. If that happens—"

"Have you canceled that Exciting Skies nonsense?" Russo interrupted.

"First thing yesterday morning."

"Then I wouldn't worry too much. As a matter of fact, I'd welcome their investigation. They aren't like the FAA, who have to wear two hats. The NTSB is fair and unbiased. They'll give us a fair shake. What's our load factor?"

"We're down to fifty percent on some of the runs."

"That's bad. Cargo?"

"Not much drop-off there. We've always had good relations with the shippers. We're fast and on time, which is all they care about."

"Then why don't you just forget the media frenzy and get on with the business at hand?"

"Frank, we can't meet our payrolls!"

"I've been thinking about that. I had a talk with Josh, and he thinks the pilots and mechanics might be willing to put up the cash to buy this airline. It goes without saying they'd be willing to take a cut in pay for a while to make their own company solvent."

"They'd do that?" She felt her spirits lifting at the thought. It was a way out she'd never thought of. Richard had mentioned it once.

"Why not? Other airlines have done the same thing. It's not much of a gamble. Hell! This is just a temporary slump. We've had those before. And if the board gives you any trouble, we'll make them an offer they can't refuse."

She looked into his strong features for a moment. He'd always been able to lift her spirits. Just like Roger. The two men had a lot in common. She supposed it was because they were both pilots. She wondered what Roger was doing today, and the thought brought back memories of that night they'd talked about the airline at her place. The night she'd wanted to keep him from leaving. She hadn't seen much of Roger since then. The disaster up on the mountain had kept her too busy. It was time to take those feelings out again and examine them. Maybe tonight. She smiled up at her brother, wondering if he had any inkling of her thoughts. "Thanks for being here for me, Frank," she said. She glanced at her watch. "Hey! I'm starving! Would you let me buy you lunch?"

"I'd planned to ask you," he grinned. "But I'm sufficiently liberated to feel comfortable about my sister buying. I've got a hankering for something Mexican. Are you game?"

"Wonderful! Let's find one where we can sit outside."
"Let's go!"

Saturday

◆

0920: Flight 47

Russo looked up into the burning blue of the sky ahead as he adjusted their heading slightly to bring them a little closer to the mountain.

"Not too close, now!" Walter Harris cautioned.

"Not on your life!" Russo said, laughing. "Once in a lifetime is more than enough."

"Last run, huh?"

"Afraid so, Walter. You're going to have to break in a new Skipper." The airline flight surgeon had allowed him one more trip before he would have to trade his left hand seat for a desk. He'd asked Janet to let him take the Honolulu run again. Behind him, in the first class section, Megan and Sean were riding as passengers. What a vacation they would have, he thought. He looked down through his left-hand window at the massive grandeur of the snow-capped summit as they passed through fifteen thousand feet. "Look, Walter! It's still there." In the brilliant glare of the morning sun on the snowfield below he could see the remains of a large X in the snow and the tracks their plane had made on its wild takeoff run down the Nisqually Glacier.

"It's still hard to believe," Harris said, looking across the cockpit. "How we managed to miss those rocks!"

"We had a lot of help." Russo reached forward and increased their rate of climb slightly. "Meanwhile," he said. "Time for a little fireside chat."

"A short one would do nicely, FDR," Harris said.

Russo chuckled as he picked up the cabin PA handset and began speaking in his rich baritone. "Ladies and gentlemen, we're presently climbing through fifteen thousand feet on our way to our assigned cruising altitude of…"

THE END